The sudden silence was deafening. "How may I help you, sir?" the cook asked.

"My man was to bring a bottle of brandy to my room, but he seems to have forgotten," I said easily. "Now I can't locate him, unfortunately. Is Dobbs about?"

A voice behind me said, "I'll find him for you, sir, and have the bottle brought to your room."

I turned and immediately heard whispers behind me as words spread that they'd just met the new master. It was sharp and somewhat disturbing, to be frank. I really did want a piece of Barrett at that moment.

"Thank you," I told the footman. I looked again and grinned. "Still here, are you?" I said in a very low voice.

Granger grinned back, his eyes sparkling. "Can't really set off in the dead of night, now can I, Mr. Munrow? I'll be going at first light."

I nodded and took a step toward the stairs, weighing my options and the number of chances I'd be taking.

Damn it all, it had been a night, and I was set to lose a little bit of control. Thus the brandy, after all. "You'll bring the bottle and glasses?" I asked, not looking back.

"If you'd like, sir." The reply was polite, the voice warm. The hand surreptitiously placed on my arse was hot.

"I'd like."

An Agreement Among Gentlemen
TOP SHELF
An imprint of Torquere Press Publishers
PO Box 2545
Round Rock, TX 78680
Copyright 2006 © by Chris Owen
Cover illustration by Rose Lenoir
Published with permission
ISBN: 1-933389-95-8

www.torquerepress.com

If you enjoyed An Agreement Among Gentlemen, you might enjoy these Torquere Press titles:

Galleons and Gangplanks by Mychael Black, Sean Michael, Willa Okati, and Julia Talbot

Ranges by Dallas Coleman, Chris Owen, Julia Talbot and BA Tortuga

Bareback by Chris Owen

Historical Obsessions by Julia Talbot

Hyacinth Club by BA Tortuga

An Agreement Among Gentlemen

An Agreement Among Gentlemen
by Chris Owen

Torquere Press Inc.

romance for the rest of us

www.torquerepress.com

An Agreement Among Gentlemen

Dedication
   For Inga, with thanks and affection
         Chris

Acknowledgments and Thanks
   I would like to thank E.K., A.T., K.B., and N.B. for all of their help and gracious guidance. Thank you for mailing me maps of England, for answering endless geographical and practical questions, for helping me with historical accuracy and modes of address, and for being lovers of words, word plays and etymology. You have been invaluable, and have made both this story and my life richer.
         Chris

An Agreement Among Gentlemen

Chapter One

It was intended to be an evening's entertainment. How little I knew.

I had, in point of fact, been looking forward to the occasion -- a ball to celebrate a milestone birthday, followed by a week in the country. The diversion came at a welcome point in my life, as I had little to do in London, and the constant reproachful looks my brother cast my way over the dinner table were weighing heavier upon me than usual. He never actually told me to make myself useful and less of a drain on the resources our father had left, or for that matter on society in general, but his opinion was obvious and one I did not share.

It was therefore with anticipation that I had accepted the invitation to Red Oak Hall, looking with a keen eye to the company I would find there. Of course, most of the assemblage would be boring in the extreme, but there was almost always something, or someone, to capture my interest there.

The journey had been easy, as the weather had cooperated for once. The carriage did not break a wheel as it had the previous year, there was no rain, and the horses all seemed to be in splendid health. Even the usual bumps and knocks were more gentle than I had hoped. So pleasant was the travel, I was almost regretful as we arrived in the late afternoon, but that soon passed as I saw a familiar shape in the entry, the light of the open door falling upon him.

Trusting my man Griffith to do his job and make sure my belongings eventually found their way to my rooms, I left the carriage and made my way up the steps. The butler, Dobbs, was as ever in control, managing to greet me, instruct Griffith where to take my cases, and direct the driver to the back of the house. With a few simple words I was made to feel welcome, assured that everything would be handled with ease, and escorted into the Hall to greet my host.

Barrett, the current Earl and master of Red Oak Hall, stepped forward with a smile and clasped my shoulder with one warm hand. "So good to see you, Munrow," he said. "I trust the journey was tolerable?"

"Pleasant," I replied, returning his smile. "Things look well in hand here." They did indeed. The Hall, from what little I could see, was already set to celebrate. There were no servants rushing about, yet the air seemed filled with anticipation, and the scent of summer flowers was strong. Barrett himself looked splendid, his smile genuine and natural, the tension I'd seen in him a few months before, gone. Yes, his hair was still grey and his skin a little slackened with middle age, but he was tall and fit, carrying his years well.

"It will be wonderful, my friend. But now is not the time to bore you with the details -- you'll see them soon enough." He cast his gaze to my left and nodded to Dobbs. "No doubt Mr. Munrow would like to rest after his travel." To me he said, "I'll see you at dinner, Munrow."

And with that, I was handed over to Dobbs, who very politely informed me that due to Lady Sophie's demand for morning light, I would be in the gold room rather than my usual suite, and would I please follow him?

I did not care into which room I was put, honestly. I knew that, as there were many guests for the next two nights -- after all, one cannot throw a ball and expect two hundred guests to make their way back to residences all over Berkshire that same night -- there would be less than a dozen for the week. As such, those of us staying on would get the better rooms.

Dobbs silently led me up the staircase and down the main corridor; I could see ample evidence of the preparations. The Hall gleamed, almost literally. Everything had been polished and cleaned to within an inch of its life, and Dobbs, when I happened to remark on something, informed me that the drawing room would be open for the gentlemen, the morning room for the ladies' cloaks, and the larger parlour was set up for card play. Of course, following him down the hall to the east wing, I was unable to see any of this, but it was good to know where I would be able to find certain people once the music started.

Griffith, for once, was already in my room when we arrived, putting my clothes away and laying out things for dinner and further clothes for the ball. Most of everything else was put away in the cabinet.

"Did you see about the brandy?" I asked, already tugging off my waistcoat, wrinkled from sitting in the carriage.

"Yes, sir. It shall be here when you return from your meal. Would you care to rest before dinner, or shall I send for water?"

I thought about if for a moment and shook my head. "I'll wash and then decide. If there is time I may rest, but

I rather doubt I'll need it. A ball is a ball, and I suspect I'll be doing far more talking than dancing."

"Yes, sir," Griffith replied. He hung up the last of my shirts and crossed to the door -- I assumed for the water.

"Griffith?" I asked, a sudden thought occurring. "See what the talk is about this ball. I'd like to know how much truth is in the rumours before I walk into anything."

Griffith, proper for the moment, didn't even blink. It was his job to do just that, and he knew it. That I was telling him the perfectly obvious must have grated, but he gave no sign of it. But, then, it was entirely likely that he simply lacked the imagination to be offended.

When, at long last, Griffith made his way back up with the jug I washed and encouraged him to speak. "Well? Is it true?" I demanded, rinsing soap from my face.

"I'm afraid I don't know, sir," he replied, hastening to add, "No one does. It is, however, known without doubt that the Earl will make an announcement, and it is wildly speculated that it will be about a marriage. No one will admit to knowing as to whom the lady may be, however, and in fact there are many wagers being made on the name. The head footman says that the Earl has been cheerful and happy for almost six weeks and that it has been driving the maids to distraction. There has been nothing overheard, which of course speaks to how well the Earl is guarding his secret."

Interesting. And worrisome, if one were in service at the Hall, but of no use to me. I knew no more than I had the day or the week before.

"Well, it could hardly be a marriage, if the maids don't know," I said. "They know even before the poor lady."

"True," Griffith allowed me. "But there really is nothing else. An announcement will be made; the Earl has invited over two hundred people to hear it. One of the footmen saw him in deep conference with the Duke, and the housekeeper has been seen with lists of the staff -- and you know what that means."

I nodded. When the housekeeper started making lists of staff, there were changes underway. Usually the sort that involved people getting their notice and the promise of references.

I checked the time. "Well," I said, "I have time to read for half an hour, then I'll dress for dinner. Make sure the brandy is here when I want it."

Griffith nodded and withdrew, and I walked to the window and looked out at the wide lawn, the sun setting over the tops of the trees in the distance. "Let the games begin," I said softly.

Chapter Two

Dinner was not obviously hurried, but there was a certain excitement in the air as we talked. There were only eight of us at the table, the rest of our party not yet arrived, and I found myself seated between Lady Elizabeth -- the rather elderly Baroness of a pile of stones in the impoverished Lake District -- and a young woman who was introduced to me as Miss Jane Wilson, of Richmond.

Lady Elizabeth and I had met before a time or two at events such as this. Miss Wilson, who was perhaps nineteen or twenty, was apparently a distant cousin of another guest, invited at the express wishes of the Earl. She seemed to be a pleasant enough woman, well spoken and polite, if a little overawed by the grandeur of Red Oak Hall. We spoke of London and people whom we knew in common, both of us searching for a topic which would capture our attention.

Lady Elizabeth seemed very much taken by the conversation of the man to her left, for she very seldom even glanced in my direction. Miss Wilson, thankfully, was too polite to let me know if she was aware of the slight, and in truth, it merely amused me. I'd had long practice at being dismissed by peers of many ranks and ages; it had become somewhat of a sport to see who would adhere to the social games we all play.

As we finished the soup, I realised that Barrett was casting more and more looks to our end of the table, his smile almost playful as he watched Miss Wilson. She seemed unaware of his attention, but I could see the others taking note, and it was most amusing to see Lady Elizabeth following his gaze. Her lips would tighten and her shoulders would become stiff; I almost felt sorry for the poor man speaking with her. Lady Elizabeth in full disapproval could be difficult to diffuse.

If Barrett saw what he was doing, the conclusions people were reaching, he gave no sign of it. Indeed, by the time we were enjoying the final course, Barrett was looking towards us even more frequently, and his smile had become almost gleeful. There was no doubt lingering in my mind that the evening's climax would be this secret announcement, or that Barrett was very much enjoying the way he had all of us on tenterhooks, waiting to see what he was up to.

When dinner was over there was almost an unseemly haste as we each made our way to our rooms to dress for the ball. Part of it was because we could hear Dobbs making the entry ready and directing the maids for the cloakrooms, the arrival of guests being expected within the hour. But I will not mislead you -- we were all most anxious to hurry the proceedings along.

I was walking the corridor towards my room, passing by a few scurrying staff, when Lord Russell, he of Lady Elizabeth, called to me. I paused and greeted him, as we had only passed a few words over dinner, but the man was in little mood for idle chatter.

"He can't be serious," Lord Russell said to me, as if I

knew what Barrett was planning. "That... that woman? She has no title, no connections. He must be mad."

"She seems very pleasant," I said mildly, privately sharing his disbelief. Barrett had never before even feigned an interest in remarrying, even though it was, more or less, his duty to do so.

One of four children, Barrett had no son, nor a nephew, nor even a male cousin. His eldest sister had remained a spinster, staying exclusively in the family's London home. The second sister had married well, producing no fewer than six daughters, all of whom had married and scattered themselves around England. The youngest sister had apparently suffered a madness in her youth and had been sent to France. That her madness coincided with the physical fact that her corsets would not tie was not spoken about, nor was the sudden replacement of the entire complement of footmen. But that had been when I was a child, and if Barrett was even aware of her current residence, he had not seen fit to share that with me.

And so, it was of pressing importance that there were to be an heir. As it stood, if Barrett were to die without an heir, the Hall would go to either some distant relative who had never even visited the place or to the Crown, and while Queen Victoria would no doubt find a relative happy enough to take the place, I knew Barrett would much prefer she not.

"Pleasant or no, there are better choices," Lord Russell insisted. "I know for a fact that the Duke has a sister-in-law who would be most suited to -- " He broke off as Dobbs passed down the hallway, and dropped his voice. "The Duke has long being trying to reach some accord with Barrett," the Baron confided. "To join the families would benefit them both. Mark my words, Mr. Munrow. There will be unpleasant reaction if he actually takes that girl to the altar."

With that, he swept away, leaving me more than a little baffled. I don't think I had ever had a stranger conversation -- certainly not with someone of his stature. I was just as common as the poor Miss Wilson, and usually I was dismissed just as she was. My valet before Griffith would take great delight in passing on to me the opinions of my social betters, and even through the malicious filters of the servant class, I admit there was always a level of truth to the conversations.

I am indeed common. Worse, I am lazy, willing to ignore certain social niceties, and I take every advantage I can of my brother. The allowance granted to me in my late father's will is enough to provide for me, and I take delight in making sure my brother fulfils every letter of the document, to the point of maintaining my rooms at what is now my brother's home, although I am there infrequently. I am a cad and a card player; I freely admit to intimates that I have no wish to marry and that most of the company I keep is a means to an end.

And for all of that, I suddenly had Lord Russell giving me his opinion in a hallway, as if there was something I could possibly do about the situation. While it was true that Barrett and I had long enjoyed a friendship, it was not that of social equals, and I sincerely doubted that Barrett would do anything more than laugh if I were to attempt to talk him out of anything having to do with his beloved Hall.

No, our friendship was borne more of shared secrets and... tastes. I was pleased to be included for this week in the country, but I do admit to wondering why. The ball was easily explained -- there were very few who were not invited to that, but the week following was to be much more like a gathering of intimate friends, an honour to which I had given much thought. But no matter how I twisted it in my mind, I could not make all the pieces fit. I had yet to claim all the pieces of the puzzle, and the more I thought on it, turning it over in my mind as Griffith fixed my cuffs and collar for the ball, the more assured I became that Barrett's game was complex and would not be known in full until he was ready.

Chapter Three

Griffith, damn him, was unable to tell me anything of substance. Miss Wilson was an unknown quantity in the equation, and below stairs was a riot of questions and speculation. The housekeeper had caught two of the footmen and a scullery maid making odds and was most unhappy. I didn't care. I wanted to know, and I wanted to know quite badly.

"Then perhaps," Griffith said sourly, "you should make your way down to the drawing room."

"Remind me why I keep you on?" I asked evenly. Even for Griffith, that was pushing the bounds of allowable.

He merely turned and picked up my coat, holding it for me. "Because you can't keep anyone else, sir."

Unfortunately, that was true. My last valet had more or less fled one morning, struck insensible when he brought my breakfast tray before I could rid my bed of an unexpected guest. The one before that had been more open-minded regarding my bedmates but had coveted the position himself, and I'd had to let him go. Griffith, at least, held his tongue when it was important and knew how to close a door without lingering.

"That doesn't mean I have to keep you," I snapped. "You will not speak to me in such a manner."

"Yes, sir," he said, brushing my shoulders. "Sorry, sir." He sounded anything but. Damn him.

I looked in the mirror as he made minute adjustments to my clothes, pleased with my reflection. The cut of the cloth was flattering, the dark colours enhancing my skin and features. In another setting, I would be more than happy to set out on a hunt of sorts, but this night was not for pleasure. For most who would attend, it would be about position and reassessing; for me it was simply a diversion. No matter this announcement of Barrett's, it would not affect me.

Finally, I broke from Griffith and readied myself to join the throng below. I could hear the music swelling, the entire house alive and full to near bursting; footsteps of guests filled the hall beyond my door, and I found myself eager to join them. Casting a glance about the room, I moved to the door. "Where is the brandy?" I asked, my hand on the knob.

"It will be here, sir. Below stairs is rather unsettled at the moment."

"I don't care. Have it here before I retire."

"Yes, sir. Will you be needing me then?"

I considered for a moment. "No," I replied, pulling the door open. "Just make sure about the brandy and have the bed warmed. I'll be breakfasting with the rest in the morning, so wake me in time."

"Yes, sir," Griffith's voice followed me into the hall. If he had anything more to say, I lost it to the chattering of two ladies ahead of me.

The house was indeed alive, and I spent the better part of two hours walking and greeting people. There were many acquaintances about, and I was introduced to many more people as time went on. Lords and Ladies, gentlemen of substance, and the occasional person whom no one seemed able to place. It was an odd assortment, really, but all seemed willing to make allowances. It was, after all, the celebration of Barrett's fiftieth birthday, and whom he invited was entirely up to him.

That is not to say that eyebrows were not raised. Everyone I met, and most whom I passed, were locked into a single conversation. Whispering speculations as to Barrett's announcement led to no new information, although it did convince me that a body of footmen, maids, and coach drivers could easily spread the word of any event in England, and it might do her Majesty good to employ the servant classes as spies.

The new element, Miss Wilson, came as a huge surprise to everyone not at dinner with us, and I began to worry for the poor thing. People were quite obviously staring at her and seeking out those of us who'd been there. She began to look uncomfortable under the attention and soon retreated with her maid to the morning room. I was heartened to see her return within ten minutes, her face set into a pleasant smile. She was made of stronger stuff than I'd given her credit.

The crowd ebbed and flowed in and out of the ballroom as I made my way around various groups of people. I caught sight of Barrett now and again, greeting his guests and talking happily with assorted gentlemen and ladies. The house was dressed finely, and the music filled the entire lower level, people moving this way and that, on and off the dance floor.

Presently, I made my way up the narrow stair on the far wall of the ballroom. It was an oddity of the Hall that such a thing existed -- an expanse of balcony in the room so one could look down upon the floor and watch the patterns made as people danced. From there I could see the entire room, from the raised dais where Barrett would, I presumed, speak, past the dancers to the huge double doors at the other end. I was, of course, not alone in my drifting up the stairs, simply one of many who took a moment to survey the scene, and no one paid me any mind.

I had been there for only a few moments when the Duke joined me. I hadn't seen him in my wanderings and was thus most pleased to greet him. By all accounts, he'd been in conference with Barrett often in the last few weeks, and as we had a passing acquaintance, I hoped he might be able to satiate a little of my curiosity. Even as he moved towards me, holding two glasses of champagne, I had to remind myself that we would all know the answer within an hour or so, and my impatience was simply that of an overactive mind. Sometimes, however, one's natural inclinations are to be followed.

"Your Grace," I said, accepting the glass. "You're looking well." In truth, the Duke looked positively syphilitic. His face was pale and drawn, and even the few stairs he'd climbed had made his breath laboured.

"You're a liar, Munrow," he said with a smile.

I smiled back. "One must, however, observe the niceties."

"No one is listening to us here, Munrow," he countered, leaning on the railing and watching the dancers.

"True," I allowed. I sipped from my glass and studied him. Only a few years older than me, the Duke was not quite forty, but he looked ages older. I wondered what ailment had overcome him, and even if he were well enough to be in attendance at all, but decided not to press the matter. Ours was not a close relationship, certainly not one which invited anything other than polite enquiries.

"I hear you've been spending time with Barrett," I ventured.

"Everyone's heard that. I'm bored of dancing around

it, frankly." His Grace frowned at me.

"What then shall we discuss?" I asked in my most mocking tone.

"Don't do that, Munrow. It makes you sound less astute than you are, and I hate to play games."

"Now you lie," I said softly. "You love to play games, Your Grace."

And then he turned to face me with such a knowing and repulsed look it made my blood run cold. "But not your kind of games, Munrow. Not your kind at all."

I stared at him, not knowing what to say. He raised his glass to me and turned to go, saying, "Nice talking to you, Munrow. Perhaps we'll speak again soon."

"I look forward to it, Your Grace," I stuttered as he left me, cursing myself for being rattled. I didn't know what he was about, and I hated to think that someone might, just perhaps, know more than they should. Certainly a someone who had influence to wield as the Duke did.

I don't know how long I remained there on the balcony, staring sightlessly down on the crowd. The music flowed over me, around me, and I saw the faces of those below, but I was lost in thought. The Duke had taken me by surprise, and I found it all too easy to recall a number of occasions when my indiscretions could have been witnessed by those I did not trust. I had been, without doubt, careless. I shook myself, brought my mind back to that place, back to the ball, and searched the sea of bodies below me for any further clues to Barrett's announcement. It was, as I've said, a futile game, but it was more diverting than actually engaging any of the players below in conversation.

They would all speak of the same thing, each of us vying for information we would have in a few moments if we would only wait. There were, of course, many who felt strongly, or perhaps merely hoped, that Barrett was not about to announce his engagement, and I could easily pick them out of the crowd. Ladies dressed to attract his eyes, fathers and brothers subtly and not so subtly making an effort to capture the Earl's attention. I knew the moves of that game well; it was all a hunt, with Barrett and Red Oak Hall as the prize.

"They are ravenous," came a voice in my ear, and I admit I jumped.

"Barrett!" I turned and smiled. "You almost sent me off the edge," I accused with a wink.

"I may yet," he replied, his eyes twinkling. "Tell me, what do you think of all this?"

I looked out over the crowd and shrugged one shoulder. "You've got us where you want us, my friend. We are all at a loss, eager and waiting on your very word."

He laughed. "Not all. But yes, I think you are right -- most here are waiting to get back to their libraries so they can consult their diagrams and see where they stand when I'm done. Hungry, the lot of them. And they think I'll feed them."

I pointed to one of the many footmen serving hors d'ouevres. "You feed us," I said mildly.

"Oh, do stop," Barrett reproached me. "Look around, Munrow. What do you see?"

I looked. I saw the elaborate gowns, the gloved hands like my own. The way the women held themselves and the way the men pretended not to notice. I saw the flow of bodies between the ballroom and the cloakrooms, the men going to smoke and the women to gossip with whomever they could find. I saw the older people taking in the dancers, the young lovers gazing at each other. And I saw the hunters, men after the Hall, women after a husband with money and title.

I said this to Barrett, and he nodded. "It wears," he admitted.

"So why do this?" I asked. "Why invite us all here and put yourself on display?"

He didn't answer my question, simply looked out at the guests below us. I looked as well, mentally cataloguing the people I knew and occasionally asking Barrett who the others were.

"That," he said at one such point, "is Mr. Granville. He has a daughter; she's here somewhere. Poor thing is terrified I'll ask for her. Oh, and the man he's speaking to is a Viscount of some small estate or other."

"And that?" I asked, suddenly seeing someone of interest. "By the woman in the frightful pink striped gown. With dark hair and an ill-fitted waistcoat."

Barrett made a noise suspiciously like a laugh. "That, dear friend, is Granger. A footman. Look at Dobbs."

I searched for a moment and found the butler to the side of the doorway. He looked like he was about to have a fit, his face pale as he made his way through the people towards the hapless footman.

I smiled, unable to help myself. "Looks like young Granger is about to find out he's lost his position."

I felt Barrett shrug. "He was leaving anyway. I suspect he wanted a little fun before he leaves."

"And he doesn't care about his references?" I asked, not able to hide my surprise. The man would not find work again in a house of this stature, not after that display. I watched as Granger smiled at Dobbs and said something, then both of them looked up at Barrett and me standing there.

"No, he doesn't," Barrett said softly, still smiling. It was then that I saw the spark, the heat in his eyes, and the way in which Granger acknowledged the look.

I laughed. It was undignified, but I could not help it; I actually threw my head back and laughed. "The servant, Barrett?"

"Like you're any better?" Barrett asked, meeting my smile.

"Tell me: is he any good?"

"Far better than most," Barrett said, watching Dobbs lead the man from the room.

I shook my head, still laughing. "And now that he's given up his position?"

"He'll find something." Barrett sounded amused and relaxed. "Granger is very resourceful."

"Imaginative?"

"Very. And willing to please."

"I think I'm jealous."

"Find him later, if you wish," Barrett invited me. "But for now, I do hope you'll stay for my announcement?"

I smiled again. "I wouldn't miss it for anything."

Barrett nodded and once more clasped my shoulder. "Soon, then. I believe I have to speak to the Duke first. Fetch yourself some more champagne; there will be a celebration tonight, I promise."

Chapter Four

I watched the dancers for perhaps another minute or so, once more contemplating Barrett and his mystery. No matter the need for an heir, I could not help but think he would avoid a marriage to a young lady at any cost. While he might see the need to lie with a wife to produce the needed child, ladies embarking upon marriage seldom saw things in the same light men of Barrett's years did.

Or men of Barrett's tastes.

No, a young lady would want more from Barrett than he could comfortably give. It made far more sense for him to select a wife of later years -- a widow, perhaps, already with a son whom Barrett could name heir. With that in mind, I made my way down the narrow stairs, watching the crowd of people in a new light.

With a smile, I noticed that the footmen, while being strictly correct in their rounds, were paying far more attention to the women in the gathering, and two footmen in particular were taking great care to be sure that the widows were well tended. I had a passing thought that the odds being laid below stairs were most like going to pay off very richly for some.

Miss Wilson was on the dance floor, in the arms of a leering Viscount. She seemed only a trifle uncomfortable, the set of her back rigid, but a smile firmly in place. She had been trained quite well, I thought, and I made a note to attempt a rescue later in the evening. I highly doubted, at that point, that she was about to be become Barrett's wife, and the crowd would abandon her as soon as that became clear. All the more luck to her.

In the card room, I found Lady Elizabeth and her Baron -- for there was little doubt who ran that home -- playing Whist with a couple I had not met. These turned out to be Sir Bentley, a pleasant enough old gentleman, and his wife. We spoke for a moment or two, and I was once more on my way, watching as groups of men in the drawing room alternately smoked and covertly assessed the value of several paintings. It is said that the attributes of a house are not noted in fine company, but that is a lie. It is not discussed, perhaps, but we are an acquisitive people, and for those of means it is a hard habit to break.

I was deep in conversation with Mr. Merrithew, a friend of my brother's, when we noted that the music had stopped after the last waltz. With an almost audible buzz in the air, we joined the flow of people into the ballroom, amidst the swish of silk and the mild grumbling of a few men who thought that the whole event was beyond the pale.

I hung back, not because I was less eager than the rest but because I feared what would happen to my person if I edged too much closer to Lady Elizabeth. She glared at me with such fierceness, I thought she might actually stop and inform me in so many words that she suffered my presence only because I was there as Barrett's guest. Really, the extent of her snobbery was becoming legendary.

I smiled at her as sweetly as I could and said, "I look

forward to spending the next few days getting to know you and your husband. I'm sure there are many things we can discuss in the evenings."

She sniffed and nodded sharply, then turned her face away from me and moved ever so slightly faster into the ballroom. I grinned and reached for a fresh glass of champagne, noting the flicker of a smile upon the footman's face.

I stood just inside the doorway of the ballroom, gratified to find that the small conversations in the room were hushed as we watched Barrett step up onto the raised section of flooring. He was backed by lush curtains which concealed the musicians, and I knew without a doubt that the colour -- a rich blue -- had been chosen for this very moment. He looked almost regal as he stood before us, a glass in one hand and a happy smile on his face.

A tremble of energy ran down my spine as the room fell silent. As one, we waited.

I was struck by how comfortable Barrett seemed as he stood easily before the large group. It made sense, I supposed, as surely he had prepared well for this. It was then that I noticed a look pass over his face, his eyes darting over the crowd as he sought to find a face. He smiled suddenly, and the corner of his mouth twitched almost mischievously.

"Thank you all for coming," he began. "Each of you has indulged me most wonderfully in this display of vanity. I admit that it is an extravagance to celebrate one's birthday so elaborately, but I hope that you will indulge me a little further. I have spent the last several months preparing myself for this day -- a half century of life lends itself to introspection, I have found."

There was polite murmuring and a bit of quiet laughter, but I could hear a nearby voice whisper, "Just get on with it, for pity's sake!" I smiled at that and watched as Barrett gestured around him with his glass.

"Red Oak Hall has been my life," he continued, "and I have great affection for it. I came to wonder, as perhaps I should have done years ago, what would become of it after I have left it." That was a blatant social lie, and we all knew it. The matter of Red Oak Hall's disposal was his responsibility and one he would have been considering for years. "It is with great sadness that I recall my dear late wife's sacrifice to that end."

Sad he may have been for the loss of an heir, although I am given to understand that the child was both a girl and not his own. However, one speaks of that even less than one mentions his youngest sister.

Barrett had lowered his eyes when speaking of his wife, and there was a hush as we honoured him, if not her, a momentary pause in the excitement. Then Barrett looked up, and the moment had passed. He paused, as if searching for words, but it was for effect. He knew exactly what he was doing.

"I have made a decision, my friends. There shall be an heir, and I shall have fulfilled my duty to this great Hall. I am going to be leaving here within the month, taking my leave and resting well in the knowledge that the Hall is in good hands."

This caused a stir, voices whispering in confusion, the sound of skirts swaying as the ladies turned to their companions. Barrett waited until silence fell once again, tension gradually building until I thought someone would cry out for an answer.

"I have decided against taking a wife," he announced, his voice clear. "Instead, I am going to give the Hall, its holdings, and its lands to one of worth. Someone whom I know will love it as I have done. I regret not being able to pass the title on, but the law is the law, after all. On this, the fiftieth anniversary of my birth, I give the greatest gift

I have.

"Do you accept, Mr. Edward Munrow?"

There was a collective gasp and the crowd seemed to part around me, everyone turning in mute shock to stare at me. And what did I do? The only thing I could, given the circumstances.

I raised my glass to the old bastard and inclined my head. "Happy birthday, dear friend," I said.

Chapter Five

After Barrett's rather unexpected announcement, my evening became a somewhat more dangerous adventure. Being at opposite ends of the ballroom, with over two hundred hunters between us, I did not have the slightest chance to speak with Barrett for some time. As soon as I had accepted his curse, both Barrett and I were beset upon by people, happy congratulations and well wishes disguising both anger and immediate plots.

It was a game. I was stunned and not really in my right mind, so it took all my wits not to make an error of any kind. I would not accept even so much as invitation to lunch for fear of accidentally finding myself betrothed to some poor girl whose father had an eye for the Hall.

There were, of course, a multitude of implied insults, both to myself and to Barrett. Many remarks were made amidst careful smiles about how we really must be saddened when a great man enters his dotage so early in life, and many more about what a shame it was that the Hall was let slip from its family. There were also those chance searching questions about how close Barrett and I were. It was those which caused me the most agony, for the Duke had already shaken my conviction that my secrets were my own.

Everywhere I walked, I was drawn into conversation. Some were brief, my companion more or less simply being seen to fulfil the obligation of greeting the new master of Red Oak; others were longer, and I cast about me searching for escape.

I needed to think. I needed to speak to Barrett without the ears of everyone else around us. I needed a moment's peace to contemplate my next move.

There was no way out of it, of course. Barrett had seen to that by having me accept his gift in front of so many witnesses that I would be ruined if I reneged. Worse, he knew that I would not -- could not. I knew full well that he would not give up the Hall without a damn good reason; he knew that I would never trap him into something he needed to escape.

I hadn't thought that he would trap me here, though.

I stayed in the drawing room for some time, hoping to avoid the looks of assorted young ladies who had suddenly had their eyes opened. Marrying the Earl was one thing -- title and money. Marrying me was another. Money, no title, and twenty years younger. They were weighing things out, and I felt their assessment keenly.

Of course, the men were no better. Those with titles were horrified that a gentleman of my breeding had more money than they did. Those with no title and little money were wishing Barrett had picked them. All were looking within for marriageable women.

It was past midnight before I could make my escape to my room, and I had not yet spoken with Barrett. The man had vanished from my sight, and every time someone pointed him out to me, he had just left that place. I resigned myself to waiting for morning. Then I would haul the man into his... my... the library and ask him why the devil he'd done this.

My brother was going to have a fit. That thought cheered me a little, and I even smiled as I closed my door behind me. The lamps were lit, and silence fell warmly over me as I started to remove my formal clothes. Too tired to take great care, I at least made an effort to not step on them or toss them about. Griffith hated it when I did that, and he had been known to take his revenge with too cold bathwater.

In my shirtsleeves and trousers, I collapsed into a chair by the window, one hand rubbing over my eyes. I reached blindly for the bottle of brandy and a snifter, my eyes snapping open as my hand encountered a bare table.

"Damn him," I cursed aloud.

With hopes of finding a wandering footman or maid, I stormed to my door and threw it open, only to be greeted by an empty hallway. I considered simply retreating and slamming my door shut, but I wanted my drink -- needed it, really. So I walked down the corridor and located the back stairway.

It was highly irregular, or course, but the entire night had been somewhat more exciting than usual. I would find the kitchen, rouse a maid, have her summon Dobbs, get the key to the liquor stores and claim my bottle of brandy. And as I walked, I plotted revenge on my wayward valet.

Below stairs was still bustling, I found, with scullery maids washing dishes and the cook counting knives and setting things to rights. I stood in the doorway for a moment, and one of the girls saw me, immediately snapping to attention and calling for Cook.

The sudden silence was deafening. "How may I help you, sir?" the cook asked.

"My man was to bring a bottle of brandy to my room,

but he seems to have forgotten," I said easily. "Now I can't locate him, unfortunately. Is Dobbs about?"

A voice behind me said, "I'll find him for you, sir, and have the bottle brought to your room."

I turned and immediately heard whispers behind me as words spread that they'd just met the new master. It was sharp and somewhat disturbing, to be frank. I really did want a piece of Barrett at that moment.

"Thank you," I told the footman. I looked again and grinned. "Still here, are you?" I said in a very low voice.

Granger grinned back, his eyes sparkling. "Can't really set off in the dead of night, now can I, Mr. Munrow? I'll be going at first light."

I nodded and took a step toward the stairs, weighing my options and the number of chances I'd be taking.

Damn it all, it had been a night, and I was set to lose a little bit of control. Thus the brandy, after all. "You'll bring the bottle and glasses?" I asked, not looking back.

"If you'd like, sir." The reply was polite, the voice warm. The hand surreptitiously placed on my arse was hot.

"I'd like."

Chapter Six

Granger, to give him his due, was obviously a smart man. I'd been in my room no more than a few moments when there was a polite rap at the door; I'd only just begun to regret the decision I'd made. It's very hard to change one's mind when the prize is standing right there.

I called for him to come in and remained standing by the foot of the bed whilst he set the tray on the table.

He glanced around the room and tilted his head at me most endearingly. He really was a lovely boy, tall and lean with a shock of dark hair and deep-set eyes. "Your man?" he asked softly.

"Hiding, I assume," I said. "Would you care for a drink?"

He raised an eyebrow but said nothing.

"Oh, please," I said with a snort. "You're no longer a footman in this house; you know it and I know it. You're here for one reason, and if I offer you a drink, it's your choice to accept or decline."

"So we're to be equals?" Granger asked with a sardonic twist of his full lips.

"Oh, no." I almost purred. He was luscious. "Never that. We are not at all equal." I stepped forward and touched his shirt, the cotton thick and heavy between my fingers. "This, for example. It is not the fabric of a gentleman."

Granger smiled, his eyes darkening a little as he reached a hand for the buttons of my own lawn shirt. "This, on the other hand, is. Are you a gentleman?" he asked, looking at me through lowered lashes.

"When it suits me to be."

"Now?"

"God, no."

"All men are equal when stripped bare," he teased in a soft, roughening voice, his fingers nimbly undoing my buttons.

I laughed, the sound choking in my throat as he slid a hand into my shirt. My prick was swelling, heavy between my legs as he touched me. Under different circumstances, a night unlike the one I had just survived, I might had lingered with him, explored and discovered. But that was not my need, not what I sought, and he seemed to know it, his head tilting back as I tangled my fingers in the hair at the back of his neck.

When I kissed him, it was meant to bruise, to lay temporary ownership to his mouth and body. He met force with force, allowing me to taste the smoke of his last cigarette, the hint of stolen whisky, but pushing back, showing his need. We made sounds, deep and animal, and soon enough we were pulling at our clothes, trying to free ourselves from every hindrance possible.

Shirts gone, and his torn at the cuff, Granger feasted upon my neck and shoulders, his hand heavy on my shaft, rubbing and massaging me through my trousers. I gasped, unable to hold back the sound in the face of his eagerness, and allowed him to push me back onto the bed. Quickly, faster than I would have been able to manage, he had my fastenings undone and was leaving a heated trail down my body with his mouth. His tongue danced over my skin, the only sound in the room our laboured breathing.

When he took me in his hand, strong fingers weighing my balls, I lifted my head. "Easy," I warned. "I don't wish to spend too soon."

He merely looked up at me and opened his mouth, lapping at the head of my prick.

I groaned and braced my weight on my elbows, watching him. He licked me, his mouth clever and wet, slicking me well before he took me in. That the boy had talent could not be disputed, and I found myself plunging into his mouth with abandon. His full lips were swollen and reddened, holding me tightly as he moved. He travelled my length over and over again, sucking and licking, making me shudder and moan with need.

He shifted his weight, and the hand which had been gripping my hip disappeared. I tried to right myself, to see him free his prick from his own trousers, but my body was not my own any longer. I thrust and rocked, sliding deep into his mouth, and he moaned around me, sending shudders up my spine.

"No," I gasped. "I will not."

His eyes challenged me, and I felt a swell of anger. He was forcing me to my climax, proving to me that I would come when he willed it. With a grunt, I pushed him off, my prick so achingly hard it slapped my belly when freed from his mouth. I growled and pounced on him, let him take my weight as I knocked him to the floor. We rolled together, each seeking the superior position, but as our erections met and rubbed, we descended into gasps and hungry kisses for a moment.

It was an effort to tear myself from him, but need was high in my blood, making my body sing and ache. I stood and pulled him up, both of us shoving at his trousers until he was bared to my eyes.

I would have looked my fill, but I no longer cared how long his legs were, or how flat his stomach. Hard, dark nipples drew me, and as I bit and suckled, he writhed in my arms, squirming free with a low cry. I pushed him hard towards the bed, and he sprawled there, arse high.

It was too much. Far too much temptation.

"Oil?" I demanded, hissing into his ear as I cupped his buttocks in my hands. Hard and rounded, skin so very smooth and warm, he was beautiful.

He did not make a reply, moving under my hands and groaning almost piteously as he begged with his body. I slipped a finger down his cleft to tease at his entrance and found it slippery, my two fingers sliding in with ease.

The thought that he had come to me from another man's bed made me freeze. "You -- "

"Did it myself," he murmured, his hips already pushing back as he took my fingers.

I was stunned. The image of him preparing himself was too delicious to linger upon if I didn't wish to spend right then, without so much as feeling him around me. I growled again, the sound moving through my chest as a low rumble. I don't recall removing my fingers, nor moving onto the bed with him; I do, however, remember thrusting deep into his body, a fast deep stroke that made us both cry out.

We took little care with each other. I pounded into him, forcing myself past the tight ring and into clinging, wet heat, and he moved back against me, getting to his knees as I took him. Our skin shone with sweat, the sounds of our exertions harsh and obscene. He spoke only to beg, wanting deeper and harder; I spoke only to demand he move faster.

I could feel my body readying. Tight and hot, the

pleasure was so high that I thought I might scream, just to let it go. Granger cursed, his back arching as I thrust wildly, his body clutching at me. He took his weight on one hand, using the other on himself, and my eyes rolled in their sockets. Watching him touch himself, the image of him slicking his body for me... it was more than any man could endure, I assure you. I felt his first spasm, the way his abdomen seized and released, and I cried out, my eyes closing as I was gripped impossibly tight.

Ecstasy, white hot and molten, flowed through my veins and out my prick, my only sound a prayer of thanks and a blasphemous declaration. Trembling, we fell upon the bed, sticky and warm, my chest heaving against his back.

When I caught my breath, I rolled away from him and lay on my back looking at the ceiling. Granger made to leave, turning away from me, but I stayed him with the touch of my hand on his back, and he settled again beside me.

We lay in silence for a few minutes, my fingers on his arm, his hand on my thigh. "You'll be all right when you leave?" I asked finally.

His head turned, and I saw a genuinely happy smile. "Yes. A few days in London to say goodbye to my sister, and then I have a ship to meet."

I was oddly pleased. Although Barrett had said that Granger was leaving anyway, I knew that he wouldn't have spotless references after his display in the ballroom. That it really was a final bit of fun before he left England came as an unfounded relief.

Granger got off the bed and crossed to the commode, wetting a flannel in the basin. I caught a flash of the silver of my seed on the inside of his thigh, the evidence of our coupling making me smile. He turned to me, gently wiping me clean with easy strokes. He matched my lingering smile and, almost shyly, asked, "Do you like your gift?"

I groaned, the entire night flooding back. "I like the Hall," I said as his hand stilled on my hip. "Although why Barrett saw fit to tie me to it is beyond me."

Granger looked crushed. "He seeks his freedom. After a lifetime here, he is doing the one thing that will make his heart whole, Mr. Munrow. James... he thought that the Hall and its money would allow you the same."

"James?" I echoed, startled at his use of the name.

Granger flushed, his hand moving again as he washed my balls, the cloth rubbing at the base of my prick. I glanced at the tray holding the brandy and snifters, my mind moving faster, reaching unexpected conclusions. "Granger?" I asked mildly, "how did you manage not only to finger yourself into readiness but fetch someone to locate Dobbs to produce the brandy, get the brandy from that someone, and be here within moments of me?"

Granger made a soft noise, almost laughter, and his hand moved over me a little more insistently as I began to thicken and firm under his touch. "The brandy was safe in my room. I'd convinced your man that I would bring it earlier tonight. I made myself ready just before you came below stairs."

"Why?" I asked, bewildered.

"The Hall is Barrett's gift to you. I have no means to say thank you, but I do have months of your name in my ears as we planned. When I saw you, I wanted. Barrett permitted this, so I expect it's really his gift as well." His words were softly spoken, but the sheer emotion in them made me breathless, and the cloth around my shaft made it hard to think.

I moved my hips, trying to get away, but the motion had the opposite effect as I fucked his hand unwittingly. I had thought that Barrett was merely playing with the footman, a common enough game, but the truth was so much sadder, so much more desperate.

They were lovers, and I had just used Granger as a plaything.

"I was the only one, you know," Granger said as he stroked me, making me harder and harder. "No one knew his plans other than me and the solicitors. It's for us, you see? When light comes, I'll be dismissed -- Dobbs will have a good morning. And within two weeks you shall have the Hall, and I'll be gone."

"I'm sorry," I said, clutching at his wrist. "Stop. Please. I don't want you to -- "

Granger smiled at me and leant down, kissing my mouth gently. "You didn't listen. I want this. Do you really think that Barrett and I could maintain any form of singularity? We like our games too much. It is not an offence, to Barrett or to me. It just is, Mr. Munrow."

I fear my eyes were wide, and I know my breath was laboured once more. Clever fingers were playing with me and a sweet mouth was kissing me, and my blood was hot. "What do you want?" I asked weakly.

"Just this," Granger replied with a smile. Then he straddled my hips and sank back upon me, still soft and wet from before. As he took me into his body again, he sighed his pleasure. "Just this."

My hands went automatically to his hips, and we began to move slowly, luxuriously. He lifted himself, his hands flat on my chest, and made love to me with shining eyes and careful whispers. He did not bring Barrett's name into our passion, but I could feel the love he felt, and I wanted to weep for it. Granger must have been almost thirty years Barrett's junior, but they were giving up everything for each other.

It was longer and shorter and sweeter and rougher. By the time Granger and I spilled again, we had moved from the bed to the floor and back again, rolling often and taking each other as high as we could before spiralling down to begin again. When I came, it was with a gasp, Granger with a long, throaty groan I tried not to hear. It was not Barrett's name, thank goodness, but it wasn't for me, all the same.

Nor should it have been. That was my gift to him.

Sleep followed brandy, and when I awoke my bed was empty, dawn just beginning to fill the room. I stumbled from the bed to open the windows, hoping that fresh air would spare me the worst of Griffith's attempts at wit, and then I retreated under the covers again, fragrant and warm.

The day could wait for me this time.

Chapter Seven

Griffith roused me from slumber with a deceptively gentle touch to my shoulder. "I trust you slept well, sir?" he said as I rolled over and rubbed at my eyes.

"Eventually," I said, struggling to sit up.

He said nothing, but I saw him take in my lack of sleeping wear and let him reach his own conclusions. I did not particularly care what he thought -- he'd been with me long enough, and in service long enough, to know what not to say. To anyone.

He moved about my room easily, setting things to rights. As I tried to force myself to full wakefulness, he opened the wardrobe and started gathering my clothes for the morning, his movements unhurried.

"Breakfast is laid in the morning room," he advised me, "and there are already a few guests gathering. The coffee is a little stronger than you like it, but the tea is acceptable."

"The Earl?" I asked, watching Griffith flatten a slight wrinkle in my clean shirt.

"Not yet, sir." He wasn't looking at me, and I realised

how drawn he looked.

"Are you all right?" I asked, pushing off the sheets and swinging my legs out of bed.

"Yes. Below stairs was in near riot last night." He smiled slightly. "No one made the odds."

"How did they take it?" I asked, pulling on my small clothes and moving to the basin of fresh water. "Am I facing a sudden staff shortage?"

"I doubt that, sir. Dobbs and Mrs. Banks seemed to have things in order fairly shortly, but I think they were as stunned as the rest. The only one gone so far is a footman, dismissed before the... event occurred."

I merely nodded and washed my face. Griffith helped me dress in silence, and before long, I was presentable to face the rest of the house. "I don't want to do this," I said under my breath. "Damn him to hell and back."

Griffith's eyebrows shot up. "You don't want the Hall?" he asked, clearly stunned at the mere thought.

"I don't want to be the next one to produce an heir for the place," I corrected. "I was quite happy the way I was."

Griffith looked at me intently, his back rigid. "Sir, if I may speak?"

It was my turn to raise my brows. Griffith always spoke, I'd thought, but then... perhaps there was a difference between the barbs and subtle rebukes and what he had planned. I found myself nodding stiffly, not really wanting to hear what he was thinking.

"Until last night you were happy, yes. But you were also playing at being a gentleman, taking all the benefits and having fun but ignoring the responsibility. No, you ran from the responsibility and buried yourself in games and trappings. Now you have far greater resources than you'd ever hoped to have, and far more to answer to. I think, sir, that it is time you grew up."

I stared at him, utterly unable to speak. No one had ever said such a thing to me before, and I found I cared not a bit for it. How dare this man take it upon himself to correct me? How dare he judge me and find me lacking?

"You will have my shooting clothes ready when I return," I said as evenly as I could. Then I left my room and made my way down to breakfast.

Chapter Eight

Breakfast was endured, not enjoyed. The ladies, of course, stayed in their rooms, doing those secret things with which women filled their mornings. The men moved about the room, selecting food from the sideboard and sipping tea or coffee, ostensibly discussing the shoot we were about to embark on and rehashing gossip gathered the night before.

The gossip was short in supply as the main topic was me.

I was given long, speculative looks, and conversation after conversation dwindled and died as time and again eyes sought me out. I tried my best, but as I could offer no explanation for Barrett's actions, we were all left wondering just what the hell the man had been thinking. No one said so, of course.

I suppose that none of the gentlemen knew quite how to deal with me. While Barrett had made his intentions as clear as possible, it was but the morning after; Barrett was still lord of Red Oak Hall and I a guest. I was obscenely grateful to those who chose to treat me as such. Still, though, I was to take possession at some point, and I badly desired to speak to Barrett.

When he arrived, he was full of hearty good wishes and seemed very pleased with himself. He strode in, already clad in outerwear, and poured himself a cup of coffee as he wished us all a good morning.

He was greeted in kind by all and heaped with praise for a most memorable evening. His eyes twinkling, he turned to where I sat in an over-large and terribly comfortable chair and said, "I suppose you wish to have a moment or two alone with me?"

"If you would be so kind," I replied acidly.

"Certainly, Munrow." He apparently ignored my tone, replying so graciously that I felt a little chagrined. "The library? I hope the rest of you don't mind; we'll be back shortly, and we can all set out. Please, feel free to go outside and check the weather. We'll be heading towards the pond and lunching just this side of the wood."

With that, he turned on his heel and we left the room, heading down the main corridor and across the entry to Barrett's personal library. There was another library, a bigger room next to the drawing room, which was free for everyone to use, but this was more private. Intimate. Less likely to entered by every footman and maid trying to gather information.

I followed along, trying not to feel like a dog behind its master. This was utterly ridiculous, and Barrett had to be made to see that I was not the man who would be able to aid his escape from duty. When we got to the library I closed the heavy doors and turned to lean on them. "Why?" I asked desperately. "Barrett, why me?"

He sighed and walked to the huge desk that dominated the room. Picking up a paperweight in one hand, he looked at me and smiled sadly. "I am sorry, Munrow. Really. I know that this is sudden, but you have to believe me. I did this for your benefit."

"It's to my benefit that you get to run away to... to... wherever it is you're going? To my benefit that now I have to somehow deal with the wolves after this place and try to find a wife who isn't utterly atrocious? I was never meant to marry, Barrett. You know that." I was fighting my anger again, frozen in place as the full weight of the Hall settled on my shoulders.

Barrett nodded. "I do know. I wasn't either, and nor was... well. Please, Munrow. Hear me out. You have the Hall. The land. The money. You will be able to do whatever you want -- travel, meet people, do things you could only wish for previously. The price is slight, really. There are many who will look the other way to a marriage in name only -- you wouldn't even have to live together once a child was born. You don't think that all married couples have fairytale lives, do you?"

"So why didn't you do that?" I demanded.

"I did," he shot back. "For my family, for this house, I married a shrew. I wed her, I took her to bed, and eventually she became large with child. But it wasn't mine, and she died anyway. I couldn't face it again, Munrow. I'm fifty years old. There will not be another of my line, and I have a chance to escape."

"So Granger told me," I said evenly.

Barrett smiled. "You saw him?"

"I took him. Twice." I meant it to be harsh, but Barrett seemed delighted.

"And you spoke? He told you?" he asked eagerly, leaning forward. God, his eyes were shining.

I sighed. "He told me he's leaving the country. I assume you will follow?"

Barrett merely smiled again, neither nodding nor speaking.

I moved to a chair and threw myself into it. "Why me?" I asked again.

There was a long pause and then Barrett stood above me, looking down. "For your father, my friend. He could not do more for you than an allowance."

My father. A man I hardly knew, he was gone so often. He was rarely in the house with us, often away on business or visiting important people such as Barrett. He had been a firm man, not demonstrative, but fair. I looked like him, more so than my brother did, but my memories of him were mostly hazy from childhood. I knew Barrett through my father; initially, anyway. Other things had drawn Barrett and me together later, when I first began to explore the private clubs in London.

My father.

I stared at Barrett, feeling the blood drain from my face. "My father?" I breathed. "You -- "

Barrett knelt beside my chair. "Why do you think I never once touched you, lad? Never once suggested you stay here unless it was with a large group? I like you, Munrow. But your father? I loved him."

And that sealed my fate, more than anything.

I do not remember a great deal of that day. I declined to go on the shoot, retreating to my room with the bottle of brandy and strict orders that I not be disturbed. I railed. I ranted, Griffith told me later. I smashed two snifters and eventually called for Griffith to prepare a bath.

When I emerged for dinner, I was more or less in control of myself. Seated at Barrett's right in defiance of all social convention, I took Red Oak Hall as my home and made plans for the week. A trip to London to speak to my brother and close my London rooms. A visit to my solicitors to arrange a meeting at the Hall in four days time with Barrett and his solicitors. A trip to the stationers to have cards made.

I had a feeling that my social life was about to take a turn for the busier.

Chapter Nine

They would not leave. Of course, there was little reason for them to do so. Barrett had invited them for the week, and frankly, my sudden and soon to be official acquisition of the Hall gave them all the more reason to stay. The men -- Lord Russell, Sir Bentley, and Mr. Phelps of Reading -- were bemused and most curious about my intentions. The women were... a trial.

Lady Elizabeth sniffed in my direction frequently -- literally. At one point, a footman offered her a handkerchief. Lady Sophie had a simply bewildering amount of nieces to tell me about, each one more beautiful, modest, and capable than the last. And Miss Wilson was everywhere. To give the child credit, she seemed very uncomfortable around me, and I placed the blame for her sudden interest in the gardens, the pond, and the library, squarely upon the shoulders of her chaperone, who seemed to have vested herself in Miss Wilson's future.

I hid, and then I fled. I spoke with Barrett and set off for London as soon as I could, making my way directly to my brother's home. He would have heard the news before I arrived, of course, but I had a duty to inform him myself, and in person.

When the carriage delivered myself and the hapless Griffith before my childhood home I could not help but feel both relief and despair. I had sought solace within those walls before and always felt as if it were a refuge, but there was no doubt that my dear brother would be most displeased with my current circumstances.

Griffith gathered my cases and vanished, leaving me to face the loving embrace of my family, all gathered nicely in the drawing room. As I walked in, my brother rose, a tumbler in hand.

"Edward," he said. "I won't ask why you're here so shortly after you left. It's true, then?" Arthur looked calm, but years of experience led me to study his jaw. I had seen it set tighter, but not often. There was some small hope of discussing the matter without our voices rising into a cacophony of disturbing proportions.

My sister-in-law, Mary, stood and gave me a smile of welcome. "Welcome home, Ned," she said mildly, crossing to the sideboard to pour me a drink.

"You saw him less than a week ago," Arthur said disapprovingly.

"And I welcomed him then, and I'll welcome him the next time he visits," Mary said. She softened her words with a gentle hand on Arthur's arm. "Please don't raise your voices too loudly," she admonished softly. "I'll see you at dinner."

With another smile to me, she swept from the room, leaving me with my somewhat disquieted brother.

We sat and looked at one another for a few moments, and then, to my surprise, Arthur sighed and seemed to shrink into himself. "Did he say why?" he asked.

"Yes," I replied carefully. "He thought it would be good for me."

Arthur snorted indelicately. "Good for anyone at all,

Ned. Why you?"

My decision on what to say of that matter had been made long before I took to the carriage to leave Red Oak Hall. "That is something he declined to share," I lied. "Does it matter so much?"

"I suppose not." Arthur sounded tired. "You really do have the luck of the devil himself, you know."

I shrugged. "What I have is a colossal home, far enough from London that it will be an annoyance, a horde of marriage-seeking families gathering to wage campaigns, and no clue how to handle any of the daily matters."

Arthur smiled. "Serves you right, you lazy blighter. Welcome to life."

"Thank you, ever so," I said sourly, draining my glass without even tasting the drink.

"What will you do?" Arthur asked me, and I stared at him, not knowing his meaning. "With the property, the money? How will this affect your family, Ned?"

I shook my head. "I haven't the faintest idea. Barrett has told me little, and we've yet to meet with the solicitors. I expect he'll be taking a sizable sum with him, and I have every intention of making sure his sisters are provided for. Other than that... well, it's rather up in the air at the moment."

Arthur nodded and looked around the room, so full of things I knew well. There was little of my own history at the Hall, and it suddenly dawned on me that it would be generations before my issue could think of anything about the Hall as being truly theirs.

Dinner was had, and I slept in my rooms, as usual. On my way out in the morning, Arthur informed me that he would be in touch soon to discuss the terms of our father's will, in light of my new circumstances. And that, it appeared, was that.

Chapter Ten

The visits to other places around London went more or less smoothly, and I arranged for my solicitors to be at the Hall shortly after my return. I was somewhat dismayed upon that return to find that every single one of the houseguests was still in attendance, their week not yet finished. I felt even more on display than I had before, and Barrett apologised for that, saying that he had picked the guests to avoid such pressure. Sometimes our closest friends can surprise us, he said, which I took as an understatement of massive proportions.

Our days passed more or less on an even keel, regulated by meal times and the entertainment of cards. It was revealed that Miss Wilson possessed a fine singing voice, and she was pressed into service one evening, to her mild embarrassment and our great pleasure.

Barrett and I spoke often, though not at length, and I was more relieved than I had expected when the solicitors finally arrived, and we all retreated to the study to discuss matters. The other guests, I'm sure, entertained themselves by discussing the same things at greater length.

Barrett had planned well and thoroughly. I read the

documents with my solicitor hanging over my shoulder, but I was not concerned with the legalities. Uppermost in my mind was making sure that all parties were provided for with adequate means of support.

After careful and extensive prodding of the solicitors, I finally gave up and turned to Barrett. "Tell me," I pleaded. "I can't get past the clauses; what's wrong with plain speaking -- "

Barrett smiled then laughed. "In short," he said, pouring himself a glass of sherry, "there will be an account set up for my sisters. They will be able to live off the returns. I am taking an amount with me, and I warn you -- it's not a small amount. A few objects will be removed from the house and taken to my sister in London, mostly things which were my mother's or that have particular significance. Three paintings will be taken as well, and I'll be boxing no small amount of books.

"But for the most part, what you see is yours. And you may do with it as you wish." His eyes shone with sincerity, and once again, I found myself overcome with his gift. This time, however, it was not fear or social terror that robbed me of my voice; it was the amount of care he must have had for me, for my father. For Granger.

I signed a sheaf of papers, and then Barrett took up his pen as well. The signing seemed to go on for a long time, with the solicitors making minute corrections to phrases, each one needing our initials. At one point, I took my own solicitor aside and gave him directives for my own will, which I suddenly felt to be a most pressing matter.

He could not, of course, simply draw it up right then and there, but he was made aware of my wishes. In the event of my early demise, the Hall and the rest would go into a trust for my brother's children. An account would be set up for Barrett, another for his sisters, if they were still alive. I would not have them wanting, if I could stop it. There would, of course, be passages for specific items and a sum for Griffith, but until I was settled in the Hall and could take my bearings, it would suffice.

Finally, the guests left. It happened in a flurry, it seemed. When Barrett and I had returned from the library there had been congratulations and toasts, and we'd spent more time than I liked dodging direct questions. Barrett would give neither his reasons nor his intended destination, and I really could not give answers to questions of my intentions.

By the time the evening was over, I was losing patience with the gentle encouragements about varied and assorted prospective brides, and I fled to my room, pleading exhaustion. Griffith, at least, did not press me for anything, simply telling me that the situation below stairs seemed to have solidified as I'd expressed no desire to replace any of the staff. There were those, however, who were feeling bound to Barrett and resented me. It would bear watching.

The next morning, the men took breakfast as usual, and the ladies came down shortly before luncheon. Once the meals were done, I was surprised to find the entry hall full of boxes and cases and the drive lined with carriages.

Within an hour they were gone, the excitement over. Mine was just about to begin.

Chapter Eleven

In the end, Barrett left almost as quickly as the houseguests had. It wasn't that same day, nor even the week after, but it was far sooner than the month he'd mentioned at the ball. He came to me one evening after supper and asked me to join him in the library. I had assumed he meant the smaller one, but I found him in the big room, seated in a broad club chair. He had brandy ready for us both, and the air seemed heavy with anticipation and something else.

"It's time," he said quietly.

I raised an eyebrow and eased myself into a chair, watching him. He looked almost calm, but his eyes were alight, like a young child about to go on a trip. "For what?" I asked.

Barrett shifted forward slightly. "Tomorrow, the boxes will be sent to London, my cases will be packed, and I'll be going to the city to see my sister, Martha. And then I have someone to meet at the docks."

"Tomorrow?" I admit I was taken aback. I had no real idea of when Barrett would go, but I had expected slightly more than a few hours notice.

"Tomorrow," he agreed.

I drained my brandy far more quickly than I should have. We spoke quietly for some time, and he finally told me that he and Granger were going to France. He was so eager, so alive and happy. So very sure that he was doing the right thing.

I could no longer find it in my heart to begrudge him his happiness, even though it left me with an uncertain future.

When he left the house the next day, the staff turned out in main force, lining the steps to bid him farewell. In a rather emotional display, Barrett nodded formally to Dobbs and bade him to care well for the Hall, and he kissed Mrs. Banks on the cheek, making her blush. He hugged me, told me not to ruin the old place, and then he left.

I was now the sole owner of Red Oak Hall, legally and forever. I had nine bedrooms, two libraries, a ballroom, a conservatory, a dining room, and God only knew what else. Oh, yes, and a staff of over twenty bodies.

It was possible that Barrett might not have been joking when he told me not to ruin the place.

The first days were busy and hectic as I tried to make my way. I leant heavily on Dobbs as he told me how things were run, and we made some minor changes. Mrs. Banks, thankfully, was quite efficient and clear in her explanations, thinking of things I simply would not have remembered myself, such as monograms on the linens and stationery for the Hall. Between the three of us, we decided that I should not open the Hall to guests for at least a month, giving us all time to prepare and get settled.

That did not, however, stop people from coming to call. Every day I would be summoned to take tea with someone, usually a neighbour coming to greet me personally. More often than not, it was someone I knew at least in passing, and I found that the visits were either fast and painless or fell into two general categories: How soon will you sign everything over to a peer, or how soon will you marry my daughter/sister/niece?

I took to spending long hours wandering through both libraries and the drawing room, finding small ways both to make myself a part of the place and to leave my own mark upon the rooms. My things had been brought from London, and I'd moved from the guest room into the suite of rooms that Barrett had held, putting my own touches here and there. My rooms were the easiest, as Barrett had taken most of the possessions from there, and aside from the furniture, I had free rein.

The bedchamber itself was large and open, with a dressing room to the side and a small sitting room as a buffer to the main corridor. There was also a very small private study, which I left alone for the most part; I had yet to really have need of it, as I was using the small library downstairs for running the household. But all in all, it was a comfortable place, and I felt easy there.

I spent a few days calling for assorted footmen to aid me in placing other objects around the house, getting my few paintings hung in the drawing room and objects from my parents' home placed where I would most like to see them. It was a curious experience, trying to meld my history with that of Red Oak Hall.

By far the most tedious task was trying to find room for my books. One would think that with two libraries and a study in which to manoeuvre I would have had little trouble finding space for my small collection, but that was the problem -- where to place volumes, whether or not I should mix my books in with Barrett's, or if I should shelve all of mine separately. I wondered if I should keep mine strictly to my study or the private library, or if I should make them freely available to guests. In the end, I took most of my collection to my study and placed a few reference books in the private library. As I had shelves cleared and reorganised, it occurred to me that there had been a particular set of history books in the main library that I thought might prove interesting, and I took my leave of Matheson, a lovely young man who gave the impression of being hopelessly unattracted to men, and crossed the hall to the larger room.

At first I thought that Barrett must have taken them with him, for the set was not where I remembered. I was walking along the shelves, absently pulling out volumes which I thought might be the ones I sought, when Dobbs came in.

"Matheson has finished, sir, so I've sent him to begin laying the table for luncheon."   .

"Fine," I replied, distracted by the book in my hands. It appeared to be a journal of some kind, although printed and bound. I returned it to the shelf and glanced around the room. "I'm looking for the set the Earl had on the Jacobite uprising of '45. Do you know if he took them with him?"

"I don't believe so, sir, but we've not had a chance to reorder things properly. Perhaps they were put by the desk?"

Together we crossed to the back of the room, and I began my hunt anew. Dobbs located a small section of dictionaries and reference books then began pulling out volumes near the encyclopaedias. I confined my search more or less to eye level beyond the desk, trying in vain to remember what colour the binding had been. There was, on one end, a collection of black volumes that had no marks of any kind on their spines. Diaries, was my first thought, or logbooks of some kind. Carefully, I eased out the first volume and let it fall open, the pages fluttering lightly before they settled. I gasped at the images laid out for me and began turning pages.

The drawings were erotic and highly sensuous, both coloured paintings and sketches. There was no text, or even a hint of the artist's name, although I was sure that more than one person had contributed to the volume. While some of the paintings were done in deep, rich hues, others were lighter, watercolours that merely hinted at the subject. In each image however, whether sketch or painting, the subject was always the same: the male form.

It was art; erotic, yes, but nothing that would seem to be decadent or unusually illicit. Each picture featured a single subject, although not the same one. In some images, the model was clothed, or had fabric draped over his body, in others he was facing away from the artist, his face hidden as his body was exposed.

I don't know how long I stood frozen in place, looking through the book. It may have been only a few moments, but I think it was perhaps much longer, as when Dobbs cleared his throat, I started so badly I almost dropped the volume.

"Here they are, sir," he said as I spun around. He handed me two volumes and pointed to the third, resting on a shelf just below a series of monographs, well away from where I had seen them last.

"Thank you," I said, reaching for the books and setting the volume of drawings on the table. "Tell me, do you know how long these have been here?" It did seem a little odd to me that Barrett would have left such a book in the main library, no matter how artistic the images.

"No, sir. The last time I saw them they were in my lord's chambers." Dobbs glanced at the shelf and nodded. "They are, however, all there in number."

Curious now, or rather, more curious, I drew down

another slim volume. This book was slightly different in matter, though not composition, featuring the models as uniformly nude and occasionally paired. Another volume, the fifth in the line, contained sexual acts, explicitly depicted between men in twos and threes, more pornographic than artistic.

In short, I was intrigued.

I took all seven volumes from the shelf and stacked them neatly on the desk. "I think," I said to Dobbs, "that these should perhaps be in a less visible space. It would not be pleasant for Lord Russell to wander in looking for distraction and find himself faced with such pleasure." I smiled at the thought, actually. It would serve the old goat right.

"Of course, sir," Dobbs said mildly. "Shall I take them upstairs?"

I almost said yes. After all, what better home for them? But something in me was amused by the idea that one of my unwelcome guests would get a shock or two, and I could not seem to let go of the idea. Still, I did concede that it would be best to not have them prominently displayed. I looked around the library for a moment, pondering where they should go. There were open cases and closed, as well as an armoire or two for storage. "Perhaps in that cupboard?" I suggested, pointing to a large piece against the back wall.

Dobbs looked at where I meant and said, "That is not a cupboard, sir."

I stared for a moment. It certainly looked like one to me, although the door was perhaps over large. "What is it, then?" I asked, feeling somewhat stupid.

Dobbs walked to the cabinet and opened the door, then stepped back so I could see. It looked dark to me, and I could see nothing at all so I stepped closer, making a small noise when I saw a narrow staircase. "Where does it lead?" I asked, more surprised than anything else.

Dobbs smiled then -- actually smiled -- which may or may not have been even more surprising than the stairway. "Come with me, sir," he said, disappearing into the wall.

We went up. I counted eighteen stairs in the dark, one of my hands on each side wall and then there was a shaft of light spilling in as Dobbs opened the door at the top. He stepped smartly out of the way, and I followed him, eager to see what room was connected to the library.

My dressing room would have proved a great disappointment, if it were not for the stunned look on Griffith's face. He sat, forbidden cigarette dangling from his fingers and a journal of some kind in hand.

"Griffith," I said evenly, as if walking out of the wall was something he should have expected.

"Sir," he replied in much the same tone. He did, however, spring to his feet.

"You'll have to find a new place to hide," I informed him. "It seems I have a shortcut from the library."

"Yes, sir. I'll do that, sir," he said. Then he shook his head and added, "I mean, no, sir. I'm not hiding."

"Then you shouldn't be smoking, should you?" I asked, thoroughly enjoying this entire thing. Dobbs remained silent beside me.

"No, sir." And the cigarette was put out. He gestured to the door. "If I may, sir?"

I nodded, and Griffith swung the door shut, not letting it close all the way. From the inside of the dressing room it did indeed look like a part of the wall panel, and between myself and Griffith no mechanism for opening the door could be found. It was uncanny, really. Finally I allowed Dobbs to show us, and as soon as he pressed lightly on a diamond shape inlaid in the woodwork the door eased open.

I was delighted.

Eventually, I decided to leave the lovely books I'd found downstairs, although not on an eye level shelf. They were placed so that one could reach them easily from the corner chair, and I made a small wager with myself on when they would first be discovered by a guest. With a smile, I went in to lunch.

'

Chapter Twelve

I could not sleep. The air seemed heavy, and truth be told, it was the first night in some weeks that I'd felt so restless. Griffith had left my brandy, but it did not help, and I found myself wandering about my rooms clad only in my bedclothes.

It was, I decided, the books, and the fact that Granger was the last partner I'd had. I did not make it a practice to take many partners, but when in London, it was fairly easy for me to access certain clubs when I had a need. Out here, it was not that way at all, and I had not done anything more than ask Griffith to keep an ear out below stairs. I had no desire to take an unwilling partner, but if one could be found who was willing...

In any event, I could not sleep, and I had no one to satisfy my base hunger upon, so I settled for the far more unappealing alternative. Taking a lamp, I quickly went down the private stairs to the library, retrieved a select volume, and retreated to my room once more, feeling like I had the first time I sneaked something from my father's shelves. Of course, that had been a novel and not a highly pornographic picture book, but the feeling was the same, nonetheless.

The volume I'd blindly pulled must have been the fifth or sixth in the series. The images contained two men, and sometimes three, the subjects creating wonderfully lurid scenes. The lines were clean, and the colours used in the paintings enhanced the eroticism. It was the sketches that drew me, however, as they seemed rougher, more base. One image in particular struck me, a man bent over a table, impaled by his partner's cock. Their expressions were ecstatic, almost pained, and my own prick throbbed in sympathy.

I retreated to my bed, taking myself in hand as I stared at one image after another, not really imagining myself in the scenes but enjoying them for what they were -- intensely arousing, absolutely filthy, and wonderfully decadent. When I turned the page to see a line drawing of a man bound, gagged and being taken from behind I spilled over my hand, the image and a memory of my pet burning bright in my mind.

By the next day, I knew it had been a mistake. I ached, need raw and punishing in me. If I'd only left it alone, I would not have desired so keenly, I was sure. But it was done; I'd unlocked the box, and I needed more than my own hand. Griffith said nothing, but even as I snapped at him as he dressed me for riding, I knew I was being unreasonable. I stomped out to the stables in a foul humour, and I'm sure that the household was happy to see the back of me.

My mood was not noticeably cheered when I got there, finding that my mount was not yet ready. I was about to take the groom to task when I noticed a young man hovering in the background, as if avoiding everyone, but my eye especially. The groom went off to ready my horse, and I walked slowly toward the lad.

"What is your name?" I asked softly. He was tall and

about twenty years old, I thought, with fair hair and pale eyes. He looked almost meek, but there was something in him that drew me. Given my state, it could have been anything. I am nothing if not honest about my libido.

"Lloyd, sir," he said, not meeting my eye. Interesting. I turned from him and walked through the stable, taking note of the horses, and asking questions of him, forcing him to keep pace. It wasn't until I stopped suddenly to avoid stepping in a puddle that I realised Lloyd was following so closely. He brushed against me, moving quickly to avoid knocking me over, but it was enough.

I looked at him, and he finally, cheeks flaming, met my eyes. I raked my eyes over him, taking in his lithe form and the hard prick pushing at his trousers and said, "Come with me."

I knew not where to go, only that I had to. My breath was already short, and my stride was not easy as I walked Lloyd out of the stable and around to a shed. He wasted no time at all in following, and I could feel the heat from his body as I practically flung the door open.

"Sir," he breathed as I pulled him to me. And then there was nothing more to say as we moved together, inelegantly and without rhythm, just trying to bare skin to shaking hands as quickly as possible.

There was no time for anything, no time to strip, no time to explore. Lloyd, no doubt, was not prepared as Granger had been, and I had no desire to hurt him. I simply needed release, and he seemed more than willing to help. Very willing to help, in point of fact, sinking to his knees and opening my trousers with rough fingers. I felt his warm breath on me and sighed in anticipation. It was not exactly what I wanted, but it was far more than I had been expecting.

He caressed me, calloused skin making my thighs twitch, my prick jump. "Hurry," I whispered. "Oh, God, hurry."

His mouth slid over me, and I moaned, already wanting to push deeper, wanting to thrust and rut and simply use him, take his mouth until I spilled. I did not; I let him set the pace, taking as much of me as he could, his fingers dancing over my balls and my arse, learning the feel of me.

He was good at this, his mouth a tight seal over the head of my cock, his tongue playing over me again and again. I stifled another moan as he swept over the crown, my balls pulling up far too soon.

"Sir!" a voice called from the stables. "Mr. Munrow? Sir! The Duke has arrived!"

We froze.

The door was open, and there was no help for it. With a groan of frustration, I pulled away from the lad and refastened my clothes. The Duke had not been expected, and I had very little hope that he was going to provide me any happiness whatsoever.

Chapter Thirteen

By the time I had more or less stormed into the house, Dobbs had seen the Duke to the drawing room and had arranged for a light meal to be conjured from the kitchen. I fairly flew through the entry, heading for the staircase, anger and denied release making my movements swift and jerky. Over my shoulder, I ordered Dobbs to see to the Duke and to tell him I would be a few moments.

When I got to my room, Griffith was already there, my clothes laid out. I sat on a chair, letting him pull my boots off, swearing a blue streak. If nothing else, my need to change had managed to save me from spouting those same words at the Duke. Griffith, however, seemed unimpressed. I informed him that there was a small treasure working in the stable and asked him to see that Lloyd was moved to the house, if he wished it. Griffith merely rolled his eyes and nodded.

Dressed and somewhat calmer, I made my way down the stairs and into the drawing room. "Your Grace," I said as I walked in, "I apologise for the delay. I was about to go riding."

The Duke was standing by the window, turning to

face me as I approached. "Of course," he said smoothly. "I hope I haven't inconvenienced you unduly."

I thought of Lloyd on his knees, his mouth around my prick, and said, "Not at all. Please, have some more tea?"

He declined, and I dismissed Dobbs with a nod, watching as he pulled the doors closed behind him.

"I'll get to the point, Munrow," the Duke said, his voice suddenly firm. I looked at him with a shade of apprehension. He stood before me, his shoulders squared, his entire countenance fit for battle. I was suddenly overcome with a feeling of dread, the apprehension growing exponentially as we moved to sit in chairs placed across from one another. He moved stiffly, I noted, and eased himself down as if he feared he might break a bone or unsettle his body if he moved too quickly.

I said nothing, although I noted that he took the chair backing the window, making him appear dark and sinister. It was an obvious, and effective, means of intimidating me.

"Speak, Your Grace," I said, keeping my voice steady and low even as my gut twisted.

"I have a sister-in-law," he stated. "You shall marry her."

I knew, of course, of the sister-in-law. The Lady Julia had been married to the Duke's younger brother, who had passed away almost three years past.

"And why would I do that?" I asked, sounding as bored as I could manage.

The Duke smiled at me, a twist of his lips that did nothing to set me at ease. "Money, of course. You have the means to keep her," he said. "I do not."

I stared at him for a moment. "You wish me to accept financial responsibility for your family member?" I shook my head. "I am not so kind a man as that, Your Grace."

He inclined his head. "Nevertheless, you shall. To speak to the truth, I am dying. I would provide for her as best I can. You, my dear Munrow, will do that quite nicely, I think. Barrett, if he had been in his right mind, would have been better, but as he's obviously taken leave of his senses, as well as his home, it is up to you."

I thought for a moment, knowing that if he was intimating that he was broke, he must be very sure that I would acquiesce to his demand. "When will you die?" I asked mildly.

"I am unsure. A few months at most. Certainly by Christmas." He did not sound overly upset about the notion, although his eyes betrayed him.

"And your house, your lands? Pray, why can you no longer afford to keep one woman in comfort?" Yes, it was cruel, but the man was about to force me into a marriage. I would not make it easy on him.

"They shall stay in the family. Julia and Robert produced a son; he will inherit the holdings along with the title. But there is no money to manage the holdings and none to be spared. It seems that my father made a few ill-advised decisions, and I've been trying to right them. Time runs out, however. You, on the other hand, have no title but a great deal of wealth. Langton will do well to inherit from us both."

I snorted, my teacup rattling in the saucer. "You have yet to tell me why I should do this at your command. To come here and tell me that I will do this, not even to phrase it as a -- "

"You will do so because if you don't, I shall ruin you," he interrupted. "I have no time for games or negotiations, Munrow. To be blunt, I can and will destroy you if you do not agree, today, to take Julia." His voice was harsh and rasping, emotion or malady making him sound very sure of his words.

I sat as still as I could, not wishing to fidget, not wishing to show any sign of weakening. I could not, however, hide my interest in this hold he felt he had over me. I said nothing, waiting to hear the rest.

"Barrett," he said slowly, "was much better at covering his tracks than you are. If I had followed the right names at the right time, you would not even be here, and he would be married to Julia instead of gadding off... wherever he is. But you? You were far more indiscreet, my dear Munrow. I had only to visit a few gentlemen in London, ask the right questions of the right men, and it was all laid out for me. One sordid story after another."

He did not look at me; instead he focused upon his teacup, spinning it slowly in his hands. "Oh, the stories I was told, Munrow. A Mr. Quigg was most complimentary, you'll be pleased to know. As was Sir George. In fact, aside from the disgusting and illegal nature of your activities, I have it on high authority that you are quite good at what you do."

His eyes suddenly met mine, black with rage and disgust. "Binding. Flogging. Voyeurism. Fellatio." His voice cracked, the volume rising as he listed the acts, until he'd reached the crescendo. "Sodomy. Trust me, Munrow. I can and will ruin you. I have evidence and written testimony enough that I could have you sentenced to ten years hard labour. But you know as well as I do that I wouldn't even have to do that. A well-placed rumour, one letter in the wrong hands, and your life would be over. The alternative? To marry a perfectly nice woman who already has a son, and never see her if you don't wish to."

I could scarcely breathe. I could not think; I could not feel. Everything laid upon me had finally become so heavy that I could not bear the weight. I rose on shaking legs and crossed to the sideboard, pouring from a random decanter and drinking without knowing what or how much.

"Think, Munrow," he said quietly. "A sensible marriage, your freedom... you will have it all. Aside from the one night to consummate the relationship, you will be able to do whatever you wish. It's really very simple."

My hand shook. "No," I whispered.

"Yes."

There was silence for a long moment, perhaps even minutes while I attempted to calm myself and school my thoughts. "I... I cannot suddenly take a wife," I said slowly. "It would arouse gossip to the degree that I would not be safe, and it would be for naught. I would still be ruined, and your nephew would be heir to two ruined legacies."

The Duke seemed to think about that. "By the end of summer," he said.

I laughed, the sound hysterical and brittle in my own ears. "And that's it? I spend the next few months courting your sister-in-law, with the governess and babe in tow, and then there's a wedding?" God, it sounded perfectly horrid, and I could feel my body rebel at the thought.

His Grace, to my shock, laughed softly, the tone not in the least mocking. "There is no governess, and the babe is almost nineteen. You'll have to come up with your own chaperone."

I seized upon the opening as soon as I saw it. "Wait. You and I both know that everyone will see this for what it is. My attaining an heir. Why then should I court the lady, if it is the son who is the crux of the matter?"

He rose and leaned on the back of the chair. "Meaning it would make more sense for you to be seen getting to know the boy, confirming if he -- and not his mother -- is suitable. That would be acceptable, I think."

I did not press. I was near to avoiding a three-month

purgatory before hell settled about my shoulders and I did not wish to chance the Duke become enraged with me.

He made his way to the sideboard, and I poured him a cognac, waiting while his brow furrowed and his eyes darted about the room. He sipped. I sipped another drink. Neither of us spoke.

When the Duke's glass was empty, he placed it carefully on the tray and turned to me. "Langton shall come here for the summer. You will treat him well. Come September, you shall marry Julia. I will destroy all documents and indications of your past. What you do after you take Julia is up to you, although I advise you not to embarrass her."

I raised an eyebrow. "You will send your nephew to me? Me? How did you put it? Flogging, fellatio, sod -- "

"If he so much as hints that you've been inappropriate with him, I'll kill you," the Duke said in a low voice. I looked once in his eyes before I had to turn my head. There was murder there, without doubt. "If you touch him, I will know. If you talk to him of such things, I will know. And you will die. Is that understood?"

"Yes, Your Grace," I said automatically.

"Very well. There is no need to sign anything," he said, his tone once more normal as he stalked towards the door. He paused and looked at me, his smile feral. "We'll call it a gentleman's agreement, shall we? Langton will arrive within the week." He opened the door and left.

I stood rooted to the spot until I heard Dobbs wishing the Duke a good day and the front door closing. Then I flung the tray holding our empty glasses to the floor, the sound shocking and right as glass shattered.

Rage welled in me. There really was only one thing left for me to do, only one appropriate revenge. I would seduce the boy so thoroughly that he would beg for me, and then I would flaunt it before His Grace as he died.

Chapter Fourteen

The house was in an uproar. When I informed Dobbs that we were to have a guest for the summer he accepted the news with his usual aplomb, and Griffith later told me that he had simply gone below stairs and informed Mrs. Banks of the impending arrival. Dobbs and Mrs. Banks had sprung into action without so much as a blink of the eye, but the rest of the staff was a great deal more vocal.

Most were speculating on why I had suddenly taken it into my head to invite the young man to stay for so long, and the rumours were fairly -- and expectedly -- bawdy. Some saw the situation for what it was meant to be, assuming I was going to be judging the boy as a suitable heir. Others were simply dismayed at the new workload.

We were not sure which day the Duke's nephew would arrive, so things moved rather rapidly. Mrs. Banks and I had a conversation in which it appeared that I chose which room to give the boy, even though we both knew it was really a forgone conclusion. It is entirely possible that even as we spoke about the matter the upstairs maids were airing the blue room, across the hall and down from my own.

Griffith also informed me, very matter-of-factly as he laid out my riding clothes one morning, that Henri Langton was a Viscount, no less, having inherited the title from his father, and as I had requested, the stable boy had been told that if he wished he could move to the house to train as a footman. The stable boy, it seemed, preferred the horses to the people below stairs, but sent thanks to sir for his kindness.

I accepted the thanks in person, taking young Lloyd rather hard over a bale of hay.

It was just after lunch, six days after the Duke's visit, that Griffith found me in my study and informed me that a carriage had just arrived. I had long decided to greet the Viscount in the private library, so I went there, knowing that Dobbs would see to the proper dispatch of the boy's valet. We actually knew nothing of the young man, although we expected he would bring his man. If he did not, Matheson had been decided upon as the best suited footman to take the task.

I found myself listening hard for the sounds of the door, for Dobbs' voice. My stomach was tight, and I could feel my back stiffening, anger slowly stirring as once more I realised what was being thrust upon me.

A soft knock came and Dobbs entered, bowing his head slightly to me. "Viscount Langton, sir," he said, ushering the young man in.

I rose and inclined my head. "Viscount."

"Mr. Munrow. Thank you for your kind invitation. My uncle sends his greetings."

I nodded, and we stood there, studying each other. He was very fair, almost pale. His hair was blond, a light golden frame around a narrow face with high cheekbones and a straight nose. His lips were a little thin, perhaps, but his eyes made up for their lack of fullness, being a deep blue that drew one's attention and held it. Tall, but not gangly for all his youth, Langton seemed to be well aware of the picture he made, standing straight and letting me take his measure.

Or perhaps he was simply terrified of being pushed onto a stranger for a summer.

"Welcome to Red Oak Hall," I said. "Would you care for tea? Or perhaps something cool to drink?"

"No, thank you, Mr. Munrow," he said, finally taking his eyes off me and glancing around the room.

"Please," I said, sitting once more. "We are to spend a great deal of time together, Viscount. I suggest we disregard the titles, if you don't mind."

His eyes snapped back to me, and he took the other chair, looking wary. Not a stupid lad, this. "Certainly. You may call me Langton."

I smiled at him as warmly as I could. "And I am Munrow. I know it is highly irregular, but so is this entire situation, don't you agree?"

I saw his mouth twitch, and he nodded slowly. No, not a fool. He knew exactly why he was in my home. "It is," he agreed. "My uncle thinks it best, however. I fail to see, unfortunately, what you have to gain from this."

I quirked an eyebrow at him. "For now, let us just say that I seek to... know you. Perhaps when we have spent some time together we can discuss that."

He nodded once more. "Certainly. I look forward to spending time here, in truth. It's a wonderful building, and I hear that the lands are lovely. I assume we'll be riding, at some point?"

"Of course," I said easily. "We could go tomorrow, if you wish. For now, however, I'll have Dobbs show you to your rooms, and you can rest before dinner. After we dine, I suggest we spend the evening in the library, and we can talk some more then."

Langton rose with me and smiled. "I'll see you at dinner," he said softly, ducking his head in such a manner that I was quite taken by surprise. He was attractive, yes, but in that one movement, he became something more. I had not expected to see hints of something I could like.

The idea disquieted me, and I firmly pushed it aside. I had Dobbs show Langton upstairs, and I retreated once more to the private library to begin my plans. I did not have much time, really, and I would need to know certain things.

Already tentatively settling on a course of action, I called for Griffith. I needed gossip.

Chapter Fifteen

W hat are they saying?" I asked while Griffith helped me dress for dinner.

He tugged at my waistcoat and frowned, looking at my cufflinks. "Mmm? Oh. Well, he didn't bring a man, so information is scarce. Mary's sister knows a girl who is in service with the Lady Julia, so all that we really know is that he's quiet, keeps to himself, and has a tendency to be bookish. He does, however, have a passion for horses and likes to be out of doors."

"That is all?" I pressed. Really, I needed more than that to get any further.

"That is all about the Viscount, yes. Would you prefer the silver links, sir?"

I nodded absently and held out my wrists. "What else are they talking about?"

"Matheson is having a mild case of nerves, unsure if he is ready to act as valet. I've spoken to him about it. Dobbs and Mrs. Banks are mostly treating the entire situation as if the Viscount is simply a long-term guest. The maids are worried because they know nothing of the lady, and they don't know what will happen to them if there is suddenly a lady of the house so soon after changing masters. The men... well, they're just watching and laying odds, as usual."

"And what are the odds?" I asked as he switched my cufflinks to the silver.

"Currently four to one that you send him home after a month. Ten to one that he stays all summer. Oh, and if I may, I suggest you take a sudden interest in one of the maids. The odds on that are getting quite out of hand."

"I beg your pardon?" I said.

"I said, I suggest -- "

"Yes, yes. But why?"

Griffith raised an eyebrow at me, a look entirely not suited to his face. "They're waiting, sir. They neither expect, nor want, you to attempt anything in particular, but you more or less ignore them. Below stairs is beginning to wonder about you and your... tastes. Simply remembering a name at this point would do you good."

I tried in vain to remember a name. "Molly," I said triumphantly. "Brown hair, brown eyes, freckles. She's in the parlour most mornings."

"Very good, sir," Griffith said sardonically.

I refrained from cuffing him.

Dressed, I headed for the door. "I'm thinking about inviting some people for a weekend. In your opinion, is downstairs ready for that yet?"

"Yes, sir. May I ask who? Or how many?"

"About eight, I think. Friday to Sunday, a week from now -- London people. I'll speak to Mrs. Banks in the morning." Then I left, smiling at the look on Griffith's face. Yes, the London people would do nicely, if I led Langton up to it well enough.

Over dinner, I was the very soul of courtesy, asking Langton about his journey and schooling, being very careful not to press and to keep the conversation casual.

He asked a few polite questions about the Hall and its grounds, once more mentioning that he was looking forward to riding the next day. I asked him about Matheson, and he assured me that the arrangement was satisfactory and thanked me for seeing to it.

It was dull and far less interesting than I had wanted to make it, but for my initial plan to work I could not seem too eager. Langton was very well-spoken and did not seem to possess the superior attitude I'd been expecting. I was well used to the snipes and jabs that peers directed to those without title, but perhaps the lad was simply too young to have started the practice, or maybe being the owner of an estate such as Red Oak conferred me some sort of immunity. It was also possible that Langton simply possessed good manners.

After dinner, I showed Langton about the lower level of the Hall, taking him through the rooms one by one and letting him wander about. He seemed to like the drawing room, saying it was comfortable and that the view of the lawns was pleasant. He said almost nothing through the morning room and parlour, although he did look impressed by the sheer size of the ballroom. It was not until I showed him into the library that he became animated.

He walked directly to a shelf, seemingly at random, and began to read titles one after another as his hands skipped over the spines. "This is wonderful," he said softly. He pulled down a large atlas and leafed through it, then moved on to the classics, and then to a shelf of mathematics and biology. "If you ever find me missing," he said with a smile, "I suspect you should look here."

I smiled, my breath suddenly short. In the half-light cast by the lamps, his face open as he reached for yet another book, he was beautiful.

I cleared my throat. "Is there a subject you favour?" I

asked, still standing just inside the door.

He glanced back at me, his smile still in place as his hair fell across his brow. "Art, French poetry... I enjoy rereading classics, however I suspect that I could happily find volumes here that I've not yet read." He turned and wandered once more, actually gasping aloud as he found an illuminated copy of a play he'd just finished. He said that the art was lovely and only added to the text.

I cannot even say what the play was, or by whom it was written. I was far too busy studying the way he moved, the way the light played over his hair and brought out flashes of gold from the yellow. With an effort, I brought my mind back from dangerous places and firmly reined myself in. To allow myself indulgences, even in my imagination, was to risk everything, so I made my way to the door.

"There is paper in the desk," I told him, "and, please, feel free to use this room as you like. I'm going to retire early, I think, but please, make yourself at home, Langton."

He smiled at me again and said thank you, but he returned the current book to its shelf and indicated that he would also retire to his room.

I held out a hand, forestalling him. "Please," I repeated. "We are to be together for many weeks; you needn't go simply because I do."

Langton looked at the floor for a moment and then at me, shaking his head. "I would rest before morning," he said carefully. "The trip was long, and I wish to be fresh for tomorrow."

There was little point in arguing, so I demurred. "Of course. We'll breakfast in the drawing room, then, and plan our ride. Goodnight, Langton."

He inclined his head politely. "Good evening, Munrow."

Chapter Sixteen

We rode most of the morning, through the meadows and along the paths through the stand of trees, around the pond and back again. Langton was very much an accomplished horseman, having ridden point-to-point at school as well as doing the usual amount of riding for pleasure. He'd spent most of his years in London, but both his father and later his uncle had pressed him to ride as much as he could.

We spoke a little, but for the most part, we just rode, both of us making ourselves familiar with the landscape. I spotted fish in the pond and found myself wondering how often it was stocked, or if was stocked at all. The footbridge, I also noted, was in need of repair.

When we returned to the house we took our luncheon, and I excused myself to the private library and summoned Mrs. Banks and Dobbs. Within an hour, I had plans made for the weekend party and had the invitations written. Mrs. Banks was set to arranging rooms and speaking to Cook about meals, and Dobbs was preparing a footman to go to London to deliver the invitations.

It was set. I had a bare week to begin. There really

were only one or two small things I wished to do, a couple of seeds to sow in the lad's mind. The party would, hopefully, cause a seed to sprout, and then there were weeks of coaxing the boy to reach for the sun and to bloom.

I avoided him for the rest of the day, making myself busy and letting him settle in as best he pleased. He spent most of the day wandering in the formal garden with a book in hand, although I did see him on the porch for a few moments, looking out toward the pond. In that bare minute or two, I could see a certain sadness in his eyes, and it occurred to me that he was as much a prisoner here as I was. More so, possibly, for he had been given no choice, simply ordered to present himself.

Mind, I had no choice either. The Duke had removed my choices by threat, and in doing so had taken his own risks. It never occurred to me that he hadn't thought that I would attempt to molest the boy in some way. The threat to my life was sincere, and I knew that he would happily kill me if some harm came to his nephew.

However, even given all that he knew and hated about me, the Duke had still sent Langton to me. The Duke did not trust me. He did not respect my word. He wanted the gift that Barrett had bestowed, and he was prepared to risk even Langton to secure it.

It made little sense. If he wanted the money for Langton, why risk the boy? It occurred to me that the Duke's disease might have reached his mind, that he was seeing only the end result he sought. It almost made me hope that it was so, that it wasn't because His Grace cared so little for Langton that he would risk him.

After watching Langton for only a moment, I backed away, leaving him to his thoughts.

Chapter Seventeen

The week passed relatively smoothly. I gradually spent more time with Langton, playing the host and not pressing him into any intimate conversation. We spoke of books, and of politics, of school and travel, and of London. We discovered a circle of people whom we both knew in passing and traded a little bit of information concerning Mr. Parsons and his business dealing with the Duke. Langton slyly told me that the Duke had been certain he'd gotten the best of Mr. Parsons, and to be honest, I would have agreed easily if it were not for the look in Langton's eyes. When Langton finally told me at great length how Mr. Parsons had cleverly -- and honestly -- bested the Duke, I was thrilled. Langton, it appeared, was just as happy as I was to know that it was possible to fool the Duke by telling the strict truth.

On the Wednesday evening before my guests were due to arrive, Langton and I were ensconced in the library, lost in our separate worlds, which were defined by the words on our pages. I was sitting in my favourite chair off to the side of the desk with a glass of cognac in hand and one of the volumes about the Jacobite Rebellion in the other. I was unsure what Langton was reading, but he was curled in another chair, quite lost in the final few pages of a large book.

The quiet of the evening was most pleasant, and the alcohol in my drink lent itself well to my rather mellow mood. Langton and I had spent the day apart, and I found that sitting as we were, simply being quiet in the same room, was comfortable. I turned a page and glanced at the boy, smiling at how intently he was reading, the light from the lamp over his shoulder making his eyes dark and hidden. He worried at his lower lip with his teeth as he read, and it was becoming full and red, swollen from his biting.

It was not easy to tear my eyes away. Instead, in fear of being caught watching him, I glanced away a little, taking in the light and the corner of the desk nearest him. As I did so, I happened to notice the section of black near his chair; the books I'd found and left for a hapless guest to find in turn. The books I had more than once taken to my bedchamber to enjoy. My prick twitched, having him so near to the images, so near to me.

I returned to my book, the printed words now mere lines and squiggles as I stole glances at Langton. He was very near to the end of his book, still lost in its pages, and he seemed not to notice me peering at him over the edge of my own volume. I sipped my drink and occasionally remembered to glance at the words before me, turning the pages at intervals set by the turning of his own.

When he closed his book and sighed, I smiled at him and asked, "Did you enjoy it?"

"Yes, thank you," he replied with his own smile. "It was very engrossing." He stood and stretched his back, groaning a little as he worked his shoulder. "Weighty, however."

"Would you care for a drink?" I offered, gesturing to

the tray on the desk.

"Thank you." He poured himself a glass of port and held up the cognac. "Would you like a little more?"

I held out my glass and watched as he poured. "Feel free to help yourself to another book," I offered. "There are certainly enough of them."

He smiled brightly but said nothing, returning to his chair. I looked at the book in my lap and once more created the illusion of being lost in Scottish history, flicking my glance to him every so often.

Langton seemed relaxed, happy enough to simply sit and enjoy the aftermath of finishing his book, but I suspected that would not last for very long. He had only been in the Hall for a week, and I was already aware of a certain tendency on his part to reach for whatever printed matter presented itself. I watched to see what he would do, not quite daring to hope that he would simply reach out and select one of the volumes I most wanted him to see. It would be pure luck if he did, and not part of my plan.

Oh, the books were part of my plan, of course, but not really this evening. No, my intent had been to start Langton's true education on the weekend, and later manipulate his discovery of the books. I was not, however, about to deny him if he happened upon them sooner.

Luck would have always played a certain part with the books; I could not very well set out the first three volumes -- those which had more tame images -- and then produce the rest. For Langton to remain free of suspicion, all seven books would have to be present as a set when he found them. If, however, he picked up the more explicit volumes first, I feared the shock would only add to the effort I would have to expend to achieve the desired result.

I forced myself to spend ever longer moments focused

on the book in my hand, only glancing at Langton fleetingly. He settled in the chair, long legs stretched out before him and a contented look upon his face as he looked around him. A little while later the look was still content, but he was shifting slightly, his fingers tapping at his glass as his initial lassitude wore away. Within five minutes of fetching the drink, he was looking towards the shelves with speculation in his eye, clearly planning his next foray.

I could not help but smile, so like a cat was he. Curious, stalking his prey, but not yet ready to stir himself to get it.

I was staring at a picture of Bonny Prince Charlie in my book when I caught movement out of the corner of my eye. Langton was turning in his chair, his arm reaching to the shelf beside him. The side away from the books I so wanted him to find. With a silent sigh of disappointment, I turned a page and carried on through the Uprising.

I glanced again and watched as Langton pulled a random book free from the shelf and then returned it. He moved as if to look at me, and my eyes darted back to my page. I looked at the words before me for a very long time, debating how much supposed interest I should feign and at what point it would be considered that I was ignoring my guest in a manner bordering upon rude.

Thus I was not prepared for the quiet gasp from Langton, the sound muffled and choked.

I glanced up quickly, and then back down at my book, not wishing him to know I had heard him. It was difficult in the extreme to stifle my own reaction, however.

Langton sat in the chair, his face suddenly flushed and his eyes wide as he stared at the book in his hand. I had not been able to look for long enough to ascertain which volume he held, only that it was bound in black and had no title. Even in the brief moment I had watched him, his face had begun to pale again, and he moved to sit up straighter, the book already closing.

It has always been my assertion that I am a lucky person.

I willed my breathing to remain calm as I sat waiting for a sound, a movement, anything that would legitimately bring my attention to him. In a few seconds I heard him at the shelves, one book put away, another drawn out. I looked up as he returned to his chair. "Did you find something interesting?" I asked in all innocence.

His eyes flashed to me, and I could see his cheeks pink once more. "Art," he said softly. "Something pleasant to study before I retire for the night."

I smiled and nodded and began to count the moments before I politely retired myself.

Not surprisingly, Langton said his goodnights early, and I had to restrain myself from reminding him that he had the run of the house and if, perhaps, he felt the need to return to the library in the dead of night to peruse a book or two it was perfectly acceptable.

But restrain myself I did. In fact, I even managed to force myself to remain in the library for almost an hour after he had left, for no other reason than to create the illusion that I was completely unassuming and simply going about my evening. However, when I returned to my rooms I left the outer door open so that I would be able to hear any movement from the hallway, and as soon as Griffith was dismissed, I put out all my lamps and sat, brandy in hand, watching the hallway.

Foolish, I know, and more than likely juvenile, but I had to know if he would venture down to take another look at the book he'd seen. I had to know if he was disgusted, piqued, or... merely too curious for his own safety.

I was a little chilly, sitting in the dark in only my dressing gown, but I did not have to sit for very long. It was perhaps a few minutes until midnight when soft steps in the hallway alerted me, and I looked up to see Langton pass my door, a lamp in hand. He also was clad in a dressing gown, his feet bare. As he turned the corner and headed towards the main staircase, I moved swiftly and quietly through my bedchamber, into the dressing room, and down the private staircase, praying that I would arrive at the library before he did.

As it happened, Langton had moved swiftly, and I had barely opened the lower door a crack when light spilled into the room, and he walked to the chair he had occupied earlier. I was hopeful that the dim light would not let him notice that the cabinet was open, and I sat on the lower stair, trying to find the best angle to see him.

I found I was holding my breath. I could see the chair and the shelf, but the desk was positioned so that if Langton sat down, I would not be able to see his lower body. At first Langton put his lamp on the desk, which further obscured my view, and I wished to curse aloud, for when he did so, I could see neither the books nor the top of the chair.

But then Langton did a curious thing. Before even going to the shelves, he shoved the chair from where it sat farther into the room, turning it slightly so the back was to the room and it faced, more or less, the far corner, so that it neatly faced the cabinet. It took me a moment to realise that even though I now had a very good view of him, or would when he sat down, he now also would be in a good position to see that the cabinet was ajar.

I eased back a little, fearing that if he lit the large lamp I would be seen, but instead he simply placed his own lamp on a small table near the chair. He then paused, as if waiting for something, or perhaps listening for some small sound that would alert him to someone's presence. Apparently reassured, Langton moved to the shelf.

I do not know which of the seven volumes he had seen earlier that night, but as I sat in the darkened stairway, he pulled the third volume out, and as if with an afterthought, also brought the second.

I was pleased. The two volumes together contained mainly images of nude men, alone and in couples, and were somewhat sexual. They lacked the artistic feel of the first volume but contained little of the stark and intense acts depicted in the later volumes. Men having sex, certainly, but nothing of pain or the more elaborate games.

I sat frozen in place as Langton settled in the chair. His colour was already high, and he shifted awkwardly for a moment before he opened the topmost book on his lap. By this time I had lost track of which was which, and to be honest, I no longer cared. It was Langton who interested me, not the pages before him.

He flipped a couple of pages quickly, too fast for my liking; it was as if he was afraid of being caught. I suppose that was entirely likely, but I was almost impatient, waiting for him to react. His fingers slowed as he turned page after page, his eyes becoming rounder and his cheeks flushed. He moved more and more frequently, unable to be still as he stared.

Slower, he studied what was before him, and I found myself almost dizzy; I believe that we were both holding our breath. When he released his with a soft moan, I exhaled, relief and arousal coursing through my body.

Langton shifted again, his breath coming faster as he turned the page again, and I waited, my prick filling as I watched him. Two more pages turned, and he moaned again, saying something under his breath.

Speaking aloud seemed to break the spell over him for a moment, and he stood to look around the room, double-checking that he was alone. As he did, I could see the line of his dressing gown disturbed by his arousal, and my own shaft jerked in response. I fumbled with my robe, quietly slipping my hand around myself. When Langton sat down again, apparently satisfied that he was alone, he opened the other volume and froze.

"Oh, Lord," he said quietly. Volume three, I assumed.

We sat for some time, me silent in the dark, my hand tight around my prick, and him turning pages slower and slower as his breathing increased. It was interminable, perhaps half an hour like that, me listening to his breath and the occasional gasp, Langton turning pages and shifting in his seat.

I rested my head against the wall, startled at how cool it felt. I realised suddenly that a light sweat had broken out on my body, that I was almost fevered. I swallowed thickly just as Langton moaned and closed the book.

I was ready for him to return the books, to leave and go back to his room. I was prepared to simply go up my stairs and masturbate in my bed, thinking about him. I was not expecting him to give in to his own needs. I was not prepared for him to lean back on the chair, books carefully laid on the floor, and to begin to fondle himself through his clothes.

I had to bite my lip to keep from making a sound as Langton's eyes drifted closed and he licked his lips, his hand rubbing and massaging his cock through the layers. My own breath was laboured, watching him, listening to him make desperate needy sounds and whimpers as he tugged at himself.

When he groaned and opened his robe, one hand wrapping around his shaft, I could do little but whimper myself, a short quiet sound that he missed, lost in his own pleasure. I stared. His prick was long and heavy, the crown swollen and tinged a rosy shade of red, lifting away from golden curls. He was stunningly beautiful, the lamplight carving every angle of his body for me to see. Langton stroked himself quickly, almost harshly, his hips driving upwards, the foreskin sliding easily.

I could hear him. Every sound he made, the slick sound of his hand as it picked up moisture. I could almost smell him, under the lamp oil and the scent of books and paper and leather. I wanted so badly to taste his mouth, his neck, his cock.

Langton came with a soft, long moan, spilling over his fingers in a gush, his hips still pushing even as his hand slowed. His face was glowing with sweat, his hair lying over his forehead. It wasn't until he was done that I was able to breathe, and it took all of my will to stave off my own orgasm. As he panted, still lying back in the chair, I eased myself up a stair, and then another, being careful to make no sound at all. I could no longer see him, but I could hear him moving after a moment, cleaning himself, shelving the books, putting the chair back. When the light shining through the crack in the cabinet door dimmed and then vanished, I breathed a sigh of relief and made my way quickly to my bed. Sleep eluded me for some time.

Chapter Eighteen

G ood morning, Langton," I said brightly as the boy came into the drawing room. "Did you sleep well?"

I was standing by the sideboard pouring tea into my cup. Langton looked to be a little paler than usual, his eyes distant as if he'd been lost in thought. At my words, he gave me a small smile and nodded. "Good morning, Munrow. Yes, I did, thank you." His voice was quiet and subdued, but he came to the sideboard and picked up a plate. "And you?"

"I had sweet dreams," I said, taking my tea to the window to look at the sun-drenched lawns. "I was thinking, if you're interested, we could spend the day outside. Perhaps go riding again, or walking. The gardens are waking nicely, and it might be pleasant to simply wander aimlessly around the grounds." I turned then and said, as if the thought had just occurred to me, "Unless you wish to spend the day in the library, of course. I'm sure you could find something to capture your attention."

Langton dropped the piece of toast he'd just picked up, his eyes flashing to me quickly before looking away.

"No," he said immediately. He swallowed, refusing to meet my eye for a moment, and added, "Being outdoors would be quite nice."

I smiled to myself and let the poor boy enjoy his meal.

By midday on Friday, the turmoil created below stairs in the expectation of guests had reached the point where even I could see signs of the activity. Maids hurried to and fro, arms piled high with linens and other things for the guest rooms, and as I walked past the drawing room, I could see the footmen shifting furniture about to make room for another card table. Langton had fled to the garden soon after breakfast, saying that he wished to enjoy the sun while it lasted; dark clouds were moving in over the tree line, although slowly.

I wandered about for a while, getting underfoot and in general being the annoying presence that straightened every back and sent dusters twitching over ornaments. I walked through the ballroom, noting that the chandeliers had been lowered and draped in cheesecloth then raised again; I had told Dobbs that I fully intended to wait a very long time before the room would be used again. However, as I strolled through the room towards the small annex where the musicians played for dances, I was struck by the fact that there might indeed be need of this room within a few months, if the Duke had his way.

Perhaps, though, I could escape the need for a large party. A second marriage for the lady wouldn't require an elaborate celebration, I fervently hoped. I shuddered at the thought of having so many people pretending to be happy for me; it would be a farce unlike no other.

I opened the door to the small music room and whistled, impressed by what I found. I'd not been in there before, and although the room was quite small, as I had expected, it was also full of light, as it backed onto the gardens and had wide glass doors to the edge of the patio. There were a few chairs scattered about, and a small piano, but aside from that, the room was empty. The walls were bare to better enable the sound of the music to reach into the ballroom, and there were thick draperies that would cover all the windows when music was being played.

But at that moment, it was simply a small room bathed in the heat of the sun, which was clinging as the clouds built up, and with a lovely view. I walked to the doors and pushed them open, smelled the coming rain and the blooms from the gardens. As I stepped out, I caught sight of a lone figure sitting on a bench in the distance, surrounded by the quiet beds. The flowering plants had not grown so tall as to obstruct my view, so I could easily stay out of earshot and watch Langton as he read.

I found myself smiling at the image of the fair head bent over the pages of his book, but after a moment, I realised his posture was not conducive to reading. He had a large book open on his lap; I could see the pages before him, but he was looking ahead of himself, not moving. He was clearly lost in thought.

I could only hope to the subject he was contemplating so seriously. With another smile, I returned unseen to the house and moved to the drawing room to await my guests.

As it happened, there were six gentlemen for the weekend rather than eight, as Sir Milton was ill and Mr. Abbott was off on some sort of business engagement. I was, however, delighted to greet my friends from London as they arrived full of smiles and welcoming congratulations for me.

Griffith had been unsurprised by my guest list, forewarned by my declaration that they were to be London people, and those below stairs were familiar with at least two of the men, as they had been friends of Barrett's just as I had been. We all belonged to the same club in London, and while it was unusual for us to meet away from there, it was not entirely without precedent.

After luncheon, Langton had vanished once more, either to his room or to the library, I was unsure which. I did not really expect him to join the party until just before dinner, so I put the boy from my mind and let myself simply enjoy my company as it arrived.

As all were single men, save one, it had been natural for those who resided near one another to travel together. As such, William Hastings, Christopher Truitt, and Robert Kirkland arrived en masse, making for an early start to our weekend. We had only just settled into our chairs in the drawing room and were engaging in light banter when the others arrived -- Stephen Fitzhugh and Thomas Lynch together, and the final guest, Sir Patrick Haight, just behind them.

As those of us in the room rose to greet them, there came a great clap of thunder, almost as a signal. Fitzhugh and Lynch seemed to take it as such, trading decidedly wicked looks as they came forward. "Well, Munrow," Lynch said, taking my hand and clasping my arm. "You seem to have landed in it, haven't you?"

I inclined my head, unable to deny that I had, indeed, landed in something.

We milled about for a time, talking in small clusters that shifted and moved as conversations roamed. There were two footmen pouring and serving drinks, and Dobbs had disappeared, presumably to set things to rights below stairs. Each of my guests would have come with a man, and I was quite sure that between the kitchen and assigning places to the valets, Dobbs and Mrs. Banks would run off their feet until dinner was served.

When we were more or less settled, and the footmen had been dismissed, I noticed Lynch looking about him in a rather assessing manner. I was unsurprised when he turned to me and asked, "So, when will the wolves descend upon you?"

I smiled ruefully. "In fact, they are already feasting, I fear."

This was met with amusement and sympathetic chuckles, although they all knew it was inevitable.

"And are you being devoured entirely?" Sir Patrick put in. "Or is it you who shall dine? We are given to understand there is a lamb in your midst."

Fitzhugh smiled, his teeth gleaming. "Yes, Munrow, where have you caged the lamb? Won't you let him out?"

"You would do well to let the lamb alone," I said evenly. "And I expect he'll be down in a while."

Fitzhugh feigned injury. "Under your protection, is he? What a shame." He rose and smirked at me, going to the sideboard. "I have every faith in your training, old friend."

"Speaking of training," came a soft voice beside me, "I have something of yours to return later."

I glanced at Truitt and raised an eyebrow, both at the subject and at his low tone. I could recall nothing of mine that he might have. He cast his eyes downward and looked at me through artful eyelashes. "Later," he murmured.

I nodded, curious but not willing to quiz him on the matter, as he so plainly wanted it kept between us. The interruption had served me well, however, diverting the subject from Langton directly and onto other related matters.

"His uncle came to see me, you know," Hastings said, joining the conversation.

I sighed. "And what was His Grace searching for?"

Hastings shrugged. "The usual. I suspect he had enough, but I felt lucky that he had nothing to use in order to pry more from me. I sent him away without satisfaction."

"As did I," Kirkland put in. "He did, however, seem very sure of himself. With me, it was all about the circle of friends I keep and looking for hints about matters I preferred not to discuss. It was a warning, and when I failed to take it to heart, he left, angry. I got the feeling that if anyone had actually mentioned me by name he would have happily used that to get whatever he could about you, Munrow."

I nodded. "Of course. He told me that he'd had tales of me from Sir George and Quigg. Blackmail in order to blackmail. However, he may have a long list of names; it would serve you all well to protect yourselves."

There was a great deal of muttering and discussion of how Quigg fit into our particular circle; neither Sir George or Quigg were members of our club, a fact which was met with some small relief. Kirkland, an Earl, knew Sir George from other social ties but had entertained no notion of the man's tastes.

"I thought you kept mainly to the club, or to your pet there," Hastings said, gesturing to Truitt.

I shrugged. "I do. Or rather, I have for the past year and a half. Still, it would be wise for you each to take care."

"Or we could just avoid your mistakes," Fitzhugh said sourly. "Like getting saddled with a house that needs an heir."

Three voices protested -- those of the Earl and the

knight, who were indeed feeling the same pressure, and that of Lynch who was actually married in name if not deed. Fitzhugh waved them off with a tight smile. "Yes, yes. I know. Withdrawn. In any event, we are here, we shall spend our time out of that blasted rain, and I suspect we shall manage to get roundly drunk on this rather fine liquor. The rest of the world be damned, until Monday, anyway."

Laughing, we raised our glasses and drank.

As I had suspected, Langton did not make his appearance until an hour before dinner, just as the others were beginning to discuss going up to dress. The first that I knew of his presence was a sharply indrawn breath beside me. I looked to Truitt and raised an eyebrow. "Just admiring the lamb," he said quietly.

I looked up and barely managed to keep my own breath from catching. Langton stood in the doorway, looking vaguely uncomfortable, as if he was unsure of his welcome. He had not yet dressed for dinner, so I knew that this was simply a short visit so introductions could be made before we all retired to our rooms. His hair was slightly mussed, as if he'd been running his hands through it, and his eyes darted about the room from man to man.

All of whom were slowly turning to look at him.

I stood to rescue him. "Viscount. Please, come in." My words seemed to break a sort of spell and the others arose as well, the peers stepping forward to be introduced.

Langton seemed to relax once the introductions were made, his upbringing allowing him to easily remember the names and ranks of those to whom he was presented. He made small talk well and answered questions about his mother and uncle with natural grace and aplomb. The gentlemen, for the most part, minded their own manners, although I did see one or two glances I was not supposed to. Hungry, speculative looks that made me smile but also gave me a certain amount of hope for my overall plans.

Within ten minutes or so, we broke up and, as a fractured group, made our way upstairs with Dobbs leading everyone to their rooms in the east wing of the second floor. I met Griffith in my rooms and began the task of dressing for dinner, more or less content with the weekend's start.

Griffith was thoughtful as he helped me dress, and distracted. Twice I had to prompt him for things, and finally I simply sat on the chair, my collar still undone and my cuffs loose. "What is it?" I asked, reaching for my water glass.

He looked at me, startled for a moment, then his face settled into its usual sardonic planes. "Well, there is little need for you to remember the maids' names now, sir. It took less than twenty minutes of having Mr. Kirkland and Mr. Fitzhugh below stairs for everyone to take the full measure of you."

I snorted. By the names, I knew he meant their valets -- below stairs the men were known by their masters' names. And those two in particular would have plenty about which to talk. "What did they say?" I asked.

Griffith looked annoyed. "To our staff, nothing. They were being indiscreet among themselves as they polished shoes and were overheard. Does it matter? If it helps, they said nothing about you, but the association was made. And everyone knew, more or less, about the Earl."

"It was bound to happen," I said. "See if you can limit the damage, however. I don't want the staff to walk out on me. We have a lot of floors to polish here, Griffith."

"Yes, sir. Indeed."

With that more or less settled, Griffith attended to my cuffs and collar, and I dismissed him. I went to relax in my small sitting room, enjoying a few moments of quiet before dinner, and I had just settled into a chair with a fresh glass of water when there was a soft knock. Thinking it might be Langton, I bade the body to enter, smiling when Truitt came in.

"Truitt," I said, standing up. "It's good to see you. Truly." And it was. He looked wonderful, though a little leaner than when I saw him last. He was still tall and young and beautiful, though, and his eyes were warm with affection.

"I'm glad you think so, Ned," he said softly, walking towards me. "It's been a long time."

"Three months," I protested.

"Five."

"Really?" I was surprised, but when I looked back over the spring, I could see he was right. "Oh, I am sorry. I didn't mean to neglect you, pet."

Truitt shrugged and smiled at me. "My training was done," he said simply. "I was pleased to receive your invitation, however."

"Were you?" I asked, stepping a little closer to him, one hand reaching for his hip. "You do know that things are different?" I whispered in his ear, fairly derailed by the heat from his body.

"Of course. But I was still pleased. And I'm very pleased at this particular moment." He turned his head. and our lips brushed together almost chastely. "I've missed your touch, Ned."

I kissed him again, careful not to crush our clothes. He tasted wonderful, clean and light with a hint of cognac on his breath. "You said that you had something of mine?" I asked, one hand drifting down his back.

He grinned then and backed away a little so I could see his hands. The right, which he'd held loosely by his side, held a short black crop. "I wasn't sure if you wanted it back or not."

I laughed. "I had no idea I'd even forgotten it," I said, taking the crop. "You've had it all this time?"

"You haven't needed it all this time?" he countered.

I shook my head. "No, in fact. I haven't." I pulled him to me again, not so careful of our clothes, and kissed him deeply, felt his prick swell against my thigh. "I have missed you, pet," I purred when I released him.

"How much?" he teased.

I grabbed his hand and drew it to my fly. "This much."

He moaned, when it should have been me, and the dinner bell sounded. I stepped back and winked at him. "Oh, dear. Time to go. Straighten your waistcoat and let's go down, yes?"

He gave me a rueful glance and did so. "You might need the crop yet," he muttered. "Your lamb is fair and would take the marks well."

I laughed again. "That is to your taste more than mine." When Truitt was set to rights, I leant close and kissed him once more, almost but not quite chastely. "I hope you enjoy your stay at Red Oak Hall," I whispered.

"As do I."

It was not until we turned to leave the room that I realised the door was open. With a smile, I watched Langton's back as he walked down the hall and wondered just what he had seen and how much he'd heard.

Chapter Nineteen

Dinner passed more or less peacefully, with everyone happy enough to make small talk about assorted matters that could easily be discussed by all. This might sound like an easy task; however, when one is at a table with three peers and four gentlemen, there are topics best avoided. Politics, which one could rightfully assume would be a point of interest to us all, were passed over entirely; opinions on the Crown and the government in general tend to make digestion much more of a chore than it should be.

Also, the presence of Langton and the footmen who tended to us made the more interesting exchanges of information about mutual acquaintances not fit conversation. Mind, my sudden rise in position still remained one of the more pressing topics at various places in London, and my guests were able to tell me a few innocuous stories of assorted reactions.

Naturally enough, talk about my new status once more brought attention to Langton; it was patently obvious why he had been invited to stay -- even if one discounted the manner in which the Duke had approached my friends.

Everyone who was paying the slightest bit of attention would know that Langton was more or less on trial as my heir.

"So, Viscount," Hastings said as we finished the soup, "how are you finding your stay here at Red Oak Hall? I trust that you and Munrow are managing to find your way about the place?"

Langton, who was seated at my right, smiled politely and said, "I have found both the stables and the library, Mr. Hastings, although I admit that is simply indulgence on my part."

"It's early yet," I put in. "Langton has been here for less than a fortnight, and, to be fair, I myself am still discovering rooms."

This earned a little laughter, and when Langton raised an inquisitive eyebrow I told him -- them -- about the music room I'd found that morning.

"Did it have a piano?" Langton asked, his tone almost eager.

"Yes. Do you play?" I admit that the thought of Langton spending his afternoons filling the house with some small amount of music had its appeal.

"No," he said with rueful shake of his head. "But my sister does; very well, actually."

I stared, my glass of wine halfway to my mouth. "Sister?" I choked out.

Lynch and Sir Patrick laughed loudly for a moment, then remembered themselves and where they were, quickly smothering their amusement.

"Lucy. She's fourteen." Langton said, clearly bewildered. "You didn't know? My uncle didn't tell you?"

I shook my head slowly, trying not to immediately start calculating the costs involved with suddenly acquiring a wife, a son, and a daughter getting ready to come out.

"No, he didn't."

This time all but Truitt and Langton joined in the laughter; Truitt cast me a sympathetic look and bent his head to the main course.

"Damn it," Lynch said with a broad smile. "You're supposed to find out all you can, you know that. First rule of business." His eyes flashed as he reached for his wine.

"I'm sorry," Langton whispered, his face pale.

"Not to worry," I said as evenly as I could. "It's hardly your fault that I didn't know. We can discuss the matter at another time."

"Yes, Munrow." The poor boy looked devastated and embarrassed. If the Duke wasn't already near his deathbed, I would have been tempted to arrange for that myself.

With the entertainment portion of our meal complete, we moved on, making vague plans for the next day. It was thought that if the weather turned and the rain stopped once more we would go for an afternoon of shooting, letting the morning be reserved for exploring the house and grounds. Sir Patrick in particular felt that if I could find one room I'd not known about, I could find another.

I do believe that he was simply thinking that he knew every small part of his own home, having lived there his entire life. I will admit to a certain excitement about suddenly having a huge new estate to explore, even it did come with such minor inconveniences as a blackmailing Duke.

After dinner, we retreated once more to the drawing room where Dobbs and two footmen had set up for cards and after dinner drinks. Within fairly short order, we had split up into two tables of Whist, with myself, Lynch, Sir Patrick, and Fitzhugh at one table. This was at my gentle suggestion; while I did want Langton's eyes opened to certain possibilities, I did not wish to see the poor boy's sensibilities shattered. Lynch and Fitzhugh in particular were aggressive hunters, and I thought that the far more restrained conversation of Truitt and Hastings would be more conducive to my plan. The only real wild card was Kirkland, whom I knew slightly less well. The man was a peer, however, and I had hopes that his social training and small affection for me would hold his tongue.

We played quietly for some time, perhaps four games at our table. Voices were muted in the room, conversation centred on the cards for the most part. I listened to Langton and Truitt, who were paired, teasing the other two as they won their rubber, and smiled. There were any number of reasons for Langton's relaxed temperament, I knew. It could have been simply his upbringing, or his level of comfort among society in general and with men older than himself in particular. On the other hand, I could not dismiss the efforts of Truitt, who at four and twenty was closest in age to Langton in years, and by personality a gentle and unassuming man. Bold, yes, and he could be ferocious when aroused, but in general he was the least overwhelming of us all.

As we finished the first rounds of our games, we each drifted towards the sideboard to fetch drinks or gathered to the side to talk quietly, allowing the footmen to do their jobs and do the fetching for us. After a moment's discussion, it was decided to set aside the rather stoic games and begin something a little more like what we were used to. Whist might have been the most suitable game for a weekend in the country, but as a body -- save Langton -- we were more interested in enjoying ourselves.

Thus, under the ever correct gaze of Dobbs, we had the tables rearranged and took our places together as a group to settle into Loo. A somewhat more lively game, if only for the fact that we could place bets, we fell more into an atmosphere not unlike at our club on St. Barrett's Street.

Langton was quiet, intent on his cards and his brandy as we began. At first I assumed he was unfamiliar with the game, or at least the rules we played under, but he assured me that he was fine, and I left the matter alone. He remained nearly silent for a few hands, only answering direct questions and looking around with curious eyes as we talked and bid.

Dobbs sent one of the footmen away and stood guard over the beverage tray, sending the other around often to make sure we were happy. We were soon becoming most happy, as the cognac and brandy were judged favourably. On top of the pre-dinner drinks and the wine with our meal, it became a most merry evening.

In deference to me, or perhaps to the footman and Dobbs -- perhaps even to Langton -- none of my guests made direct allusion to our club, what happened there, or any past relations between assorted people present. I smiled as I looked over our assemblage and attempted a mental chart of relationships. It would, I feared, take many sheets of paper and a maze of crossed lines. To my knowledge, none of us had been with all of the others, but if one were to count degrees of separation, I doubted that one would use any more than three fingers.

As I have said, no one spoke of it. But there are many ways to communicate, and the spoken word is only one. There were a myriad of touches happening around our little table. Kirkland's fingers lingered over Fitzhugh's wrist. Sir Patrick, Hastings, and Lynch were engaged in a long and passionate argument about bee keeping, of all things, and their talk of honey was making the room most warm. And under the table, a foot brushed against my boot but did not return. When I glanced across the table,

I received an apologetic look from Sir Patrick and heard an in-drawn breath beside me. It seemed that Lynch was not going to be fetching his own drinks for some time.

Langton, the dear boy, seemed oblivious to the growing charge in the room. He had been drinking far less than the rest of us and was not being distracted as the others were. Thus, he began to win -- a great deal, as a matter of fact. He'd lost the first few hands, not badly, but a loss was a loss. The first hand he won, I'd been looking mostly at Truitt, judging the heat in his eye and the way he was running his finger around the rim of his glass. The second hand was won during the beginning of the bee keeping discussion, which he had initially taken part in -- before it devolved into a discussion of sweetness versus the thickness of the syrup.

By the time everyone at the table had noticed that the silent young man was quite good at cards, each and every one of us had lost money to the lad. I looked on in admiration as Langton's colour rose, and everyone settled down to at least one round of rather cutthroat card playing in an attempt to recoup their losses. When Langton, instead of backing down and falling out of the round, kept playing and bidding, the restraint in the room seemed to evaporate.

"Where did you learn to play cards, Viscount?" Lynch asked politely, the glint in his eye somewhat less friendly than his voice.

"I went to Eton," Langton replied, not looking up.

I smiled, feeling rather proud of his tone.

Lynch snickered and leant over towards Kirkland. "Which means, of course," he whispered loudly, "that the boy does indeed know what to do with it."

Langton's cheeks flushed, but his voice remained steady as he said, "Knowing, and choosing to best you at cards instead, is one of the advantages to my upbringing.

School can only teach so much, don't you think?"

The room filled with howls of laughter, and Langton tried to take it as best he could, attempting to be cool and aloof when he'd so clearly marked Lynch.

Langton won the hand easily, clearing me out and taking most of what Truitt had on the table as well. As he gathered his winnings, Langton smiled at everyone, thanked us all quite politely, and bade us each a goodnight. When he'd left the room and I turned from watching his retreat, I was suddenly faced with six men all looking at me with various degrees of amusement. I gave them an exaggerated nod and dismissed Dobbs and the footman, saying that I would ring when we left the room for the night.

Having taken care of the little niceties of playing lord of the Hall, I returned once more to my guests and found them more or less comfortably grouped in their usual ways, the hidden touches more pronounced now that we were alone. As I sat in my chair, Truitt took his former spot, just behind me, his hand over my shoulder.

Kirkland was behind Fitzhugh, a possessive hand resting on the older man's hip. "So, Edward, darling. The lamb might have teeth."

I shook my head. "He may play at it, but I have no fear, in truth. What he may or may not have seen at school is nothing really -- boys at play."

Lynch snickered, falling silent as Sir Patrick gestured to him. I had to smile and shake my head at them -- Lynch, always vocal, always blustering, and never one to shy away from challenging any room of people... that Lynch was constantly at odds with his other side. The side that belonged almost solely to Sir Patrick; unless they both belonged to Hastings-- these matters are hard to judge, really. The only thing that was well and truly known to those of us permitted into the inner circle was that Lynch

-- bold and brash and drivingly self possessed -- was well and truly under the control of his lovers, in and out of bed.

Fitzhugh gestured towards the door with his glass. "Tell us. What is your intention, really? To marry the mother and have the boy live here? That's a dangerous game -- perhaps more dangerous than you think."

I shook my head. "I have some small hope that I'll wriggle out of this with my home and money intact. Aside from surviving this summer without bursting into flames at an inopportune moment, I have no plan."

This was greeted with raised eyebrows and general disbelief. Behind me, Truitt laughed quietly.

"Oh, please, save us the outright lies," Hastings said with a smile. "You are like a cat spying a bowl of thick cream and planning how best to get it. Remember, however, that when cats taste the cream they wear the evidence without thought, and all can see their crime. The Duke will not tolerate -- "

"Allow me to deal with the Duke," I said firmly, a frisson of anger rising in my blood. "It is me whom he chose to blackmail and my estate he holds ransom. What I do will be for me, and me alone, and he shall pay the price for his attempt."

Lynch and Hastings shook their heads but did not press the matter further. Kirkland and Fitzhugh seemed willing to let it drop as well, although they seemed more amused than anything else. Sir Patrick, oddly, looked pleased, and said, "Whatever you do, Munrow, please be careful. I'd hate to see you taken from us due to carelessness. Make sure the lamb is worth the price of the Hall and your good name."

"My name is good?" I asked innocently.

"It is when I say it," Truitt murmured for me alone, his fingers briefly rubbing along my neck.

The others did not, to my knowledge, hear him, but they laughed and started making preparations to withdraw for the evening, gathering the cards and finishing their drinks. Kirkland and Fitzhugh were the first to leave, whispering together and sharing a brief kiss in front of us all before leaving for their rooms. I had made sure that they were next to each other; the shorter the walk, the less chance that they would run into a stray maid in the middle of the night.

Once they had left, the others waited for me to ring Dobbs and we all climbed the stairs together, catching sight of Sir Patrick and Lynch's valets as they carried fresh water for their gentlemen.

The goodnights were perfunctory, and I stood by my door and watched my friends all separate with friendly words and then disappear into their rooms. Griffith had my lamps lit and was waiting patiently to help me change for bed.

"How was your evening, sir?" he asked politely.

"Passable," I replied, letting him fuss with my assorted hooks and buttons. "How were things during dinner?"

"Manageable. Cook and her helpers seem well used to having so many for dinner below stairs, and Dobbs kept all under control. There was some discussion on where to sit, seeing as how Matheson is acting as valet but is really a footman. The valets for the other peers objected to him being seated to my right, but Dobbs and the Viscount's rank secured him the place."

I nodded and shrugged off my shirt. "And how is Matheson handling his new duties?"

"Well enough, I suppose. The Viscount has not said that he is displeased, but I think Matheson is feeling his lack of training most keenly. I saw him in quiet conversation with Mr. Truitt and Mr. Sir Patrick. They were discussing shoes, I think, or possibly linens. I was in rather a rush."

I didn't much care, really. Langton was certainly presentable, and I suspected that even a polite creature such as Langton would complain if his gentleman was more hindrance than help.

With instructions regarding my waking time, I sent Griffith off to his own bed and had him put out my lights as he went. The rain was still falling against the window, and I let the sound of it carry me off to sleep, sure that I would wake up long before morning when a lean body slid between my sheets to wake me with a familiar touch.

As it happened, it was a sound that stirred me, not a touch. I smiled and rolled over in my bed, trying to see through the dark as muffled curses filled my ears.

"Bloody hell, Ned. What is this thing?"

"It's a chair. Having trouble?"

"Let's see. Strange house, strange room, big pieces of furniture...can't you put on a damn lamp or something?"

I chuckled to myself and pushed the blanket off, kicking the lump of bedding to the foot of the bed. "No, I think not," I said with a smile. "Hunt me, Truitt. It's not that hard is it?"

"Hard, yes, although not the hunt." He was closer, and I laughed aloud as he suddenly climbed on the bed and sprawled over me, arms and legs winding around my body. He was like a monkey, or maybe a cat, all limbs and wiggling skin and nuzzling mouth.

"You're dressed," he complained.

"You're not," I observed.

"Thought it would save time. If you would prefer I could go back to your evil chair over there and fetch my robe. I warn you, however, that the chair might win this time and then your bed would remain cold."

I licked a line along his neck and shook my head. "My bed is not cold, pet. But I think I'll keep you here, just the same."

"Not cold?" he asked, moving against me, his fingers playing with the buttons on my bedclothes. "Someone got here first? I'll have to give Dunwiddy his notice for keeping me so long."

I lay still and let him work my fastenings, simply enjoying his touch as he bared my skin. "Would it bother you?" I teased. "If, say... Lynch had made his way in here ahead of you?"

Truitt laughed, his fingers stumbling. "Like his keepers would let him go. This is not the club, dear heart; he is not available to play. Nor, I suspect, are any of the others, which you well know. So, as the only one here without a claimed bed partner, it falls to me to make sure our host is content, no?"

"I do believe you have a point," I replied, smiling to myself. The point was currently making itself known against my thigh.

In truth, I had not really considered the matter in such depth, simply inviting the men I felt closest to, or the ones whom I had shared a certain level of pleasure with whilst I lived in the city. That Truitt would make his way to my bed was not a surprise and certainly not unwelcome.

"It's my duty," he whispered in my ear, quite earnestly.

"Only duty?" I asked, my breath catching as Truitt finished with my buttons and let his fingers drift across my chest to torture my nipples.

"One I would beg to have if it were not... thrust... upon me." I could feel his smile against my neck.

I laughed softly, finally moving to draw him to me, pressing his body against mine. "How I've missed you, pet. You make me smile."

"I could make you scream," he suggested, one hand sliding over my stomach, a finger dipping into my navel.

I shook my head. "Not tonight, I think. It's late and we have a full day tomorrow. I think perhaps something quiet tonight."

He nodded and immediately slipped against me, his mouth going to the nipple he'd been playing with and licking gently. I knew he would do as he was told -- that was his training -- but I knew he was disappointed as well. I made up my mind to make it up to him, either the next night or as soon as I could make it to London. A special treat, just for Truitt, something he would particularly enjoy.

I let a soft sound escape as his lips and teeth pulled at my nipples and a warm hand cupped my balls. As my prick began to fill and swell, he answered my sound with one of his own, his hips rocking a little, pushing his own hardness against me.

Feeling him, his need, set a fire in me that had been quietly simmering since everyone had arrived... since I had kissed Truitt before dinner, since I had witnessed Langton masturbating. I hardened rapidly, my hands petting and stroking Truitt's back and shoulders, urging him down.

I could feel him smile, the deliciously wicked one that would have his eyes sparkling with a sultry light if only I could see them. But knowing it was there was enough, and coupled with the hungry licks and open-mouthed kisses he covered my body in, I was almost writhing by the time he flicked his tongue along my hip bone.

"Don't tease, Truitt," I admonished.

"I'm not," he protested. "I'm simply not rushing. Five months, dear heart. The least you can do is let me take my time." And then he did it again, a long lingering play of his hot tongue down the join of my leg and hip, the tip curling around the base of my cock for a brief moment.

I groaned and let him arrange me, shifting my legs apart as his fingers dug into the muscles, digging deep to make me feel, to make me let go and relax. It was a special touch, just strong enough to make me gasp, not hard enough to hurt. It was a natural talent, and one I'd often chosen to appreciate and not take for granted. His tongue was still lapping at me, soaking my balls and dragging over my flesh again and again.

I did not realise that I'd been clutching at him until he stopped massaging my thighs and gently but firmly removed my hands from his shoulders and placed them on the bed. I fisted the sheet in my hands and tried to smile at him, but he'd gotten the reactions from my body that he'd wanted -- I was hard, my pulse making my cock twitch and jump with every beat of my heart.

We said nothing; there was no need. He moaned once against my hip and returned to his task with fervour. I could only stare into the inky darkness and feel, letting him do as he wanted; seldom have I been so happy to do so. One hand wrapped tightly around my prick, not stroking yet, just holding my length as he licked and suckled my balls and the soft skin below. Without thinking, I drew my legs up, bracing my feet flat on the mattress as I rocked my hips against his mouth. Hot and wet, so smooth it made me ache, Truitt's mouth was like a gift.

I heard a long, hungry moan, a sound so needy and full of lust it made my aching shaft pulse. The vibration as Truitt's sound tore through me made me gasp and cry out his name, almost had me undone as I thrust into his fist. It seemed to loose something in him as well, or perhaps his need for me had simply grown too large for his control; he made a hungry cry and urged me to curl up, pushing the back of one knee until I had drawn the leg up to my chest, exposing myself fully to him.

To his tongue, his heat, and his questing mouth. Such

pleasure I had not often experienced and never before from a partner so fully intent on only my satisfaction. I gasped, utterly unable to draw breath as he licked around my opening, leaving biting kisses on my buttocks and returning to rasp his tongue over me again. I could not control my hips, the sensation was far too intense, the heat more full than ever before. I began to fear I would spill too soon, fire trying to force its way out of my shaft.

"Christopher," I gasped, forcing air into my lungs. "Pet... oh, Christ. More, God, give me more."

And Truitt, always obedient, always quick to please me, did. I thrashed on the bed as his tongue entered me, my hips jerking as I tried to push into his fist and back onto his tongue at the same time. Wet heat, soft and firm at the same time, the gentle rasp of his teeth on my most tender flesh... it was far too much and I could not get enough.

"More," I begged. "More, more, more."

He fucked me with his tongue, his hand pulling at my prick, and my entire body began to tingle, right from my feet. I could feel the heat through my body, I felt every drop of sweat as it formed and beaded on my skin, and I pushed every breath out as if it were my last. When I thought I would surely die if the pressure grew any further, Truitt pushed his tongue deeper, squeezed harder, and I screamed.

"Oh, God," I cried out. "I'm going to -- Oh, God!" My prick throbbed and jerked against his palm as I spent, great jets of seed landing on my chest, my chin, my shoulders. I trembled and shook like a newborn colt, complete control of my reactions gone. Truitt, my dear pet, stroked my shaft until it had stopped, then pulled me into his arms and kissed my face as I rode the last effects of my orgasm.

It was minutes later before I came to my senses enough

to kiss him and reach for his erection. He accepted the kisses and met them with his own affection, but he stayed my hand. "I fear I've made a mess of your sheets, Ned," he said shyly.

It took the admission and the dampness of his thighs for me to realise that my own satiated and sleepy kisses were returned with the same; his affection was tempered as mine was, with satisfaction and release.

"Sleep, my pet," I whispered. "I will plan something special for you, to thank you for this night."

Truitt did not reply, save for another kiss, but his arms tightened around me momentarily and then he drew the sheets up and over us, warming the bed in the dark of the rain.

Chapter Twenty

Griffith woke me by pulling the drapery open and announcing, "The rain has stopped, sir. Breakfast is laid out in the morning room rather than the drawing room, as you requested. The gentlemen are there already."

I blinked rather blearily and sat up in bed, looking to the windows. The rain had indeed ceased for the moment, but the sky was dark and foreboding. "Is it cold?" I asked, rubbing a hand over my chest as Griffith brought clothes from my dressing room.

"Not particularly, sir. I believe that you may be able to take your party riding this morning, although shooting may not be possible in the afternoon. Would you like luncheon later in the day? I believe that dinner is to be late this evening, as you had discussed with Mrs. Banks."

I nodded slowly, making my way to the dressing room to wash. "Luncheon at three, I think, dinner at nine-thirty. When we are done here please go ask Cook to arrange something light for about noon. Oh, and I need fresh linens."

Griffith snorted. "As does half the house, sir."

I stopped, one hand reaching for the flannel and water basin, and turned to look at him. "Oh? Do tell."

Griffith shrugged and picked up my fresh shirt, shaking out imaginary wrinkles. "Fresh linen is needed by Mr. Kirkland for Lord Robert, and by Mr. Haight for Sir Patrick. It appears that Mr. Lynch did not stay in his bed at all, following his man in this morning by a few seconds. Mr. Truitt apparently slept as the dead or was in his own bed for less than an hour, according to his man." At this, he shot me a knowing look that was very near a smirk, and then he added, looking at my clothes, "Matheson says that the Viscount was stammering and blushing this morning, unable to look him in the eye. When Matheson was ready to see to the tidying up, the Viscount finally blurted that he would need fresh linens. So, four sets of sheets, two barely used and one set untouched. It's a wonder any of you can get out of bed this morning."

I shook my head and let the impertinence slide, knowing that if I called Griffith out every time he spoke his mind he would soon stop giving me the snippets of information I needed. As I washed, I thought about what he'd said and smiled, knowing exactly what had happened. Fitzhugh and Kirkland had used Kirkland's room -- which I knew to have a large bed, and the other three had made their way to Sir Patrick's room, which was the gold room Barrett had given me the night of his ball. Truitt, of course, had slept next to me until dawn, and Langton... well, the lad was young.

Satisfied with the weekend's progress so far, I made my way down to breakfast, knowing that the others were waiting. I found them gathered in the morning room, discussing the chance of rain and how we should best fill the afternoon if we were not to be out of doors. At my suggestion, we decided to leave the matter open until we had returned from riding. At this point, there was a brief discussion about the library, although I am unsure how the topic drifted, and as a body we made our way to the large room.

"Oh, this is wonderful," Hastings said, his voice almost as animated as Langton's had been when he'd first seen the room.

"You've not seen the room?" I asked, curious. Hastings had been one of Barrett's closer friends at the club, and I had assumed that Hastings had been to the Hall before.

"Not this room," Hastings replied, distracted by the wealth of volumes before him.

Lynch tugged at my sleeve and whispered loudly, "Barrett would not allow it for fear of losing our dear Hastings altogether, buried under a mountain of words."

I smiled as Hastings turned on his lover with a frown. "For that, my dear friend, you shall do without me for the morning, I think. I'll save my bottom from a few hours in the saddle and ensconce myself in that chair by the window."

Given the tone and the words it was simply a declaration of intent -- it was, after all, a holiday weekend and one should try to make oneself as happy as possible on holiday -- but it was so much more than that. I was not privy to the inner workings of their relationship, but by the devastation in Lynch's eyes, I knew that he was being punished.

Lynch sighed and turned to leave the room. "Yes, William," was all he said, but he did gather a sympathetic look from Sir Patrick. Curious, I thought. It had been my impression that Sir Patrick was in charge.

Unexpectedly, Kirkland spoke up and announced that he would be staying back as well, although it wasn't so much the books that drew him as a desire to stay out of the damp air. "Get enough of that in London when I can't stay in, so I think I'll manage right here as well -- I'm sure there are some books of interest even to me."

I could not help but look at Langton, who was suddenly pink.

"Langton?" I asked politely. "I hope that you will come ride with me?"

"Of course, Munrow," he replied immediately and then pinked further. Behind him, Truitt grinned at me and winked.

I smiled at Langton, looking as innocent as I possibly could, then called for Dobbs. Once I'd made sure that Kirkland and Hastings' needs would be met, I had him send someone to the stables to let the grooms know that our party would be ready to go within half an hour. It was simply a matter of finishing coffee then and stopping back in our rooms for riding boots and heavier coats.

After Griffith had helped me into the tight riding boots, I left word with him to make sure my guests knew I was already in the stables, and then I started down the stairs. I had just reached the bottom when Langton, in his riding clothes, came out of the drawing room and met me in the entryway.

"Are you ready, Langton?" I asked.

He smiled and nodded, and I found myself most pleased to make the short walk around the Hall with him beside me. The sky was still thick with clouds, but we were blessed with a lack of strong wind, and I was sure that we would be warm enough for the relatively short time we would be on horseback. As we walked, I happened to glance at Langton and found him looking at me out of the corner of his eye.

"Yes?" I asked with a slight smile. "Was there something you wished to discuss?"

He blushed and shook his head, then looked around. I could hear voices in the stable, and the smell of hay was strong on the light breeze. "I was simply wondering," he began, his voice hesitant. I looked at him when he stopped, and he shook his head. "I'm sorry, Munrow, it is not the time. Forgive me."

I stopped walking and reached for his arm. "Langton? Is there something wrong?"

"No," he protested vehemently. Then he smiled and said it again, calmer. "Nothing wrong. I have questions I want to ask, but not right now. About the Hall, my uncle... about many things, in truth. But this is not the time, I apologise for bringing it up like this."

"We can talk anytime you wish it," I said honestly. "Perhaps tomorrow afternoon, after the others have left, if you would like?"

Langton smiled at me, his eyes lighting up. I had not seen this smile before; and for a moment, it was as if the clouds had cleared and the sun was beaming down on me specifically, warming me through. "Tomorrow, Edward." Langton agreed.

It was not until we had returned to the house a couple of hours later -- soaked to the skin from a sudden downpour which caught us on the far side of the pond -- that I realised it was the first time he had called me by my Christian name.

As we were all wet and somewhat bedraggled when we returned to the house, it was natural for us to separate and go to our rooms to warm, clean up, and dress for luncheon. The ill weather had forced the lamps to be lit in the dining room, and even in the drawing room, where the large windows simply allowed the grey to stream in rather than light. It was, all in all, a rather gloomy day.

My guests all insisted that they did not mind the loss of shooting -- and as they were mostly city living, I chose to believe them. They seemed quite happy just to sit and talk quietly or wander between the drawing room and the library, although they did extract the promise of a proper tour between luncheon and dinner. Hastings had actually dozed off in his chair in the library, and I noticed that he and Lynch had a very brief, very quiet, conversation before joining the rest of us in the library.

Seeing them together suddenly reminded me that I had something to plan for Truitt, and hard on the heels of that was the memory of his tongue in my arse and the way he'd made me feel. Oh, yes, he would need something very special. Intense.

"Munrow? Are you well?" Kirkland asked suddenly.

I looked up, startled, and realised that it was altogether possible that he'd been speaking to me for some time, sitting in a chair not far from my own, a brandy snifter in hand. "Sorry, Kirkland," I said. "My mind was quite taken with something."

"So I could see," he said with a raised eyebrow. "You were quite flushed. Your lamb?"

"My pet."

Kirkland smiled broadly. "Ah. And what new tricks does our dear Truitt offer now?"

"I would tell you," I said seriously, "but, truly, this is something you'll want to experience."

Kirkland looked intrigued. "Really? I must speak with Fitzhugh, then. You looked at rather a loss."

I smiled and leant back in my chair, surveying the quiet conversations and the game of Whist going on around us. Truitt and Langton had yet to make their way down from their rooms. "I am trying to come up with a suitable reward, actually," I confessed. "Something to Truitt's tastes; something that will take him utterly out of himself."

Kirkland nodded thoughtfully. "Well, really. That

shouldn't be too hard, should it? You know exactly what his tastes are; you may possibly have created some of them yourself. I doubt anyone knows Truitt as well as you do."

"That's the trouble," I said. "I know him too well, or rather, he knows me too well. I can't make him forget as completely as I would like."

We sat silently for a time, nodding to Langton when he came in, speaking occasionally of outside matters, such as how Mr. MacDowell's import of Indian spices would affect the prices that Mr. MacDonald set. But as we talked of London and businesses that were not our own, there was an undercurrent of thought about Truitt.

When Truitt came in a few moments behind Langton, Kirkland stood up. "We will discuss this later, Munrow," he said. "I believe I might have an idea, but I will have to speak with Fitzhugh and Hastings first."

Bemused, I nodded, and he left me, going over to watch the final few hands of Whist. Langton and Truitt were standing by the window, peering out at the rain, and I moved to join them.

"Sorry about the weather," I said mildly.

"You should be," Truitt teased. "Your lack of ability to change it makes me wonder if you really are as talented as you say." My eyes widened slightly, but my pet was in rare form, and he kept talking. "Not able to change the weather, not able to fly to London for supper at the club, not able to make a carriage wheel that rolls smoothly over cobblestone and gravel both... really, you are a huge disappointment to me."

I raised an eyebrow and murmured, "And yet you seem not only willing to come to me here, but beg me to sprout wings and fly to London. I hate to think what would happen if I pleased you, poor boy."

Langton was smiling at us both, seemingly enjoying

the play. "And you," I said cheerfully to him. "Not able to protect your library from the grasping hands of an Earl and a... gentleman. Have you taken inventory in there yet?"

Langton shook his head with a smile. "I am very sure that if they absconded with a book or two you would find out which. They didn't seem overly interested in the plays or the French poetry." Then he gave me a most devilish grin and backed away, putting the glass he'd been holding on a table as he turned. "I'll see you at dinner," he called as he walked from the room.

I stared after him, rather taken aback, startled out of my stupor by Truitt's hand at my elbow. "Yes," he said softly. "Teeth. You'd best be careful, dear heart; he may present more of a challenge than you had bargained for."

"Or more of a reward," I said to myself, quite lost in thoughts of young Langton's surprising blooming.

Truitt merely chuckled.

Dinner was as the night before, a meal filled with politely restrained conversation that was somewhat less then inspiring to us all. Oh, we did pass over subjects of interest, but aside from a titbit about one of the businesses I remembered seeing mentioned on some of the papers Barrett had left me, it was unremarkable. I had a quiet word with Dobbs to remind me to go over a folder of information when my guests had gone, to see if one of Red Oak Hall's investments needed a second look, and dismissed the matter from my mind.

It was not until after dinner, indeed after we had adjourned to the drawing room and had had a relaxing drink, that I finally led my guests through the lower level of the Hall and showed off the various rooms. I fear that the lateness of the hour roused the ire of the footmen, who were obliged to go ahead and light lamps for us, but then, I'm fair certain that their expectations of me were already lowered. The parlour, the ballroom and its music room, the smaller library... all were visited, and bypassing the library, we returned once more to the drawing room. As everyone save Langton refreshed their drinks, Kirkland drew me aside for a quiet word.

"It's a wonderful Hall," he said, "but there doesn't seem to be a room which would provide a certain... atmosphere. I've spoken to the others, and if you and Truitt are willing, I think we can assist in some small way as you return a favour to him. But it will require room for us all and a strict need for being uninterrupted."

I raised an eyebrow at him. "I don't do orgies," I hissed under my breath.

He snorted. "None of us do, Munrow. But you do put on the occasional show, and we don't believe that Truitt has had the pleasure."

I thought on that for a moment, sipping my brandy. It was true, so far as it went. There had been rare occasions at the club when two or three close friends had been invited to witness specific events; I'd been witness to a small number myself. I had never shown Truitt, not even when his training was complete, and to my knowledge no one else had, either. There was a certain level of trust necessary, and I doubted that he had found such with anyone else.

I nodded finally. "I'll let you know. Give me... an hour."

Kirkland smiled slightly and moved away, going to stand by Sir Patrick and talking quietly in his ear. Sir Patrick glanced at me and smiled as well, his eyes bright. And suddenly there was an undercurrent in the air, something indefinable yet impossible to ignore. One by one, the others picked up on it, looking about them until their eyes met with mine, or their current bed partner, and it was as if the temperature in the room soared. The brandy became smoother, and yet more smoky, and the lamps cast flattering light on each face I looked into.

I ignored Truitt, beginning the game.

Clusters of quiet conversation formed, two or three men gathering for brief, intense conversations and then splitting up. I moved from man to man, not really talking of anything in particular, but letting my body language become eloquent. A stroke on the back of a hand, or the brushing of one's arm against another's. The lingering of fingers along a wrist, and in a spectacularly bold move, edging behind one of my guests and pressing my partially stiff erection against him.

Langton, when I looked at him, was looking from one man to another in confusion and then in mild alarm. Within half an hour, he approached me and bade me a goodnight, saying that he was quite ready to retreat to his room with a book to enjoy a bit of quiet.

I smiled warmly at him and clasped his arm, just above his elbow. "Of course," I said. "Sleep well, and if you need anything, please know that you can send Matheson for it."

His eyes widened a little at my touch, and he licked his lips as though they were suddenly dry. "Thank you. I think I shall simply fetch something from the library, however, and make my way to bed."

"Of course. Goodnight, Langton," I said, squeezing his arm and then releasing it.

He nodded and left the room, casting one more look at me from the door with vaguely troubled eyes.

Three minutes later, Hastings and Lynch appeared, looking guilty and apologetic. I looked at them in mild confusion -- I'd not seen them leave. "What happened?"

I asked.

Hastings flushed and looked at the floor. "We were in the library, talking about something from this morning -- ironically enough, we were actually discussing the bounds of appropriate behaviour."

I actually smiled, thinking about the way that Hastings had disciplined Lynch before we'd gone riding that morning. "Yes?" I pressed.

"And we reached the point in the discussion where all parties were agreed," Lynch said.

I waited.

"Langton came in."

I could not help but smile. "What did he see?" I asked evenly.

"Nothing more than a kiss," Hastings said quickly. "Well, a rather involved kiss, but at least we were fully clothed." He sighed. "Sorry, old friend. I'm not sure how slowly you wanted to break in the lamb -- "

"Oh, no," I protested. "I do believe that you may have helped -- unless he panics, that is. Did he say anything at all?"

"He simply begged our pardon and left. Quickly, and with a lovely rosy blush, but that was all."

I tilted my head. "It may have been enough," I said. "I'll let you know."

Lynch smiled broadly. "So you do intend to train the boy?"

"No," I said firmly. "I intend to keep my Hall, that's all. Langton may or may not play a part in that." It was all I would say on the matter.

Hastings shrugged and glanced around the room. "Truitt is starting to sulk. Are you going to put him out of his misery?"

I laughed. "He isn't sulking. He's anticipating. I promised him something special, and I do believe that he's trying to figure it out." I looked at the clock on the mantle and then at the assembled men, who seemed to note a change in my stature. "Gentlemen," I said. "The hour grows late, and I'm sure that we are all about ready to rest. You have some distance to travel tomorrow, and I fear the weather will make it less than pleasant. I suggest we retire now and get a good night's rest."

There were murmurs of assent, and those with drinks quickly drained them as we made our way to the stairs as a group. To Sir Patrick I murmured, "My rooms, an hour past midnight." He nodded and moved ahead a little to speak with Hastings, and I fell back to Truitt. "I have something for you, pet," I said, my hand on the small of his back.

"Oh?" he asked with a slight smile. "And what would that be?"

"It's a surprise, of course. Come to my room later -- say about one o'clock." Without waiting for a reply, I moved away from him and reached the top of the stairs. "Goodnight, my friends," I said as I opened my door and stepped through. Their replies were lost as I hurried into my room to begin preparations.

Truitt was a few minutes early, which did not surprise me in the least. Of his many charms, his eagerness had long been one of my favourites. He came to my rooms barefoot, dressed only in his trousers and shirt, his eyes dilated and eager. I smiled at him but didn't say anything, other than to tell him to sit at the foot of my bed whilst I gathered a few things from a cupboard in my private study.

There are very few tools that I have used with any consistency when it comes to pleasure, and fewer still that I keep near me. I have never been given to excessive bindings or using instruments to remove me from my partner; when I need to strike I prefer to use my hand, and when I desire restraint I use my tone of voice and my will to achieve it. For all of that, however, I do have a few favoured possessions. The crop which Truitt returned to me was one, and the fact that I had not even missed it speaks to how rarely I indulged him with it. The other items were simple, really, but quite effective. As I brought them out and laid them upon the bed, Truitt's breathing sped, but he said nothing.

I had just finished putting the things next to him when a quiet knock announced the arrival of the others. I had been unsure how many of them there would be, but when I opened the door and allowed them into first my sitting area and then the bed chamber, I was gratified that they had all chosen to come. I was further pleased to see that they were all still fully dressed including shoes and coats. It would make the experience that much more intense for Truitt; there is simply something inherently vulnerable about being naked before a company of others who were clothed.

As I led the others in Truitt's eyes widened and he stood up. "Ned?"

"Hush, pet," I said gently, taking his chin in my hand so he could look only at me. "Do you object?"

His eyes searched mine carefully for a moment before he smiled shyly. "No."

"Do you trust me?"

"You know I do."

I nodded and bade him sit once more, and with another nod to Hastings we brought in enough chairs from the sitting room so that all would have a place. No one spoke. Once the gentlemen were seated the room was somewhat crowded, but there was room enough for what I wanted to do.

Truitt was still sitting on the bed, looking at the men with something akin to wonder. I smiled at him, stepping in front of him and blocking his view. All he would see was me.

I was curious, I admit, and knowing the gentlemen as I did I could be sure that a certain level of questioning would be forgiven -- at least in that particular situation. "How many of the men in this room have you lain with?" I asked, keeping my voice soft.

Truitt looked confused for a moment, then said, "If you mean how many I had any level of... play... with, four. How many have been allowed into my body? Two."

I was pleased and let him see it in my smile. I did not ask who, or who besides me had taken him; it did not matter. There were two at least who had never seen Truitt in his ultimate beauty, and a fair chance that I was the only one who had seen him at his most wonderful, the moment when he utterly lost his fine hold on control.

I traced his cheekbone with my finger and kissed his warm mouth softly. "This is for you, and you only. I promise it will be what you crave, what you miss. Will you submit?" I asked him seriously. I no longer could command him at my will, and I would have his permission.

"Yes," he whispered, and I found myself having to swallow, the affection in his eyes taking me by surprise.

I stepped away from him and reached for the thin strap of leather on the bed. As I fastened the collar around Truitt's neck and tied the leash to the head of the bed, I said to the others, "You may comment, if you wish, or ask questions of me. You may not speak to Truitt, and I will tolerate no disrespect of him." They nodded in acknowledgement, as I knew they would -- it had been a formality, after all, and a standard practice at our club.

I looked at Truitt, schooling my smile into the one

I'd used when I was teaching him his control. He looked so lovely -- his trousers dark, his shirt light, and the dark band around his neck. The leather was no more than a symbol, not strong enough to hold a spaniel, let alone a strong man. As I've said, I prefer to guide through my will.

I urged him farther up the bed, on his knees, and had him turn to kneel with his back to the headboard. He could see them, see the other things on the bed, but his eyes did not leave mine.

"You will make no sound until I say you can," I said. "Nothing at all. If I hear you before I allow it, you will be gagged. Do you understand?"

Truitt smiled and lowered his head a fraction, acknowledging my word. I picked up the strip of black cloth and bound his eyes, creating the separation he would need for this to work as I intended.

As I looked at him, taking in the flush on his cheeks, the line of his prick as it swelled against his trousers in anticipation, everything began to fall away from me. I was aware of the others watching, but they were at the periphery of my consciousness. All that really mattered was Truitt and making him feel so much that he became lost in pleasure. "You're beautiful, my pet," I whispered. And he was, a study in light and dark. I wanted to see more definition, the hollows and planes of him, so I moved about the room turning lamps down and lighting candles, setting the atmosphere for my benefit.

The others, all five of them, were still and quiet, simply watching. When I had the lighting set to show off my pet to his very best I got on the bed with him and touched his face lightly with my fingertips.

"There are limits here," I said softly, dragging the pads of my fingers down his throat to the top button of his shirt. "I cannot use the crop, although I know how much you like it. There is no room, and no matter what I ask of you, it would be impossible not to cry out as it fell. We'll save that for another time."

Truitt swallowed but made no sound as I began to unbutton his shirt, caressing his skin as it was revealed. He was warm and smooth, the skin soft but unyielding under my fingers. I moved the fabric a little and bared one shoulder, pausing to kiss it as I slid a hand into his shirt and circled one tight nipple. When I brushed my thumb over it, again and again, Truitt shuddered silently. I smiled into his neck and undid the rest of his shirt slowly, touching and stroking as I went.

He smelled wonderful -- a hint of smoke, a bit of musk, and something under that which was his own. I could feel the heat from his skin, and on impulse, I licked at his collar, wetting the leather and adding its scent to Truitt's blend.

With the shirt unbuttoned, I let it fall from his shoulders and paused to look at him, the white fabric pooled around his waist, the leash leading away from him and his eyes bound. His chest was suffused with blood, his nipples were hard and dark, and his lips parted as his tongue darted out to lick them.

"Lovely," Hastings said.

I smiled as Truitt flushed darker, and I knew that if I could see his eyes, they would shine with pride. "Let me show you," I said quietly, reaching for the oil.

I rubbed oil into his skin until he glistened, the light playing over his flat stomach and sculpted chest. Every touch was special, my fingers and palms sliding over him, arousing him even as it drew out our play. His arms gleamed, his back twitched, and his tongue did not stop its delicate touches.

"Up," I said softly, and Truitt lifted his arse from where he'd been resting on his feet, going to his knees.

I undid his flies easily, slipping his clothes down and exposing his strong thighs. With a minimum of shifting, I was able to rid him of the garments and lay him down on my bed, reaching once more for the oil.

Where I had lingered over his body before, I now used my hands with purpose. I massaged his legs, digging my fingers into Truitt's thighs and spreading the oil until he was slick with it, hot and slippery under my fingers.

He moved. Truitt was like a dancer, shifting and undulating, but silent; even his breath made no sound. As I touched his hip, his calf, his foot, he would twist and twitch, his body telling me where to go next to increase his pleasure. The only part of him I avoided was where he wanted me most, and he expressed his want in the best way he could, arching his back and subtly thrusting his hips up, his heavy prick lying on his belly like a rod of steel.

I crawled over him, my legs straddling his hips, and I dipped my head to taste his mouth. His kiss was wild, enthusiastic in the extreme as he bit at my lips and plunged his tongue past my teeth. I let him take control of the kiss, let him take my mouth as his hips bucked, and he rubbed his engorged shaft against me for a moment, before I lifted off, leaving him gasping. He panted, but he did not moan. Really, his control -- his ability to obey my wishes -- took my breath and made my heart pound. His hands were fisted in the sheets, the tendons in his arms straining against reaching for me.

I rolled away from him and stood by the bed, watching him writhe, looking for contact. One of the others, I didn't look to see who, shifted in his chair. I moved to the bed once more and took up the oil again, settling between Truitt's spread thighs. With newly slicked hands, I cupped his balls and stroked the soft skin underneath, pressing up slightly.

Truitt held his breath, and I could hear nothing at all in the room save for my own heartbeat. "My pet," I said softly. "Mine to touch, to taste, and to tease. Mine, Christopher. Right now, here in my bed, you belong to me." I pressed harder, the fingers of my left hand stroking his hidden places, those of my right dancing over his prick and smoothing the droplets of his seed into his skin.

He rocked and moved, the heat of his erection filling my hand, but I would not hold him, would not stroke his length. I was waiting for him to break, to beg me, to make some sound; only in making his need vocal would Truitt break, forget where he was.

I heard Fitzhugh's voice sigh, and someone moved again. I could hear fabric shifting and sliding against itself, but it was not the sound I was waiting for; it was not my pet. I glanced back at them and smiled. Every eye was on Truitt; to a man they were lost in him. Sir Patrick and Hastings had Lynch between them, and I could only guess that it was one of them who had moved -- for certain, they were all leaning towards one another, hunger making their eyes over bright and dark. The other two were as they had been, Fitzhugh's face as flushed as Truitt's.

"They want you, pet," I whispered. "They are all aching to be where I am, touching you. They are looking and wishing, smelling you, wanting to taste you..."

Truitt shuddered and bit his lip, his prick twitching hard enough to rise off his belly. His balls were heavy in my hand, and I squeezed them gently. Before I even knew what I was going to do, I let them go, my fingers sliding over his skin so smoothly, oil warm and slippery over us both. As I pushed two fingers into him, I groaned, the sound echoed behind me by more than one voice.

I wanted to rub myself against him until I spent. I wanted to lie on top of him and plunge into his heat, stab into him again and again, until we were both sweat-slicked and hoarse from screaming. I wanted to fill him with me and bite down on his neck and claim him as mine.

Instead I fucked him with my fingers, reaching for the hard nub inside him and brushing against it. I was panting with him, both of us in fast rhythm with my fingers, with his hips as he pushed back and rode them. I wanted. I wanted. I wanted. With my free hand, I reached for the last item, holding it in my hand.

"Speak," I said, my voice loud in the room.

Truitt's back arched off the bed, bearing down on my hand. "In me, in me, oh, God, dear God, please, Ned, in me now," he screamed in one breath.

I pulled my fingers out and pushed the toy in, watching as the polished wood slid deep into him. It was long and smooth, thicker around than my own prick, and something Truitt loved as a special treat. He had seen it, knew what it was, and as he thrust madly, riding and fucking himself on it, he cried out again and again, begging for deeper, faster, harder.

I slammed the toy into him again and again, my fist smacking against his arse, his balls, and still he begged for more, his words blending and mingling until they were confused and a simple repetition of "please" and "yes".

Then I leaned forward, angled the toy to rub him at his core, and took his prick in my mouth. I sucked once, very hard, at the head. When I lifted off, rubbing his gland with the dildo, he came in a great fountain, his mouth open and once more silent as he shook.

I could hear soft sounds behind me and the sound of someone moving. I paid no heed, not when I had Truitt to care for. I carefully freed him of the toy and lay next to him, holding him close to me as I removed the blindfold and then kissed the tears away. It was then that I heard the door to the hall close and looked up to find Sir Patrick and Hastings standing just inside the bedchamber. The others had replaced the chairs and gone already.

I looked at them, met their eyes and accepted their smiles of approval. Truitt had let go and had been rewarded.

Chapter Twenty One

In the morning, Griffith was silent after his initial words to wake me until I was ready to go down to breakfast. As I walked towards the door, he cleared his throat and I turned, the question in my eyes rather than voiced. I was impatient; my guests would leave soon and I wanted to take my measure of how the weekend had affected Langton, and thus my plans.

Griffith looked at me, his mouth twisted in a knowing grin. "Another full day for the laundry, sir," he said.

"Mind your manners," I replied mildly. "At least they are happy guests."

"Quite, sir."

In the morning room, I found everyone assembled and enjoying their breakfast. The sun had seen fit to appear, and although the roads would most likely be muddy and rough, at least they would not get worse as everyone made their way home. Each of them made a point of thanking me for their weekend, and there were a few quiet words of praise for Truitt and more than one suggestion of what I could do with Langton. The poor lamb seemed unaware of the imagination he inspired, which was probably for the best.

When breakfast was cleared away, the carriages were brought around, and we could hear some activity as the cases were loaded up. I had a few words with Lynch about a business matter, and soon enough the party broke up, and more farewells were exchanged. It took some time to extricate Truitt from his corner of the room; it seemed that he and Langton had found something to talk about, and the rest were more or less forced to await the conclusion of their rather animated discussion.

They finally stood up, however, and I watched as they shook hands, both of them smiling warmly as they said goodbye. I believe that it may have been that exact moment that my plans began a fateful shift.

Truitt came to me, his travelling companions already out of doors and ready to go. "Munrow," he said warmly, his hands on my arms. "Thank you." It could have been taken to mean for the weekend, and for the ears of the staff, it was intended to, but I knew otherwise.

"Thank you," I said back to him, sharing his tone.

"Promise me you'll come to London soon. Have dinner at the club."

I nodded. "I suspect I'll be into the city sooner rather than later. Business matters and all that. I'll be sure to let you know when."

He smiled at me and then turned to smile again at Langton. "Soon, Munrow," he said, and then they were gone.

The house seemed so much quieter when they had left. Langton had vanished almost before the carriages had left the drive, and I went to the library, assuming he would have taken his usual place there, but found it empty. I was disappointed, but I had hope that he would let me know when he was ready to speak of the matter he had almost raised the day before. I went to the smaller library and spent more than a few hours going over some papers and making notes on things I had learned over the weekend that could be of importance to Red Oak Hall.

When next I noted the time, it was late afternoon, and my back was aching along with my eyes. When one is not used to sitting at a desk for long lengths of time, it wears on one's body. Of course, when one's body had spent the night before in the state mine had... well, a nap seemed like an appropriate thing.

I did not see Langton until dinner. As we sat in the dining room, which suddenly seemed far too big for just two people, I studied him, and found that unless I was asking him a direct question he would not look at me. He was not rude, but he was clearly distracted and possibly troubled. I wondered if he was upset with me specifically, or if his unease was brought about by what he had seen over the two days, or if it was something else all together.

"Langton?" I asked as we finished our meal.

"Yes?" He looked at me and then away when I did not immediately ask him a question or make another comment.

"Are you quite all right?" I asked softly. "You seem worried. Is there something -- "

"I'm fine, thank you," he said hastily, then flushed a little. "I apologise. I am... thinking rather heavily upon a few things, and I feel we really should have a serious discussion soon. But not tonight, if you don't mind."

My curiosity was piqued, but I could not press him on the matter. "Of course," I said easily. "Please, simply let me know when you are ready, and we can talk about anything you wish," I added sincerely. There was little chance that what Langton wished to speak about would lead to the sorts of things I wished to speak about, but I was beginning to quite like the boy.

We finished our dessert in companionable silence, and I was somewhat surprised when Langton said goodnight immediately after and retired to his room. He was truly avoiding me, it seemed, and for some reason that bothered me more than I'd thought it should.

I spent some time in the library, but after a day of going over books and files, I could not settle and had no interest in reading, so I retired early as well, thinking that an early night would do me well after a weekend of having Truitt in my bed.

And thus I missed Langton's trip to the library in the middle of the night and would not have known of it except that as I went down to breakfast I overheard the footmen in the hall below discussing how the chairs in the library needed to be shifted if someone was going to keep moving them. Suspicious and thrilled, I went to the library immediately and found that the books were misplaced -- grouped yes, but in the wrong order. It seemed that Langton was up to volume five. Smiling, I carried on to the drawing room. Langton did not come down to breakfast, having slept quite late.

He found me in the garden. I usually pay little attention to gardens, other than to note that they smell nice and whether or not they are in bloom, but for some reason I'd had an urge to wander through the formal beds in the warmer weather and bright sunshine. The gardens around the Hall were extensive, a combination of hedges and flowers, a small orchard, and the lawns. At one point, long ago, I'd thought that Barrett was considering putting in a hedge maze, but it had obviously not happened. There was certainly space for one.

I was walking along a path near the larger of two fountains, trying to gage the distance to the pond, which I could see clearly, when I heard a step behind me. Turning, I saw Langton. "Hello," I said with a smile.

He smiled back and ducked his head as he had done when we first met. "Munrow," he said softly. "May we sit for a time? Perhaps talk?"

Finally, I thought. I looked around and spied a stone bench, fashioned to look like some kind of ruin or artefact. "That... looks uncomfortable," I said thoughtfully. "Tell me, do you mind sitting on the grass? We could go out on the lawn, if you like."

He smiled again, bright and open, his eyes the same colour as the sky, and I felt something break inside me. It was as if my plan made an audible noise as it shattered and left me stunned.

There was no way on God's earth that I could seduce this boy.

Chapter Twenty Two

I am unsure how long I stood in shock, although it could only have been a moment or two. Langton was walking towards me, his smile still happy and open, and I forced myself to act as calm and relaxed as I could. I needed to think, to be away from him while I considered this new situation, or, to be more accurate, my new understanding of the situation. It was as if I suddenly realised that beneath my anger at the Duke, under the single thought of making him suffer for forcing me into this comedy, there was Langton. Not a means to an end, but a young man on the verge of awakening. A man whom I would have taken, lied to, used, and then destroyed.

The thought of what I would have done -- what I had already set in motion with such forceful intent -- shamed me. I held my place and watched as Langton moved to my side, gesturing out to the lawn where there was a cluster of the oak trees the hall was named for, and I was grateful that I had done nothing overt to begin my seduction. I had made him aware of some things, yes, and exposed him to books and people, but I had not myself said or done anything to make him realise I desired him.

I only hoped that it was enough of an omission to save us both from the inevitable pain I had unthinkingly begun us on the road to reaching.

We strolled in silence. I was lost in thought and fighting to maintain a polite interest in whatever it was that Langton wanted to discuss -- most of me praying that it wasn't the weekend newly over. All I could do was talk to him and hope that I had not done too much damage; planning and fixing my previous deeds would need to wait until I could escape to my rooms or the privacy of my library.

I was not so lost in thought that I did not immediately notice the change in his posture, his demeanour, as we walked to the trees and settled ourselves in the cool grass, next to each other and facing the pond. He had begun to look a little uneasy, his eyes not quite settling anywhere and his hand rubbing over his thigh now and again. He caught his lower lip with his teeth time and again, and by the time I had rested my back against the trunk of the tree, his brow had furrowed, making him look most distracted.

"Langton?" I asked quietly. "If you are not comfortable we can go back into the house."

"No," he said, finally looking at me. "I wish to speak openly, and whilst I know that I am supposed to be somewhat more than a guest here, I do not really wish that the servants know all of our business."

That was a sentiment I could heartily agree with, although it did make me somewhat more on edge regarding the topic of our conversation. I merely nodded and looked upon him calmly. "Of course. What is it you wish to discuss? We can be as frank as you like."

Langton took a deep breath and closed his eyes. "I've been thinking about this for almost two full days, and I still have no idea where to begin. I hope you know that

I do not mean to pry into your private affairs, but where they affect me I feel that I really must speak up."

I suppressed a sigh and braced myself. "By all means, Langton. Please, speak your mind and I'll try my best to answer your questions."

He looked at me then, and smiled slightly. "Thank you. I suppose that the place to start is why I am here. My uncle has obviously forced me upon you, and while I'll not go so far as to ask what he is... holding over you, I do need to know what you intend. Are you playing for time, Munrow, or do you actually intend to marry my mother?"

I said nothing for a long moment, trying to find the balance between truth and being too blunt. "I am very angry with the Duke," I finally said. "He had been trying to arrange a marriage between Barrett and your mother, without success, and when I was given the Hall, he wasted no time at all in making my position plain to me. However, he does have a point. I do not wish to marry at all, and yet I must. It would be better for me to marry someone such as your mother, with a son ready to step into the place of heir. So, both are true. For the sake of appearance and because of my anger with him, I am playing for time. And yes, I strongly suspect I will eventually ask your mother to have me."

Langton picked at the grass between us, nodding silently but not looking at me. I waited, not sure what to expect from him; I had confirmed blackmail at his uncle's hand, more or less said that a marriage with his mother was personally repugnant, if he hadn't already assumed that, and told him that it was to happen anyway. He had to be angry with me on some level, but he was almost nineteen and had been raised in a well-placed family -- he well knew the games we play, and how little control any one of us had.

"I think it is time we stopped playing at this, then," he said quietly. "If I am to be heir of Red Oak Hall, I want to know about it, its business, and what we are dealing with. I am not a guest, not really. I am as much a pawn as you are -- more so -- and I will not allow myself to be manipulated like this."

I stared at him, wondering where the shy boy had gone and where this pragmatic and proud young man had come from. My respect for him grew exponentially as he looked at me, his blue eyes almost flashing in the sun. He sat taller and nodded sharply at me, as if he'd made a decision. "I would like it very much if you spent some time with me in the next few weeks going over the Hall's investments and your plans, so that I might have a better idea of how best to care for the place, and also my own property when it falls to me. I will, most likely, be Duke before mid-winter. I hope that I shall not be master of Red Oak for many, many years, but I would like to know it -- and you -- as well as possible."

I could not help but smile at him and reach for his hand. Langton was perhaps the most amazing man I had met in years, and in a few well-chosen sentences he had just made damn sure that the Hall would be his. "Whatever you need, Langton," I said. "We can begin as soon as you would like -- now, or tomorrow. We will also have to go to London soon, I think."

His smile was radiant as he shook my hand, and I fear I got lost in it, holding onto him for much longer than was proper. When I realised I still had his hand in mine I dropped it as gracefully as I could, looking away as a blush crept up his cheeks. I moved to rise, planning to escape into the house while we were more or less at a point we were both pleased with.

"If there is nothing else?" I said, placing my hands to lift myself from the ground.

"Actually," Langton said then hesitated. I glanced down to find him quite pink and studying his hand most intently. "Never mind," he said quietly. "It's nothing."

I debated. I could walk away, and, honestly, I felt that I should do so. I had a vague impression that if I stayed I would be making a massive mistake on a personal level, but I was so impressed with Langton that I could not in good conscience simply leave him. He needed an ear, and whilst I freely admit to being a cad, I am not, I hope, intentionally cruel. With my conscience pricking me and my stomach in a knot, I settled once more and tried to prepare myself. "Langton? What is it?" I asked softly.

The self-assurance seemed to have vanished, and once more he was refusing to meet my eyes. His mouth opened twice, but he said nothing, and I sighed. "Please?" I said. "If I can help set your mind at ease…"

Langton laughed quietly. "I feel rather alone at the moment," he confessed. "And once more unsure where to begin." He said nothing further for a moment, then he shook his head. "No, it is perhaps better if I say nothing."

I could not be completely sure of what turmoil was going through his mind, but I could make an educated guess, and as it was my fault I had little choice. "No, I would prefer to know," I said. "You are to be here for the summer, and if there is something bothering you, I hope you know that you can speak to me." I took a breath and added, "Does this have anything to do with Saturday night, and what you saw of Hastings and Lynch in the library?"

Langton looked at me, his eyes wide and his cheeks flushed. "They told you?"

I nodded. "They said that you saw them kissing and apologised to me for their lack of discretion."

"They apologised to me before they left," Langton

said. "Or at least, Mr. Hastings did, for both of them. But Munrow, they were not merely kissing -- or at least not in any way I'd seen before. They were... passionate, intense. It was... it made me regret disturbing them."

I smiled before I could help it. "Yes, I suspect it was quite something to walk in on. They were having a discussion about something that had happened in the morning, and were, in effect, ending an... argument."

"Are they always like that?" Langton asked. "I mean, the entire weekend was rife with undercurrents, not them alone. How do they manage to live their normal day-to-day lives if that sort of passion is under the surface?"

"They have no choice," I said simply.

Langton looked at me and nodded, then ducked his head again. "That's it, isn't it?" he whispered. "What the Duke is using to force you into this? He knows and would hurt you."

I closed my eyes and leaned back. "Yes."

"I won't," Langton said, still speaking so quietly I had to strain to hear him. "I won't hurt you with this."

"Thank you." There was nothing more I could say, really.

"The others?" he asked. "Are they... ?"

"That is for them to tell, Langton. But you have eyes and ears, and you -- " I broke off as he flushed red. "Langton?"

He stared very hard at the ground in front of him. "I went away to school," he said softly. "I am not entirely innocent; boys away from their homes tend to experiment. But that was the crude fumblings of children, playing against their father's rules, and something left behind as we moved on. This, what I saw here and heard... it's more. It's real and terrifying. Did you know that you have books in the library that could be seen as perverse and are possibly illegal?"

I blinked and sighed again. "Yes, I do," I admitted. I would not have him know that I had seen him.

Langton may not even have heard my reply. He went on, his voice still quiet but more intense, and I knew that he was restraining himself for fear of drawing attention from the house or the stables. "Is Mr. Truitt... is he... I mean, he was so nice to me, and the others were not cruel, but the way they looked at me... he was different. He talked to me."

I was unsure what exactly he was asking. "Truitt is a very kind man," I said cautiously. "The others are good men, but more worldly, perhaps."

Langton shook his head and appeared to be thinking again, unsure of how to proceed. He sighed again and looked at me, turning to face me fully. "I saw you with him," he said boldly, his blush rising.

I froze, thinking naturally of my bed and Truitt laid upon it in his leash and nothing else. But as soon as I drew breath I knew Langton did not mean that, he meant on the Friday, which was confirmed as he went on.

"I did not mean to intrude," Langton said quickly. "I was going down to dinner and heard your voice. I thought to wait, as it seemed to me that you and Mr. Truitt would be going down as well. Your door was open, so I stepped into the doorway and I saw you kiss him." His cheeks were stained again, and he dropped his eyes. "I'm sorry."

"Don't be," I said automatically. "I should have had the door closed, or not done it at all."

Again he looked at me through lowered lashes, unconscious of the effect such a pose had on me. "Are you in love with him?" he asked shyly.

"No," I replied honestly.

"He loves you," Langton accused.

"Ah, but that is not what you asked, dear boy. Loving

and being in love are two different things." He looked like he was about to accuse me of semantics, so I held up a hand. "Truitt and I have a rather complex relationship based on attraction, admiration, and trust. I do love him, and I'm sure that he loves me, but we are not in love, nor are we committed to one another. It may not be the most romantic thing, but it is all we can have."

Langton frowned. "Is it enough?"

I shrugged. "We have no choice. Look, Langton. Our lives are more or less dictated by convention and stolen moments. There are tools we can use, such as our club and weekends like the one just past, but for men such as Truitt and myself, we cannot ask for more. Unless we give up our homes and flee the country," I added, thinking of Barrett and Granger.

Langton did not look happy. In fact, he looked rather upset and disquieted. I stood and offered him my hand. "Let us leave this for now," I said. "If you would like to discuss it further, I am willing to answer questions, but please know that I cannot betray any trusts."

I pulled Langton up, letting go of his hand at the appropriate moment that time. He held on. "Munrow, I... I am very confused."

"About Truitt?" I asked, looking at the hand Langton still held.

"Yes," he whispered. "And you."

My gaze shot to his eyes. "I am not a nice man," I said softly. "You don't want to become too... confused about me."

He looked at me intently, searching my face and eyes for something. Finally, he let go of my hand and stepped back. "Too late," he said. Then he turned and walked away from me, leaving me to curse my stupidity under the oak trees.

Chapter Twenty Three

There was little I could do. Langton was determined to know of Red Oak Hall's business and history, and I could not deny him. In point of fact, I welcomed his interest, and over the next few days we spent hours in the private library going over investments and obligations, discussing income and expenses. Having his ear helped me form opinions and strategies, for which I was grateful, and I discovered that for all his youth and inexperience in such matters, Langton possessed a keen analytic mind.

I had thought him bright, I admit, but I had expected him to be more chaotic of thought, more artistic. Instead, he was highly disciplined and linear, following one thought to another in logical patterns. He could weigh choices and reach decisions -- offered as suggestions, of course -- rapidly and efficiently. With each suggestion, he made clear the benefits to the Hall above all else and noted the personal effects as well. He was politically and socially aware, seeming almost amused at the stumbling blocks thrown in my path. Being a gentleman of means was one thing; being a gentleman of great wealth and holding lands that traditionally belonged to a peer was another.

However, our time in the library was not all admiration and easy discussion of business. Langton, even in the midst of trying to sway my mind to one investment over another, seemed to be overly aware of his own body. Several times during our first day in the library, he leant forward in conversation, his eyes locked with mine as he spoke, and suddenly backed off. I had quickly noted that when he was involved in a discussion he moved closer, engaging me with his eyes and his voice; it was an effective means of debate and seemed to be unconscious. The pulling away, however, was very conscious and reactionary. I did not comment on it, or on the fact that each time he did it he became flustered.

I knew what it was, of course. He would be talking, arguing a point, and suddenly my proximity would register and he would force himself to retreat. I could not fault him for it, and I knew it was for the best. I also could not help but wish that he would be at ease, my baser desires wanting nothing more than to throw him on the desk and taste his mouth, to feel the press of his lips on my skin.

The second day, he began to start whenever our hands brushed together over the files, or when he found himself leaning over me pointing to something on the register. I was hard in my trousers, feeling him leaning against me, and I did not even notice the sudden silence, coming into my senses only when he backed away, his colour high.

The third day was a reversal, marked by a lack of blushing but an increase in the casual touches, which I pretended not to notice. We made lists of people we wanted to speak with concerning investments and sponsorships, and Langton wandered around the office making his suggestions and passing me files and slips of paper, his fingers sliding over mine.

I was an utter wreck by the time we had planned our agenda for London.

I had a discussion with Dobbs, giving him our list of intended stops so he could send someone to London to see about our lodging and make appointments. I could suddenly see where one could use the services of a secretary and decided to think on that a little more. Barrett had employed one, but for some reason I had thought I could do without. Dobbs expressed no opinion on the matter.

The night before we were to leave, I was in the main library after dinner seated at the large desk. I had the Hall's letterhead out and was penning a note to Truitt, inviting him to the club for dinner the following night. Once we were in London, I would have the footman run it to Truitt's home and, barring a business engagement, I was sure that Truitt would accept. I needed him to accept. Langton had me so on edge that I needed Truitt to bring me back into my senses, to distract and ease me.

I had almost finished the note when Langton himself strode into the library, his shoulders back and his eyes flashing. I looked up, surprised. It was not unusual for him to be in the library, not by any measure, but I had never seen him like quite like that, with so much energy and turmoil. He was angry, it was clear, and apparently the focus of his rage was me.

"My mother?" he accused, still walking towards me. "You will send me to my mother?"

I stared at him, surprised. "You don't wish to see her?"

"Of course I wish to see her, and Lucy, too. But I do not wish to be treated as a child, sent off to my mother's home for the evening." He paced before the desk, his hands flying through the air. "We have two days in London, Munrow. Two days and two nights. I will not be shunted off to the side as soon as dinner is finished. I have not done anything to warrant this. Do you have any idea what it is like there? With my dear uncle in the house, dying? My mother quietly lamenting her lot in life? Lucy being sent to her rooms at half of nine? And I know full well that business as much as pleasure is discussed at night -- half of your business for the Hall will be done in private conversations, and I'll get it all second hand." He stopped pacing and leaned forward on the desk, mere inches from my face. "I am not a child, Munrow."

I was impressed by his speech, but there really was no help for it. "I know you are not, Langton. But where did you plan to stay? My brother's home? Even I won't stay there, not when I can be elsewhere." As soon as I said it, I knew it was a mistake.

"And where will you be?" Langton asked quietly, his eyes hard. "At your club, I assume. With Mr. Truitt?"

I raised an eyebrow. "At my club, yes. With whom is up to me, don't you agree?"

Langton stepped back from the desk and turned his back to me, his hand raking through his hair. "Of course. I apologise."

I sighed and stood up, walking to the front of the desk and leaning on it. "I am not trying to treat you like a child, Langton. Please, there are things to consider."

"Like what?" he demanded, turning to face me. He was still animated, his body tense.

"Like your uncle," I shot back. "Do you know what he would do to me if he knew you were in the city and didn't go to see him?"

Langton waved it off. "I shall see him; I just don't want to spend two nights locked up with him. I would much rather be with you, and I had hoped that I might be able to see Mr. Truitt as well. At the very least, keep me with you through dinner and send me to my mother's later in the evening."

"I can't take you into my club," I insisted. "If your uncle heard so much as whisper of such a thing he would kill me, and in all honesty, I'm not so sure of his sanity as to think that you would be safe from him."

"And who would tell him?" Langton asked. "Seriously, who? Not you or me. Not Chris -- Mr. Truitt. Your club is by its nature secretive."

"And someone, most likely several someones, have been talking. Don't you see, Langton? That's how I wound up like this in the first place -- your uncle got his information from somewhere."

"Not from the club," Langton insisted.

I froze. Langton looked at me and sighed, the fight seeping out of him.

"What do you know of it?" I asked calmly. Remarkable, considering the way my guts were twisting.

Langton sat in his usual chair, looking miserable, withdrawing into himself. "Not very much," he said quietly. "In point of fact I only put it together a couple of days ago, when Matheson was telling me about... well, he was gossiping. And it occurred to me that just before I was sent here my valet at home had been telling me about a sudden rash of household reorganisation." He quirked an eyebrow at me. "Four or five men had all let their valets go, and a slew of footmen had been tossed as well. Timothy -- my man -- said that it was due to talking to the wrong people about the wrong things. I had assumed he meant that they were speaking about their gentlemen, but in hindsight, I suspect it was about their gentleman and you. To my uncle's people."

I thought about it for a few moments. I had been having trouble with the notion that any of the men I'd been with had been so indiscreet as to either name me or to let themselves be in a position where the Duke could blackmail them for information. He said he had letters, but I hadn't seen them; it would make sense that while he was taking tea with the masters that his groom, his footman, his page -- any of them could be talking to the kitchen staff. Gossiping. All it would take was one or two less than loyal men, and the whole house of cards would fall.

Upon me, apparently.

"It doesn't matter," I said. "The point is, people talked, and they would mention you being there. Trust me."

Langton growled in frustration, his hands once more waving as he sat in his chair, his head tipped back so he could look up at me. "I just... Damn it, Munrow. Can't you see? Are you really that blind to me?"

I growled right back at him. "I am not blind in the least, and I think you should know that you are playing a very dangerous game. Your uncle -- "

"Oh, leave off," Langton interrupted. "What about you? What about me? You fight for what you want, don't you? You make your arrangements, and you live the best you can. Why can't I?"

"Because you shouldn't have to," I insisted. "God, what do you want me to say, Langton? What do you want from me?"

"This!" he practically yelled. Reaching to the side and grabbing blindly, he pulled out one of the black volumes and threw it at me. "This is what I want!"

I caught the book only by reflex and had to force myself not to look at it. I shuddered to think about which volume it could be, and it didn't matter as he had hardly been paying attention when he clutched at it. I stared at him, my jaw open, and watched as he stood up, trembling in front of me.

"Langton -- "

"Don't you dare. Not one word about how I don't know what I want, or that I'm too young to know, or anything else. I won't hear it. I know exactly what I want, have done since I walked into this house. I've only recently come to the point where I know it isn't impossible."

I shook my head. "I am not a nice man. Trust me. You may very well be attracted to me, but I won't be responsible for -- "

"I am not a child," Langton said softly. His voice was calm and the nervous energy was gone. He seemed to be in complete control once more, and he met my eye steadily. "I know what I want, Munrow. I think it's time you figured out just what you want as well. Now, I am going to bed, and I'll see you at breakfast. I would greatly appreciate it if you would give the matter some thought."

I stood speechless, still holding the volume he'd thrown at me, as he walked away from me. I don't recall moving for several minutes after he left, and when I did, it was to put the book back on the shelf.

Volume four. A personal favourite, damn him.

I sat at the desk and added two lines to the note for Truitt, signed it, and dripped wax over the edges to seal it. Twice.

Chapter Twenty Four

Sleep was impossible.

I wandered about my rooms, my mind a whirl of activity. Thoughts were piling up, one on top of another, crashing and melding. Names of those whom I suspected had talked to the Duke were mixed with faces from my club as I tried to sort out the acts that had become the Duke's weapon. It was brought home to me by Langton's idea that it had been solely the talk of servants, and I had begun to feel a sense of dread on behalf of my fellow members. If one of us could be blackmailed, any of us were open to a number of dangers. It was oddly reassuring to hold hope that my trouble lay not within the club but in the few occasions I had spent time with friends at their homes.

Intermingled with the names and faces and thoughts of betrayal was the constant thread of Langton. What he'd said, how he'd looked, how insistent he was that I see him as a man. That I look upon him as a man of passion and needs and desires. That I look at him and see that he wanted me.

The irony almost choked me. I had, effectively,

succeeded in my seduction without really trying, and mere days after deciding not to act. There were choices for me to make, ones that it would be impossible to undo if I chose wrongly.

By three hours past midnight, I was still awake, pacing from my sitting room to my dressing room, attempting to look at the problem logically, then by weighing my emotions, and then simply by my desire. I had very little control over that, I'm afraid; no matter how I looked at it the only image that hung before my eyes was Langton throwing the book of pictures at me and saying that was what he wanted.

He had been stunning at that moment -- so vibrant and alive, his eyes dark and shining, and his hair lying over his brow in golden swirls and locks. He had shone, and I had wanted him so badly it made me ache to picture it hours later.

I left my rooms and walked down the hall to Langton's door. I stood there, my hand raised to knock, and I could not. Not like that. If Langton wanted me, if he truly wanted to explore a different sort of relationship... he deserved better than a late night visit brought on by my libido. I went back to my bed and attempted once more to sleep.

In the morning, we did not linger over breakfast. I was overtired and not in the best of moods, as my doubts over Langton's choices came back in the light of day. I wished him a good morning, which he returned without much feeling, and went to my library to make sure all the papers we wanted were ready to go. Dobbs came to inform me that the carriage was at the front and ready to leave, so I sent him to tell Langton and made my way to the other library for a moment, picking out a book at random and then another with conscious choice.

"Travel well, sir," Dobbs said as he held the door for

me.

"Thank you, Dobbs, I'll try," I said, walking down the steps. "Is Viscount Langton ready?"

"Yes, sir. In the carriage."

I nodded and waved, then stepped up into the carriage, tossing myself rather abruptly onto the bench as the footman closed the door. Langton was across from me, looking out the window with his hands clasped in his lap. I knocked on the roof and called for us to leave.

Langton bit his lip. "Griffith?" he asked

"He's staying here. I'm actually quite good at dressing myself, and I assume that your mother keeps enough staff that you -- " Langton ground his teeth, so I stopped. "Did you sleep well?" I asked as the carriage started down the lane.

Langton shook his head. "Not really." He did not turn to look at me.

"Nor did I," I said. "I had rather a lot on my mind."

Langton crumpled a little at that. "I'm sorry," he said softly.

"For what? Speaking your mind?" I asked mildly.

Langton shook his head and turned from the window to look at his lap. "For being so... blunt. I should have just left it alone."

"Ah. Does that mean you've changed your mind about wanting to have dinner at the club?"

Langton looked up, his face confused. "I thought... um, no. No, I would like that."

"All right," I said, reaching for the tied bundle of files. "You and I will dine there this evening, and if he can make it, I expect Truitt will join us. Now, we have some time, so I thought it might be a good idea to go over the account with Forsythe again."

Langton looked somewhat baffled, but he shook it off easily enough, and within a few minutes we were passing papers back and forth as if nothing had happened.

Throughout the journey, I made every effort to maintain a businesslike attitude with Langton, more for his benefit than mine. He was clearly regretting his words of the night before, even if he still felt them, and I thought that some normalcy would go a long way to setting his mind at ease.

That is not to say that I utterly ignored the undercurrent of tension; I simply did not draw too much attention to it and I did not reject him outright. I met his eyes when we spoke and listened attentively. I did not move away when we chanced to touch and was somewhat gratified that he did not either. He even graced me with a smile or three along the way.

When we were finally done with the accounts I bound them again and set the bundle aside. "May I ask you something?" I said, leaning forward. "About the men who dismissed their help."

Langton nodded but said, "I'm unsure what I can tell you, really."

"I only want to know their names, if you remember. I've a theory I'd be happy to see proven or dismissed."

Langton's brow furrowed and then smoothed as he figured it out. "Certainly, let me think." He closed his eyes for a moment and said three names, then paused and added two more. When he opened his eyes, I was nodding my head. I had met two of the men at parties, which had gotten rather out of hand, and the other three had been partners in the distant past.

Langton gave me a small smile. "Not the club. As I said."

"Quite. Not the club. However, I was not speaking lightly when I said your uncle would have my life if he got word of anything inappropriate between you and me," I said seriously.

Langton sighed. "I know. I didn't mean to put you in an awkward position, Munrow, really. I just... I needed you to see. All weekend your friends were looking at me, making jokes at my expense -- or did you not think that I would hear about my new name?" He gave me an almost pitying look. "This lamb has ears and eyes, and I was well aware of the wolves."

I couldn't help but grin. "And you have teeth, it appears. You bore it well."

"I had little choice, although I did get rather a jolt when I walked into the library. You will be happy to know, I'm sure, that the walls of Red Oak Hall appear to be quite soundproof."

I threw back my head and laughed. "I'll be sure to pass that along," I said, making him blush. A glance out of the window told me where we were, perhaps an hour or less from our first stop. Looking at Langton, I made another choice, one that I had been debating since I'd stepped into the carriage.

It was time to test the lamb's restraint. If he could deal with this, he could very well deal with anything, and it would go a long way to making me feel more certain about his own choices.

Moving the bundle of files to the floor I picked up the two books which had lain ignored next to me for the journey. Langton was looking out the window again so I cleared my throat to gain his attention, smiling when he turned to look at me. "I thought you might like something to read," I said, passing him the book I had brought at random.

He took the volume and looked at the flyleaf, then raised an eyebrow at me. "You thought I would be interested in botany?"

I shrugged, still smiling. "Sorry. Perhaps this is of more interest?" I held out the plain black book and waited for him to take it.

His mouth fell open and his cheeks flushed as his face took on an expression best described as accusatory. "Why are you doing this?" he asked hoarsely.

I moved across the carriage and sat next to him, quite close. "This is the one you threw at me last night," I explained.

His eyes were locked on the book in my hands. "I was trying to make a point."

"As am I," I whispered in his ear.

Langton swallowed, and moved as if to turn his head to face me but stopped. "You wish me to... to look at the book with you?" he asked softly.

"If you'd like. Since you threw it at me, I wondered if there was something in particular you wanted me to see." I kept my voice soft, speaking into his ear.

He shook his head minutely. "I don't even know which one it is," he said absently. His fingers touched the book in my hand, almost caressing the cover as he took it from me.

"Have you looked at all of them?" I breathed, my thigh pressing against his.

"No." He swallowed again. "Which is this?"

"Four. Open it, Langton. Look with me."

The tip of his tongue swept across his lower lip, and he looked around us. "Here? In the carriage?" He sounded vaguely outraged at the suggestion.

"Here. In the carriage. No one will see in, Langton, and if they do, we are simply looking at a book. I'm not about to strip you bare and have my way with you."

"Oh." The poor lamb looked rather crestfallen. But his breathing was a little shallower, and his fingers were not quite steady as he opened the book to a random page near the beginning. He stared at the pages and turned them almost mechanically, his eyes so fixed that I knew he wasn't really seeing the images, was going through the motions. I let him, watching his eyes for reaction as his hand slowed and he began to focus. Every once in a while, I would glance down, wanting to see as he did.

Men, always paired in this volume, and by this part of the series entirely nude and aroused. Kissing, fondling, and in some cases with their faces drawn in ecstasy. I breathed against Langton's neck, inhaled his scent, and listened to his breathing, becoming aroused myself by our sheer proximity and his growing attention to the images.

"Oh," he said again, staring down at the pages.

I glanced at the book, needing to see what had dilated his eyes and made his cheeks flush anew. Two men, facing each other with their legs entwined, each masturbating the other. I smiled and leaned in to whisper once more. "Would you like that, Henri?" I whispered. "So close you could feel the heat of my body, smell my need? Held so close to me that our balls press together as I stroke your prick? Do you want to feel my hand around you as I kiss your neck? Do you want to know what I feel like in your hand and hear me as you touch my cock?"

Langton moaned and nodded, his breath coming even faster as he bit his lip.

"Turn the page," I bade him, shifting on the bench and pressing even closer. I could smell him, the musk and salt of his desire, and it made me hard, probably as hard as he was.

Langton turned the page with shaking hands, and there were two men sucking each other. Another page, and there was a man being taken from behind. A third, and a man was astride his partner, both of them masturbating him as he rode. Langton whimpered, and I took pity, turning the page myself as he shuddered beside me, his eyes fixed on the book.

"Oh, God," Langton whispered. He touched the

image with a shaking finger, along the back of the central figure.

"Three?" I asked with a smile. "Tell me, which is you?"

"This one," he whispered, touching the man being sucked off by the one in the middle.

"And who are you kissing?" I asked, pointing to the third man, the one sliding his prick into the man on all fours, who was sucking the figure Langton imagined himself as.

"You," he said, almost panting, his finger tracing "my" chest and belly.

"And the third? Whom shall I fuck whilst he takes you in his mouth?" I whispered, my lips brushing Langton's ear.

"Christopher."

I smiled and closed the book, putting my hand on his thigh. Immediately his own hand clamped on my wrist. "Please," he asked, barely making a sound. "Don't touch me. If you do, I fear I shall embarrass us both, and I won't go to Forsythe reeking of sex and wearing soiled trousers."

I had to relent; how could I not? I eased away from him and put the book under the cushions, moving carefully. My own trousers were somewhat less than comfortable, and it occurred to me that I might have done too good a job. We were perhaps ten minutes from our first stop, and I wanted release far more than I wanted to simply let the hunger die down.

I sighed and gave Langton a rueful smile. "I seem to have become caught up in this," I admitted glancing down at myself. "We are in a state not quite fit for polite company."

Langton gave a ragged laugh. "You really are not a nice man, aren't you?"

"Indeed. However, I have faith in your youth and your control -- I'm sure that you've some experience in willing away inconvenient erections?"

Langton rolled his eyes and then leant his head back, ignoring me for not a few moments. I could only assume he was concentrating on something distasteful, and as I had my own libido to contend with, I left him to it. Happily, by the time we arrived at the offices of Mr. Forsythe, we were both calmer, and any dishevelment could be blamed upon spending so long in a carriage. We gathered our papers; I sent the carriage around to Truitt's with my note, and we set about the other reason for our trip to the city.

Our business day was very short, due to our time travelling, but I was extremely pleased with the results. One of the investments had yielded higher returns than expected and remained promising, and another was renegotiated with comparative ease. The bright light, however, was Langton, who conducted himself in a most exemplary manner. He listened attentively and kept to the background, but when I asked a question or his opinion, he did not hesitate to give it, even if it was contrary to my intentions. When I questioned his postulation in one case, he backed it up with facts and logical inference, impressing both me and my counterpart.

I was feeling more than content when we finally arrived at the club on St. Barrett's Street. Langton was happy, I was happy, and I felt safe within the confines of the large building, surrounded by leather and dark hues. I was greeted by name, had my cases sent to my favoured rooms, and logged Langton as a dinner guest. He frowned once more, knowing I was resolute that he would not stay with me for the night, but did not complain. With a hand on the small of Langton's back, I led him to the dining room.

"It is possible that Mr. Truitt will be joining us," I told the servant who led us to a small table discreetly set into an alcove.

"Yes, Mr. Munrow. I can check for a message, if you would like."

"Please," I said with a nod. "And we'll start with a bottle of red, I think."

"Certainly, sir."

Langton was looking around the room with interest and trying very hard not to look like he was curious.

"What do you think?" I asked, sitting across from him.

He blushed a little and ducked his head in that endearing way of his. "It's much like any club, isn't it?" he observed. "Although I didn't expect quite so many people."

There were perhaps a dozen others in the room, at small tables of two or three, and there was seating for half as many again. We had passed the library and games room, and I estimated that there were probably three dozen men present in total, aside from the staff.

"I think the club boasts between sixty and seventy members," I said, "although it is rare that all would be here at one time. Few of the men here will stay the night; it really is simply a Gentlemen's Club, where we come to talk and drink and play cards. The only difference is the strictness of confidentiality and what happens behind closed doors."

Langton nodded and glanced around the room again, looking at the walls of all things. "It's quite comfortable. The design and colours are all very masculine, yet there is a sense of privacy and intimacy."

I nodded, happy that he was in tune with the general

feel of the room and with the club at large. Our wine appeared at the hands of the steward, and I was informed that Truitt had left a note that he would indeed be joining us for our meal. I smiled at Langton and winked as the steward poured. "You will be a pleasant surprise for my pet, I think."

Langton glanced at the steward, who pretended not to hear, and ducked his head again. When I had approved the wine and the bottle was left to us, Langton raised an eyebrow at me even as I raised my glass. "Your pet?" he asked.

I merely smiled and sipped my wine.

A shadow fell across the table and I looked up to see Mr. Ludlow smiling at me most apologetically. "I'm very sorry to interrupt, Munrow, but I'm off to Birmingham in the morning and I wondered if I might have a quick word before your meal arrives?"

I nodded and stood up, as did Langton, and after I made hasty introductions, Ludlow and I excused ourselves to the library. "I suggest you avoid making social obligations to anyone, Langton," I advised with a smile. The remark earned me another pretty blush, along with a scowl. The boy was feeling contradictory, apparently.

I was gone for almost twenty minutes, in which Ludlow made a business proposition I said I would consider, a pass I declined, and a heavy hint that his niece would make a fine mistress for Red Oak Hall, which I politely dodged. He did not remark upon Langton at all, and I had not expected him to, discretion being what it was at the club.

When he finally released me, I went back to the dining room to find that Langton had been joined by Truitt, the two of them sitting close together with their backs to me. I stood for a moment watching them talk earnestly, their heads bent as they spoke quietly. Truitt had his arm around the back of Langton's chair and seemed to be doing most of the talking; Langton was doing most of the blushing. Really, for a man as forward as he'd proven to be, one would have thought he'd have better control over that.

Smiling as I watched them, I walked over and touched Truitt on his shoulder before taking my seat across from them. "Good evening, pet," I murmured.

Truitt withdrew his arm, and he looked at me, smiling wickedly. "There you are, Munrow. Langton was just telling me of your day. The travel was smooth?"

"There were one or two points of excitement, but it was a good day, yes," I said. "How have you been?"

Truitt laughed quietly, his attention as focused on me as mine was on him. We were playing, and Langton was designated as spectator. "In the week since I last saw you? Terribly lonely." He pouted most beautifully.

"So sorry," I said with overdone sympathy. "I'll have to see what I can do to make it up to you."

"Ah, another promise."

"You know I always keep them, however."

"One of the highlights of my life, dear heart." Truitt glanced at Langton, and his smile broadened. The lamb was studiously attempting to melt into the woodwork. "And how do you like your rooms, Langton?" Truitt asked.

Langton frowned in my direction and opened his mouth, but I spoke first. "He's not staying," I said firmly. "I'm being entirely cruel and sending him to his mother's. I'm afraid the lamb is rather upset with me."

Truitt cocked an eyebrow at me and returned his arm to Langton's chair back, presenting me with a united front. "What on earth for? Not on my account, I hope."

"Not at all. It is more a matter of not tossing my life away upon his uncle's sword. Or pistol, or whatever the damned man would use."

Truitt waved the idea away with his free hand, the one about Langton dropping to touch the boy's shoulder lightly. "You'd rather play it safe than see if the lamb is ready for games?"

Langton's eyes widened, although I was unsure if it was for the comment or the fingers now caressing him. I narrowed my eyes at Truitt and lowered my voice. "Pet, you're pushing."

"I know," Truitt said, matching my tone and sliding his foot along mine. "It's what I do best."

I was saved from further comment by the arrival of our meal, and the three of us set aside the banter in favour of enjoying the food and each other's company. I have never been one to use food as a tool for seduction; it is messy and too often falls into farce if the wrong note is hit at the wrong time. That is not to say that I deny the effects of certain foods, or even that which a good meal can create; rather, it takes too much effort at too high a risk.

Truitt did not share my view, and it became apparent within moments that Langton tended to think as Truitt did. It was my great pleasure then, to enjoy dish after dish of a wonderful meal whilst I watched them flirt and play with one another. It would have been all too easy to be drawn into the game, but I made a point of staying outside it, other than to return a few comments to each. In Langton's case, I earned one blush and one wide-eyed stare; in Truitt's, I garnered two smouldering glances and another foot rub.

The real treat, however, was watching them together. They talked -- God, how they talked. About anything, it seemed to me, beginning with the wine we shared, then to wine in general, to grapes, to France, to poetry, to literature... they flew over and around topics, all the while apparently sharing an innocent meal. I knew differently.

It was not in their words or even their topics, although I did happily enter the discussion of literature with allusions to Langton's preferred reading material. It was more the way they looked at each other as they sipped the wine or tasted the asparagus. Langton actually grew rather pale watching Truitt eat his asparagus tips, dipped in butter. My pet was not terribly subtle, I'm afraid, but as a lesson in fellatio, it was quite competent.

Langton countered with his marinated baby carrots, which he took forever to eat as he was midway through his thoughts on a particular poet. Each sentence was punctuated with a flick of his tongue, the carrot not quite making it into his mouth before he had to speak again to follow his thought. Truitt sat frozen during that particular display, his eyes locked on Langton's mouth. I was fairly sure that Truitt was within seconds of launching himself at Langton when finally the carrot disappeared and was eaten, Langton showing no signs of knowing what he'd done.

They shared bits of their salad, sucking at slices of tomato. They had a long discussion about cucumbers which made me worry that they were going to descend into comedy, but they left that soon enough and moved on to talk about brandy, a leap which I didn't follow well, distracted as I was by the way Langton's eyes were dilated.

Dessert was served -- a selection of small pastries. As they smiled and each reached for one, I shot out my hands and grabbed their wrists. "There will be no feeding each other, is that understood?"

Identical looks of surprised innocence were turned on me, but I merely tilted my head, not letting go. Langton caved first, of course, having little experience with either me or the entire situation. As his eyes dropped, Truitt sighed and nodded. "If you say so, Munrow. I do think you're being perfectly unfair about it, though."

I smiled. "Of course I am. But it would do little good for any of us if you two wound up having sex on the table, now would it?"

Langton gasped, honestly astonished, but Truitt laughed. "I doubt it would have gone that far," he protested.

"You underestimate yourself, pet," I said, sitting back and smiling at them both. "I know you well enough to know exactly how hard you are, and I strongly suspect that Langton is ahead of you, given what he did to the carrots." I didn't really see the need to point out my own degree of arousal, though it would be apparent if I stood up.

Langton reddened as Truitt turned to look at him, not able to speak. A subtle change came over my pet as he studied Langton, and with a glance at me, Truitt leant closer to Langton, his arm once more around Langton's shoulders. "Are we merely flirting, Langton? Or this the beginning of a greater game?" he asked quietly. He was serious, I knew, and I could tell that Langton knew it as well, his eyes going to me and asking questions.

I leant across the table and selected a pastry. "Not tonight, Truitt," I said. "And not here. But perhaps you would like to come to Red Oak Hall for the weekend?"

I could not see Truitt's other hand, and I dearly wished I could. Langton was looking at Truitt now, his eyes wide and glazed over, his lips parted a fraction. Truitt stayed exactly as he was, turning only his head to face me as his arm moved ever so slightly in a steady rhythm. "Another weekend party?" he asked.

"No," I said, studying the pastry. "Just you."

Langton made a soft noise and closed his eyes.

"Not on Friday, I'm afraid. Perhaps Saturday to

Monday?" Truitt offered.

I thought about it for a moment and nodded. "Langton? Does that suit you?" I asked.

Langton drew a shuddering breath and nodded. "Perfectly."

Truitt beamed, leaning a little closer to Langton, looking for all the world like he was imparting great secrets as he whispered in the boy's ear. If I'd not been in Langton's position myself a time or two, even I wouldn't have known what was going on. Truitt talked for a few moments, his own eyes drifting closed, and then Langton's breath caught, the tendons in his neck standing out as his body stiffened.

"Very nice," I said softly, my own prick throbbing.

"Very," Truitt agreed, kissing Langton on the nose. "Five days, lamb. I can't wait."

Langton took a deep breath and composed himself, surprising me by staying calm and even eating a pastry. He was able to join in the conversation in fairly short order, and he seemed to have no particular embarrassment about what had happened.

He was not, however, very happy with me when the meal was done, and I had the steward call the carriage around to take him to his mother's.

"Listen to me," I said soothingly. "I will be there first thing the morning to collect you. We have business to attend to, and we won't be able to linger. I'll speak with the Duke, if he is there, and we'll be off. There are appointments set, so your escape is assured."

Langton sighed and nodded. "I don't want to be there," he said quietly. "I want to stay with you."

It was my turn to sigh. "We'll be home in two days, Langton. Do you seriously think that you'll be able to avoid me once we are?"

He looked at me across the table and gave me a small

smile, humour returning to his eyes. "It's a big house," he said. "I suspect I could hide."

"I'm a very good hunter," I replied, smiling myself. Langton's eyes darkened slightly, and I knew we'd found a new game.

"The carriage is ready, Mr. Munrow," the steward said at my elbow.

The three of us sighed and stood up, Langton's napkin wrapped inside Truitt's. I smiled at the sight and spared a thought for the poor laundress. We walked to the door, pausing in the entry before we would be seen through the small window. "Goodnight, Langton," I said softly.

He turned to face me, his hat in hand, and I reached to touch him, tracing his cheekbones. "Sleep well, Munrow," he replied. He leaned forward and kissed me softly. I smiled at him, terribly pleased, and let him say goodnight to Truitt. Their kiss was just as gentle and sweet, and I found I wanted to see so much more. Five days.

Langton backed away and was out the door, walking towards the carriage. I took Truitt's hand and laced our fingers together, tugging him gently away from the entry. "Will you stay?" I asked.

"God, yes. Need you. Now."

I tugged on his hand again, and we moved to the stairs, perhaps a little more quickly than was strictly necessary.

Chapter Twenty Five

As soon as the door was closed and locked behind us, Truitt fell upon me, his kisses deep and passionate. We tugged at our clothing, shedding coats and waistcoats, shoes and adornments, with as much haste as our fingers would allow.

"God," Truitt gasped, "Only a week and the lamb has turned lion. What on earth did you do to him?"

"Later," I growled, my hand at the placket of my trousers. "We'll talk later, pet." I was more eager for Truitt's touch than I could remember being in a very long time. Watching him with Langton, watching them flirt and tease, had inflamed me so that I was near the brink before I had even managed to fully undress. I was still in my shirt and trousers, my chest heaving and my prick full and heavy between my thighs.

Truitt was no better prepared, still in his unbuttoned shirt as he leaned over the edge of the bed and reached for the pot of oil. "You should have brought him up," he said. "We could have tutored him by making him watch."

"I said later." I was almost snarling, and poor Truitt's bare arse was too tempting as he stretched. Before I'd thought, before I'd weighed any options, instinct and my lust took hold and I smacked it, my hand falling heavy on his seat with a loud clap.

I froze, as did Truitt. For a heartbeat, we remained just as we were, my hand stinging and Truitt looking at me over his shoulder.

"Do you think he would like to watch?" Truitt said carefully, testing my reaction. His eyes were dilated and hot, longing for me. Spanking was something he greatly enjoyed, although for me it required a certain mood, and he was checking to see if that been attained.

I spanked him again, and he groaned, his legs locking and thrusting his arse higher in the air. "Or would he be unable to sit still?" Truitt pressed. Again, my hand fell, and this time Truitt's head dropped between his shoulders.

"Not now," I ordered, my hand striking him again. "We will speak of him later."

Truitt choked back a laugh. "And give up this punishment? I think not."

I wrestled with my fastenings with one hand, the other landing again and again as Truitt held himself still, looking utterly wanton, half dressed and clinging to the bedpost. "You are going to be most tender, pet."

Truitt's back arched as he moved into my hand, his breathing harsh and as sharp as the sound of my hand on his flesh. "Think of it, dear heart. His hands on you, so unschooled and shaking, not knowing where to touch first."

"Hush," I said, although I suspect I did not say it aloud. My hand continued to fall, the rhythm natural and easy even as my hand stung and Truitt's skin warmed and became rosy.

"His hand, too loose around your cock, kisses too tentative... he'll tremble in your arms, and you'll have to teach him everything. Those first tender moments will make you so hungry, the fumblings even more erotic than the touch of the most knowing lover."

I growled again, my fingers delving between his legs for a moment to cup his balls and tease at his entrance, making him groan and move with my hand.

"Yes, Ned. Please." Truitt's voice was breaking, words coming between panting breaths and I reached for the oil. He hissed when he saw me fetch the pot and then added fuel to the flames. "He's ripe and eager, so ready to be taught. The wonder in his eyes as you touch him for the first time -- "

His words were cut off as I drizzled oil over his cleft, spreading it with quick fingers and sliding one into his body. "Ned, please!" he begged. "I'm ready; I'm not the young virgin -- God, just shag me!"

If I would have had had any mind left I would have laughed, but all I could do was try not to spend as I heard the raw need in his voice. I slicked myself swiftly and parted his reddened buttocks, the heat coming off him in waves. We both cried out as I breached him, the intensity of our pleasure threatening to overwhelm us.

Control was hard won and quickly lost as I moved. Too soon, far too soon, I found myself unable to control the depth or speed of my thrusts, plunging towards completion in mere moments, with one hand gripping his hip and the other tightly wrapped around his shaft.

I was beyond words, and Truitt was almost beyond breath as he spilled over my fingers, his body clamping down hard on me and wringing my climax from me. Trembling and gasping, he clung to the bed, and I held onto him, not trusting my legs to keep me up. Carefully we shifted, parting to fall upon the bed, our clothes tangling on our limbs.

"Haven't done that in a while," Truitt said after

he'd caught his breath. "You've not lost any strength by spending your days as a gentleman of leisure."

I groaned and rolled over, kicking my trousers off and fighting with my shirtsleeves, tossing the garments to the floor. I was satiated and utterly boneless; sleep was calling to me as I gathered Truitt into my arms and pulled the blankets over us.

Truitt, on the other hand, was apparently energised by the experience; or perhaps his arse was too tender to be comfortable. In either case, he was more than happy to lie with me, dropping soft kisses on my chest and shoulders, one warm hand heavy on my hip. "So tell me, dearest," he said with a smile. "What have you done to Langton?"

"Nothing!" I protested. Then I sighed and rubbed at my eyes. "I fear I've made a rather large error, pet."

Truitt made a sympathetic sound and kissed me again. "Tell me all, and let's see if we can get this sorted before morning, yes? I think Langton's patience will wear out before long."

I nodded and gave him a brief smile. "I think I had forgotten to take into account what young men are like, how driven they can be."

Truitt laughed softly, and I held him to me as I told him everything of my initial plan, starting with the Duke's visit and blackmail and ending with my resolution in the garden to go no further and to leave Langton alone.

"So what changed?" Truitt asked. "Why did you decide not to pursue him?"

I thought about it for a moment. "I made the fatal mistake of seeing my prey as something other than just prey, I think," I said. "He had done so well over the weekend, picking up on the undercurrents and handling it with grace. I had not really counted on becoming enamoured with him."

Truitt made a delighted sound. "There is so much there to be enamoured of," he declared.

"His curiosity and passion for literature," I agreed. "His ability to think and articulate."

"His smile, the way his eyes widen. His shoulders," Truitt countered.

"The way he's taken a full interest in the Hall."

"His tight arse."

"His adaptability."

"His prick, which -- by the way -- has a slight curve and might be larger than mine," Truitt said, peeking under the covers at himself.

"Oh, do shut up," I said.

"You like him," Truitt said.

"I do," I sighed.

"All right, then," Truitt said, once more ready to talk. "You decided against using the boy and tossing him away at the end of summer to retaliate against his uncle. That doesn't explain what happened tonight. He was more than eager."

I nodded. "Yes. I made my choice and was ready to leave things as they were. However, Langton has his own mind and had reached his own decisions. And for some reason, he's decided that he wants me. Not only that, but he wants you as well."

Truitt began to laugh. "He's seducing you?"

I groaned and made to smack him again, but he was too quick, rolling away as he kept laughing.

"He first told me, not half an hour after my resolve was made, that he was confused about his feelings for you, and for me. He then spent some three or four days flirting with me, which I attempted to ignore, and then last night he burst into the library and accused me of treating him like a child. When I denied it and asked him what he wanted from me, he threw a book of pornography at me and said he wanted that."

"Oh my. The lamb has style. And pornography? Where did he get that?"

"From my own library, actually. It was Barrett's."

Truitt grinned madly, delighted with the teeth of our lamb. "What did you do?"

"I got very little sleep. Which then led me to do something very foolish in the carriage this afternoon." I could feel the colour rising on my cheeks.

Truitt looked at me with undisguised curiosity, so I took a deep breath and described the entire scene in detail, including the picture of the three men and Langton's hopes regarding same. When I was done, Truitt was both hard against me and thoughtful.

"I think you have some more choices to make, dear heart," he said seriously. "You must know that regardless of Langton's reactions thus far, particularly to me bringing him off in the dining room, he is most likely having a quiet breakdown at this very moment. I suspect that his experiences at school were... perhaps varied, but I doubt he's really handling this double attraction as well as he appears."

"I know," I said quietly. "But I didn't know what else to do. I didn't want him to stay here tonight; I couldn't."

"Why ever not? And don't tell me it's about his uncle again, because that's rot and you know it."

I sighed and closed my eyes. "I didn't want... I won't... " Words failed me, and I looked to Truitt, pleading with my eyes for him to understand.

"You didn't want to share your first time with him," he said with a broad smile.

"Forgive me?"

"Of course, dear. Don't be silly." He kissed me sweetly and laid his head on my chest. "Now, answer me this. I suggest you make an arrangement with him, like you did with me. He's young, and I suspect his head is filled with his heart at the moment. You and I both know that declaring undying love would be foolish, but if you don't place some limits, he'll get very hurt come the end of summer. Let him know that it isn't a one off, but that it may not be forever either."

I thought about it for a while, relaxing into the warmth of Truitt's body. "It wouldn't be the same arrangement," I said finally. "You knew what you wanted, exactly. Langton, for all his eagerness, is not quite as aware of himself yet. But, yes, I will talk to him, certainly." I kissed the top of his head. "And what of you, pet? What do you want your place to be?"

"Oh, I expect I'll be around for some fun," Truitt said lightly.

I shook my head. "I don't know if I'll be happy with that, pet. I've missed you. More than I had realised, I admit."

Truitt raised his head, his eyes serious. "What are you saying, Ned? I need to know."

I shook my head again. "I'm not sure, exactly. We extended our arrangement once; why didn't we do it again?"

"Because we are both greedy sods and wanted to taste everything at the banquet instead of limiting ourselves to our favourite food," Truitt said honestly. "Really, if Langton had not brought this up, would you be thinking about this?"

"Perhaps. I think it was the weekend more than Langton, to tell the truth."

"So what do you want?" Truitt asked. "If you want Langton and me, and he wants us both... "

I nodded. "It sounds lovely to me. I know you can't move out to the Hall, but I will have a house in London, or at least rooms. Langton will have the Duke's house, and you are here. It could work for us, in the long term."

"You're thinking about a permanent arrangement before you've even lain with the lamb," Truitt pointed out with a smile. "I think you're losing your hold on your heart."

I smiled back and took a kiss. "I think I lost it a year or so ago, pet," I whispered.

Truitt kissed me back, his hand moving from my hip to my arse. "Talk to Langton. When I come for the weekend the three of us can see where we are. But for right now, I have more immediate concerns, dear heart."

"Oh? Like what?" I teased, licking at his lips.

"Roll over," he said with a filthy smile.

I smiled back and rolled, saying, "Be gentle, love. It's been months."

"Good."

Chapter Twenty Six

In the morning, I had a hasty breakfast in my room and had the carriage brought round so that I might make my way to the Duke's house and collect Langton well before our first appointment. The day was starting out somewhat grey, but there was hope for sun before noon, and I was sure that we would be able to conduct our business fairly easily, barring catastrophe.

When I arrived at the Duke's London house, where Langton and his mother and sister lived, I was admitted by the butler, who took my hat and led me to the drawing room. "Viscount Langton is taking his breakfast now, and His Grace will be with you shortly," the dour man said as he backed away.

"Of course," I murmured, walking into the room. Langton was sitting in a chair to the side of the door, sipping tea and looking at the floor. At my voice, he looked up and offered me a somewhat paler smile than usual.

"Good morning, my lord," I said glancing about the room to the footman by the sideboard.

"Good morning, Mr. Munrow. Help yourself to tea

or coffee, if you'd like." His voice was soft, almost tired, and I looked at him with some concern. He was neat and presentable, but dark marks under his eyes suggested that he'd another night of little sleep.

"Thank you," I said, crossing to the tray and pouring a cup of coffee. "I trust your mother is well?"

"She's not here."

I turned, startled. "She's not?"

Langton looked at me, his eyes searching. "No. She and Lucy are in the country, apparently. You didn't know?"

"No." Of course I didn't know. I wouldn't have sent him to that place to be alone with his uncle if I'd have known. "How was your evening?" I asked cautiously, trying not to be overly concerned in front of the Duke's staff.

"It was fine," Langton said, not looking at me. Meaning it was anything but.

I took a step forward, about to assure him of how sorry I was, when the Duke appeared at the door. "Munrow. You're here early."

"Your Grace. No earlier than I said I would be," I said mildly, taking a sip of my coffee and tearing my attention from the dejected countenance of Langton. "You're looking well."

"Your lying hasn't improved overly," he replied, not moving from the door. He did, in fact, look pale and weak, worse than when he had been to Red Oak Hall. He held a cane in one hand, although he was not noticeably using it to bear his weight. "It's a shame that Julia is not here; it would have been well for you to meet her."

"You might have sent word back to me that she would not be in residence when I informed you of my intent to be in London. It would have been good for my lord to know," I rebuked him, gesturing to Langton.

The Duke didn't bother to glance at his nephew, and he shrugged it off with a falsely apologetic gesture of the hand. "It had slipped my mind. How are you two getting along, if I might ask?"

"Fine," I said. "The Viscount has a quick mind."

"My nephew tells me you had guests last weekend."

I inclined my head. "I did. The weather was against us, unfortunately, but we had a good weekend despite it. We missed the shooting, but got a bit of riding in, around the pond."

There seemed nothing more to say, and I dared not take my eyes off the Duke to see how Langton was bearing up.

"I trust Henri did not make a nuisance of himself?"

That was quite enough, I thought. "He was a most pleasant companion. And now, if you'll excuse us, we have a full day of business ahead of us and then a long trip home." I turned to Langton and said, "I hope you don't mind, but we'll be heading back tonight instead of tomorrow, so someone should collect your cases and have them put in the carriage immediately."

Langton blinked at me and rose at once, but the footman was already on his way, nodding to the boy as he went. "Certainly, Mr. Munrow," Langton said quietly.

The Duke did not look pleased, but he had no leverage with which to counter me. I set my coffee cup down and gestured to Langton. "If you could take your leave, we really should hurry. I don't wish to be late."

Langton nodded and stood in front of his uncle, both of them inclining their heads as they said goodbye. "Thank you, Uncle. I expect I'll see you again soon. Please tell Mother that I was here, and that I will write soon."

The Duke merely nodded and in so many words told Langton to behave himself in a respectable manner. Langton looked to me, and I moved towards the door, fully intending to simply brush past the Duke without comment. Langton preceded me, crossing to the door just ahead of the footman with his case. As I passed, however, the Duke grasped my arm, and I was stopped.

"One hand on him," the Duke hissed, "and you will pay."

I looked at him coldly and tugged my arm away. "You will see him before you die, but only the once. I promise you."

In the carriage, I found Langton huddled into a corner, looking miserable.

"What happened?" I asked as I joined him, sharing his side of the carriage and putting my hand on his shoulder.

"Nothing," he protested. "He was cold and angry, pressing me for details over and over. He wanted to know everything you said, looking for some hidden meaning somewhere. He wanted to know what you were like towards me, if you'd ever been improper or even rude, although he seemed more interested to know if you were kind or not."

"I'm so sorry," I said again. "You won't be going back, and if I'd have known your mother wasn't there, you would not have been there last night." I wanted to know what Langton had said, but was afraid to ask. Not because I thought he would have said anything about our carriage ride, or our attraction, but because if I asked I would hurt him, would make him think I didn't trust him. All the same, I wanted to know.

"You really didn't know?" Langton asked.

I shook my head, wishing he would look at me. "I had no idea, lamb. I would have spared you, I swear. Tonight will be different."

Langton snorted. "Yes, spent in the dark in a

carriage."

"No, at the club. I have no intention of travelling at night."

Langton turned to me, his eyes widening. "Really?"

"Yes. We'll go on today as planned, then dine at the club and stay there tonight. Are you all right? Do you want to talk for a while?"

Langton looked dazed. "Talk?"

I held his chin and brushed my lips across his. "Talk. I'm sure you have a great deal on your mind, and we will discuss it all at length. But we have some time right now if there is something pressing. Your uncle, last night, anything."

Langton's eyes softened, and he smiled shyly at me, some of the light coming back into his face. "No. I put him off, told him only the truth whilst keeping to myself what he was truly after. Tell me about your night?"

I smiled. "My night was lovely, in contrast with yours. Truitt is quite taken with you."

Langton beamed, his eyes dancing. "Is he? Is he really coming to visit?"

"I doubt we could stop him now, lamb. Are you happy?"

"I will be," Langton said, giving me a saucy look. "But if I start thinking about that right now I shall be unfit for business. Who are we seeing first?"

That, it appeared, was my cue to turn my mind to business.

We had three appointments in the morning, all of which were uneventful. We then stopped at a few shops, where I ordered some items as gifts, and had an early luncheon. After we ate, we discussed music for a time, watching the people pass by and avoiding each other's eyes. It was insanely easy to put our mutual desires aside when in the company of others; when left to our own devices, however, we quickly fell into a pattern of speech and mannerisms that were not suited for our surroundings.

I began to fear for my good judgement. The very idea of having him more or less on his own in the vastness of Red Oak Hall had a great deal of potential for havoc.

In the afternoon, we paid a visit to Barrett's sister, Martha. The lady was gracious, which surprised me a little, considering that I had more or less swept her heritage away from her. I made it plain that if there was anything at the Hall that she wanted, I would have it sent, and I spoke to her regarding her allowance. I knew the terms of her father's will in regard to that, and also what Barrett had set up for her, but I wanted to make sure that she herself knew and understood how much she had. She did, and even though she had solicitors to handle the money, she paid close attention to her situation, and I told her that if she needed more I would be more than happy to discuss the matter.

She finally sent us away, full of small cakes and assurances that she was just fine, thank you very much. She did call to me as I left the room, pulling me back to say that she had a letter from Barrett the week before.

"He's well?" I asked eagerly.

"He's happy," she said with a warm smile. "He has purchased a small house and has been spending time in the garden. He and Granger are settling in very well."

I smiled and inclined my head. "Thank you."

"Thank you, Mr. Munrow. It is most wonderful to have one's family happy and healthy."

I was still smiling when I joined Langton in the carriage, and we made our way to our final appointment, a simple accounting with my solicitors. All in all, it was a most pleasant day. Dinner and our evening promised to be even more so.

Chapter Twenty Seven

Our conversation flowed easily as we ate, the business of the day still high on our minds. We had done well for a day and a half's work, taking the Hall out of one deal that looked to be going sour and checking on two more commitments that were doing well. Langton had a theory about something he'd overheard, and he spent a good amount of our time coupling his information with some other things he'd gathered from the newspapers and listening to his uncle. It occurred to me that I might perhaps take more interest in the financial climate of Britain and how it would affect me, now that I had something for it to affect.

I loved watching him like that. His eyes danced as he put the various parts of his idea together, creating counter arguments as he played his own devil's advocate. He seemed to be almost oblivious to where he was, in the middle of the dining room at my club. The room was full tonight, and we were seated in the least secluded area there was. Langton had been patient as I greeted a few of the gentlemen, seemingly missing the appraising glances he received.

By the time I had accepted the wine and we'd been served, Langton was in mid-flight, tossing comments and ideas to me as soon as he'd had them, his voice light and happy, then thoughtful by turn as he weighed variables. He talked throughout the meal, my own comments serving to keep him on track and encourage his line of thought. I was curious to see what his final recommendation would be, but for the most part I was simply enjoying seeing him like that, in contrast to the shattered young man I had collected from his uncle's clutches that morning.

When dessert and coffee arrived, he suddenly stopped, blushing furiously and apologising for monopolising the conversation.

I could not help but laugh indulgently. "I like listening to you, I think," I confessed. "You have such passion when you are arguing with yourself."

His colour deepened, and his eyes shot to the table we'd occupied the night before and then to his plate.

I shifted in my seat, leaning closer to him across the table. "And not only in argument," I added quietly.

He looked up at me through his eyelashes. I wondered if he knew how that looked, how coquettish; I suspected he might. "I found myself wondering if it was real," he said. "Last night, when I'd gone to bed. It seemed so... unlikely."

"Unlikely?" I echoed, amused. "Oh, it was real, and not in the least unlikely. But I can see how it might have been overwhelming. Are you all right with it?"

He nodded, looking at his plate once more. "I... I wanted it. But after -- when I left, and then this morning, it just seemed like something outside of me. I felt like I had lost control and done something you wouldn't respect." He wouldn't look up at me, and his voice grew even quieter, just above a whisper. "I don't want for you to think badly of me."

"I don't," I tried to assure him. "I most certainly don't. Langton, look at me, please."

It was a long moment before he finally raised his eyes, but he did, meeting my gaze steadily and letting me see a certain amount of his fear.

"Truitt suggested I have a long talk with you, about several things. How you are coping with things, concerning him and me, and about what you want. He went so far as to suggest I seek out an agreement with you, as I did with him. But before we even get to that, I want to know if you are willing to discuss matters. I know that it can be difficult, and I don't want to press you -- "

"Yes," Langton interrupted. "Please."

I smiled, relieved. I had not dealt with anyone like him before. In the past, all of my relationships -- and indeed my trysts of too short a duration to be called relationships -- had been dictated solely by following my desires or emotions until such a point that things either settled or a discussion was needed, such as with Truitt. But Langton was young, and I had found myself in the singular position of having involved myself emotionally before knowing what was returned, what was wanted, or what was expected. Given his age and the differences in our experience, I was feeling nervous about each step, half-afraid I would scare him away or push too hard and take advantage of his youth or his unsettled mind.

"Shall we go to the drawing room then?" I asked, standing up.

Langton nodded and followed me down the hall and into the room, staying close to me as I paused to speak to Stevenson, who was in charge of keeping the rooms and more or less acted as the head of house.

"We're going into the drawing room for a spell," I told him, "but the Viscount will be staying for the night so we'll need a second room. One next to mine would be best, if it's possible."

Stevenson shook his head apologetically. "I'm sorry, Mr. Munrow. We're full tonight, I'm afraid."

I stared at him, astonished. "It's mid-week," I protested.

Stevenson opened his mouth but a voice behind me said, "My fault, Munrow. My boy, Daniel, is being presented this evening, and there are a large number of people staying over after. We've quite taken over the place."

I turned and shook hands with Mr. Royston, whom I'd not seen in months. "I see," I said after our greetings. "Oh, dear."

Royston smiled, his gaze flicking to Langton. "You should come to the Green room at ten or so. Daniel has done very well; it'll be well worth your time. Bring your... young friend."

I blanched at the thought. I knew Royston's tastes, shared a few of them, but if he was presenting Daniel for the first time it would be a full out show and would set Langton's mind to doing cartwheels. "Thank you, but I think we'll have to decline."

"Shame. Fitzhugh and Kirkland are here; they always like to see the presentations."

I felt my blood flow speed downwards, recalling the last presentation those two gentlemen had seen in my own room, and found I could not look at Langton at all. "I don't suppose they asked for separate rooms?" I asked desperately. Lord knew they wouldn't use both, if they did.

"No, sir," Stevenson said, coming back to us. "I've just asked a few gentlemen who were unsure if they would actually be staying the night, but it appears that we are well and truly booked."

I sighed. "Thank you, Stevenson. Could you have his

cases taken to my room, please?"

"Don't bother," Langton said quietly. "I'll go to my uncle's."

"You most certainly shall not," I said emphatically. "You'll stay with me; we'll be fine."

Royston smirked. "Most fine, Munrow," he said, slithering away down the hall.

Langton was white. "I don't want to be a bother," he insisted.

"You aren't," I said, feeling that I'd lost complete control of the evening. "Are you well? You're pale, and… bugger, let's go up, shall we? Give you a shot of brandy and talk in peace and quiet."

Langton said nothing, didn't even nod, simply followed me as I headed for the stairs and up two flights. My rooms were just as I'd left them, although my clothes from the day before had been hung up and the bed remade. Langton's cases had not yet arrived, and I crossed immediately to the small table by the window and poured us each a snifter of brandy. Langton had still not said anything and took the glass without a word, not meeting my eye.

"Langton?"

He ignored me, turning his back and moving to the foot of the bed, where he stood looking at… nothing, I assumed. I sighed and tried again. "Langton? What's wrong?"

"I seem to have made a mistake," he said, his voice tight and low, so low I almost didn't hear him.

I set my glass down and undid my overcoat, draping it over the back of a chair. "What do you mean?"

Langton turned and looked at me, holding his snifter carefully in his hand. He spoke quietly still, but his words were sure, his voice steady. "It's perfectly obvious that you would rather I were not here. You don't want me,

Munrow, and I'd really prefer not to stay, to be honest."

I stared at him, wondering when he would smile, when he would make this into a teasing prod and not a pronouncement. He stood there, back straight and shoulders set, apparently waiting for my reply. I admit it took me longer than it should have, but I was so stunned by his misreading of the situation I did not know where to anchor my reply.

"Did I imagine myself in the carriage yesterday?" I finally said. "Or at dinner last night?"

Langton raised an eyebrow. "You mean when I looked at pictures and you spoke of my senses and my desires but said nothing of your own? When you watched me with Truitt? You have not touched me, Munrow. Instead you send me away, time and again, treat me as a child, and refuse to see me for what I am -- perfectly capable of making up my own mind and not so very innocent."

Again I stared, watching as he set his glass down and advanced upon me, stepping slowly, carefully. Hunting. God, he was beautiful.

"You don't see, and if you do, you don't want me. I'm more than able to accept that, Munrow, but I find myself unwilling to play these games, this tease and release."

I stood as he walked to me, his pace not changing as he came abreast of me and moved to walk past to the door, clearly intending to leave me. I let him pass me, let him even reach the door, but I had no intention of letting him open it. As his hand touched the knob I spun him around, his back hitting the door with a solid thump as I pinned him there.

"Blindness all round, I think," I said, holding him there with my body, one hand on the door beside his head the other on his hip. "You refuse to see courtesy, me giving you a chance to have somewhere to go. What you see as me rejecting you is respect, Henri. You may very well have had hands and mouths on you before, but 'twas nothing like it will be."

I leant close to him, smelling his hair, the brandy on his breath. His breathing was quickening, clearly not through the shock of having me suddenly ambush him. His eyes widened, growing dark as he pushed against me to no avail, succeeding only in pressing his body closer to mine.

"No more teasing, lamb," I whispered as I insinuated my leg between his thighs, my own heartbeat quickening as my blood flowed faster. "You say I only spoke of what you desire? That I don't want you? I want you on your knees, Henri. I want to feel your mouth on me, your tongue as it slides over my skin, over my shaft. I want to taste your sweat, to smell your passion." I nuzzled his neck, licking at the pulse points as he gasped. "I want to hear my name on your lips as you gasp for breath, and I swear you'll understand. You'll know that the clumsy, hidden touches you've had before are nothing, not even shades of what you can feel."

"Ned," he said hoarsely, shifting against me and rocking on my thigh.

"Hush, lamb. Listen to my voice." I scraped his neck with my teeth, and he shuddered again, his hands suddenly hard on my hips, pulling at me. "You think I don't want you? When all I can see is your eyes? When all I want is to spread you out on my bed and to feast upon your skin? I think about you around me, moving under me. I imagine you astride me, pushing down upon my prick...God, you're going to be so tight, so hot inside when I take you -- "

"Ned!" It was more of a gasp than a cry, but the way that he shook and trembled in my arms nearly made me spend as well, and I had to close my eyes against the beauty of him. His head against the door, his hips still

197

moving restlessly as he strained against me; he took my breath and almost shredded my control.

"No, no more teasing," I said quietly. I kissed his neck, just under his jaw, inhaling the scent of him and growing ever harder. "Get undressed, lamb, and into bed. Now."

He stumbled as I let him go, his eyes vague and unfocused. I stood to the side and watched as him as he stripped, wordless and clumsy as he struggled with his buttons and hooks. His cheeks were flushed as he used a flannel to clear away the evidence of his spending, his body angled away from me so I could not see him. He looked at the bed, and then back to me, as if waiting for encouragement.

I nodded, and he climbed onto the high mattress, burrowing under the covers until I could see only his face. He watched me intently as I undressed, taking the time to hang my waistcoat and shirt. I had just bent to remove my boots when there came a soft knock at the door.

Langton's cases.

I glanced at the bed, smiling as Langton vanished under the blankets. Bare-chested, I opened the door and took the cases from the man, not allowing him entrance. His face was familiar, one of the footmen who served the club, and he took my state of undress in stride, simply wishing me a good evening before retreating down the hall. When I'd set the cases aside I resumed stripping, as if nothing had happened.

Langton was still buried, hiding under the sheets and blankets, a tight ball in the middle of the bed. I shook my head and smiled, quickly stripping everything to the foot of the bed and leaving him bare on the bed. "No hiding, lamb. Not from me." I uncorked a bottle of oil, let him see me leaving it within reach of the bed.

He didn't say anything for a moment, looking up at

me warily. He did, however, unfold himself, not quite stretching out for inspection but making the effort not to hide. "I wasn't expecting the knock," he said finally. "It startled me."

"I'm sure it did," I said, my shoes finally off and set aside. "But now it is just you and me here, and you shall not hide." My fingers worked at the fastenings of my trousers, drawing his gaze. "Truitt wants me to talk to you," I said conversationally as I stripped.

"Does he?" Langton asked, staring at me and sounding quite distracted as I removed my clothes.

I nodded, folding my trousers and placing them on the chair. "But that is Truitt -- he's very much interested in rules, limits, and obedience." I gestured at Langton, removing my small clothes and finally stood nude before him, my erection heavy and thick before me. "You, on the other hand, are more about knowledge and not being dismissed."

He swallowed as I approached the bed and lay down next to him, not yet touching him. His fingers twitched, his eyes still fixed on my shaft, and he rubbed his hand on his stomach, a soft, slow circle. I watched his prick as it began to swell; youth has its distinct advantages. I stretched for show, my back arching slightly off the bed, and Langton made a low sound, his fingers stilling on his stomach.

"And you?" he asked, his voice thick as he dragged his gaze up to my eyes. "What do you need?"

"For us all to be safe," I said seriously. He held my look, his eyes searching my face, and I knew he took my meaning. He nodded slowly, acknowledging the promise and all that lay behind it, including the precautions that we would need to take to assure ourselves of that safety. He would do as he was told and would not demand more than I could give.

I rolled onto my side and let my hand settle on his hip, pulling him to face me. His eyes were wide once more, and I could see nervous energy building in his face. "You liked it, didn't you?" I asked smoothly, keeping the conversational tone. Langton off balance was lovely. "At school, with the others. More than they did, and that worried you, correct?"

He shook his head, his hands restless and floating, unsure where to settle. "I... had to hide it," he admitted. "They used each other, hands rough on fevered skin, seeking merely for release and then were shamed. I wanted more, wanted to lose myself in it, the warmth of bodies. But I couldn't; I dared not."

I nodded, catching one of his hands in my own and bringing it to my mouth to kiss the palm. "'Tis dangerous to show such needs." He watched me with parted lips, shifting on the bed. "But things change, yes? Like seeks out like, and safe places are made." I licked his hand, biting lightly at the inside of his wrist. "As you have discovered."

He made another soft sound, air drawn into lungs with a hiss. "Yes. You, your friends. This place..." His eyelids fluttered closed. "Ned," he sighed. "God, please. Show me."

There was more I wanted to say, questions I wanted to ask, but everything faded away at the sound of his voice, the ache in it. I admit that part of the reason I stayed my words, put off conversation, was because my body was crying out for him; control only extends so far, and when one is hard and hungry and wanted... well, resistance crumbles like so many dried leaves.

My hand gripped his hip harder, digging in around the bone until his eyes opened to look at me, the blue once again losing focus. "Kiss me," I said, leaning over him. He lifted his head, one hand at long last finding its way to me, tangling in the hair at the back of my neck.

Langton kissed me with his entire body, his mouth and his tongue merely hot points that flashed while his skin took over everything. I don't recall him moving, and I'm most sure I didn't pull him to me, but there he was, warming me from lips to ankle. He didn't writhe or push against me, nor did we have a rhythm, but he was kissing me with every fibre of his being, each touch and brush of our limbs incendiary.

Langton was hard again, his prick hot against mine, thick and full. I tore my mouth from his before I was lost, holding onto a fine edge of control. This was for him, and it was my responsibility to make sure it was nothing like what he'd experienced before. I pressed him to the bed, my hands on his shoulders, and bent my head to his neck.

"Lie back, lamb," I whispered. "I'll show you."

He moaned, the sound coming from the back of his throat, and he tried to kiss me again. I smiled at him and left him wanting, beginning to make my way down his body. Each time he tried to rise, to reach for me and pull me back, I pushed him back, laughing. Finally I had to kiss him again, just to make him stay.

"Now," I said into his mouth, the weight of my body pinning him down. "Stay." I reached for the bottle of oil, and watched his eyes widen anew.

"I've never..." he whispered.

"Good." And it was. My task, my right, my gift.

I took a pert nipple between my lips, and Langton gasped, twisting on the bed. One hand went to my hair again, the other slid down his body on a direct route to his shaft. "Ah, ah," I chided. "No."

"But I need -- "

"Let me."

Langton growled, a most wonderful sound, and

grabbed at the sheet we lay upon, his fingers struggling for purchase. I rewarded him with a scattering of kisses across his chest and down his belly, being careful not to spill the oil. Now Langton writhed, his body shifting and twisting under me, but he did not attempt to rise. He made sounds constantly, little growls and whimpers that made me smile against his skin, and his legs twitched every time I brushed against him.

Heat filled me, warming me through like no liquor could. Langton's skin was hot and tasted like salt, the sweetness of butter and cream overlaid with smoke. He sounded like music, and he felt like softest velvet laid over stone. I traced his hipbone with my tongue, and he begged.

"More. Please, Ned. Touch me."

I kissed his stomach and knelt between his legs, sitting up to spill oil onto my palm.

"Will it…" Langton swallowed, watching my hands as I spread the oil, warming it. "Will it hurt?" he asked in a rush.

I smoothed the oil over his thighs. "I'll try not to. But I can't promise you won't be uncomfortable at first, and you may not really enjoy the journey home in the morrow. Would you prefer to wait until we are home?" I teased the soft skin behind his balls with my thumbs, and he gasped, shaking his head.

"Now. Please," he choked out, his legs spreading by reflex. Such a wanton picture, so beautiful and pale on the sheets, his cock dark and heavy, rising from a thatch of golden curls.

I slid down the bed, my fingers sliding over his skin; legs, belly, hips, and balls, my fingers caressed and stroked, bringing forth sweet cries and the most incomprehensible language. I nuzzled him, lost myself in the scent of his skin, his musk, his need. When I licked at his balls and traced the veins in his prick, Langton swore and clutched at the bed again; when I took him in my mouth he groaned, his hips lurching once before he forced himself to be still.

I smiled to myself and sucked a little harder, my hands going under his arse to urge him up. I traced a slippery finger down between his buttocks, waiting for him to thrust up into my mouth before I teased at his entrance, simply circling the soft skin.

"Oh, God," Langton gasped.

I pulled more of his flavour into me, the passion leaking steadily from his rigid shaft. He was too close; I was too close, my prick throbbing with my heartbeat. I let him slide from my mouth and reached for the oil once more. "Roll over, lamb."

Langton looked dazed, and for a moment, I thought he would refuse, but he nodded slowly and turned, arranging his legs on either side of me again. I leant forward, newly slicked fingers gliding over him, and kissed his back. "Breathe, Henri." Slowly I breached him, as carefully as I could. "Relax as much as you can," I whispered, one finger pushing and gliding back.

Langton breathed and relaxed, and he pushed back, his body asking for more. More kisses, words a constant whisper against his skin... I would not rush, no matter the insistence of my own need. Concentrating on Langton -- his breathing, his sounds, his every move -- helped to temper my need to rush. It took time, and far more care than I was used to, but soon he opened to me, my fingers moving faster and deeper as I readied him.

Langton was sweating, whimpering into the sheets as he lifted his arse into the air. I smoothed my free hand over his hip, slick with moisture, and found his prick no longer achingly hard, his erection deflated but not flaccid. Three fingers now, and my own need was soaring; he needed to be brought back to me. I had avoided the hard smooth spot inside of him until this point, knowing the pain and discomfort would lessen his passion; that deep touch inside of him would bring it back.

The effect of my fingers brushing the spot was immediate. Langton's head snapped up and a sharp cry filled the room. "God, again! Oh, God, again!"

I growled, scraping my teeth over his spine, tasting his sweat, and did it again, picking up a heavy rhythm as he moved back onto my fingers, moaning and swearing. "Henri," I said, my voice harsh. "Henri, I need."

"Please, God, yes. Ned, please!"

I stroked him again, his erection now full and heavy once more as I worked oil into him. I let go of his prick, and he moaned, unable to reach for it himself as he balanced his weight. "Let me... I'll..." Words fled me as I smoothed oil over my shaft. "Henri." I tried again. "I need you to relax and let me in."

Langton whimpered, his legs trembling. I withdrew my fingers, and he inhaled sharply, the sound almost a sob, and then I was pushing in, as slowly as I could. I'd never been anywhere so tight, although the heat was expected. I could barely breathe for the feeling, sinking into him, into that beautiful, perfect body.

"Ned," he gasped. "Full."

"Hurt?" I could barely manage the one word and wasn't at all sure I'd be able to pull away if he said yes, if he told me to stop.

"More," he demanded, and then he thrust back, impaling himself upon me and stealing everything from me in that one movement.

I swore and gripped his hips, holding him to me as I tried not to spend. I ached, heat was blossoming in my belly, my legs were on fire, and I knew there was very little chance for me to fend off my climax for more than a few moments. I kissed his back again, breath coming in harsh pants, and found his cock with my hand, stroking him slowly.

Langton keened, the sound high and desperate, and I thrust into him, not gently. He begged, praised, demanded; words flowed from us both and I remember none of them, aside from a repetition of "please", and me telling him how beautiful he was. My hips met his buttocks with sharp sounds, and I could feel his body tense as I thrust and pulled, his legs quivering even as he forced himself back onto me again and again, his voice louder with each rocking of our hips.

Fire raced up my legs and out of my prick as I came with a shout, pushing deep into him and shaking so hard I feared I would topple us off the bed. He met me, crying my name and spilling over my fingers onto the sheets, his body clamped tightly around me. "Henri," I said again and again, "My beautiful lamb. My Henri."

We fell onto the bed, gasping and shaking, clinging to one another. It was minutes before I could ease away from him, waiting for my cock to soften enough that I could slip from his body. Even then, he moaned, and I pulled him into my arms, turning him to face me. I scattered kissed on his face, lapping away his tears as I searched for pain under the euphoria. "Are you all right?" I asked him softly.

"I'll be fine," he whispered. "Just don't let go, please."

"I won't," I promised him, our legs tangling. "I won't."

We slept for a time, waking when we were cold, only to stagger off the bed and wash with soap and lukewarm water and to have something to drink. Then we climbed back in and drew the covers up over us as we kissed and took our time exploring one another. Langton delighted me by taking a certain amount of initiative, his hands skimming over me again and again before he dove under the blankets to take me in his mouth.

Truitt was right, the touches were arousing in their lack of finesse, the slight tremble as endearing as the growing confidence. He was also wrong; there was nothing untalented or unschooled about my lamb's mouth. Between the kisses, the likes of which I'd never experienced, and the way he feasted upon my prick until I startled us both by climaxing again, I was beginning to suspect that Langton had an oral preference nearing on obsession. More the luck for me. I could hardly wait for Truitt to arrive at the Hall, five days hence. But then again, that was five days in which I would have Langton to myself. .

I considered the entire trip to London to be a rousing success.

Chapter Twenty Eight

When I awoke, the sunlight was streaming in through sheer curtains and Langton was lying by my side, peering at me in confusion.

"Good morning," I said softly as I stretched. I sincerely hoped the boy wasn't about to jump out of the bed in a fit of nerves. I could think of much better ways to start the day than soothing a panicked lover. Much better ways -- indeed, parts of me were already quite insistent about the matter.

He blinked at me and then smiled shyly. "Good morning." He seemed unsure of what to do, pulling away slightly as if to rise, and then leaning forward again. Colour began to creep into his cheeks, although he was still smiling.

"How did you sleep?" I asked, rolling onto my side and snaking my arm around his waist and pulling him to me. Oh, he truly was well awake.

"Fine," he gasped, his eyes widening slightly. Then he gasped again as I dipped my head to nuzzle at his neck.

"Oh, good. Do you happen to know the time?" I asked casually, my hand dropping to his arse as I thrust gently against him.

"Half eight. Oh. Ned -- "

I smiled into his neck and bit lightly. "Not much time then," I teased, pushing him to lie on his back and covering him with my body. I braced myself, arms to either side of him, and looked down upon him to judge his reaction.

Face flushed, eyes wide, tongue slipping out to lick at his lower lip -- he was delicious. I rocked gently against him, eliciting a moan and an answering thrust.

"Shall we greet the day properly?" I asked, still watching his reactions.

"I'm not sure that this is quite proper," he replied. But his legs spread a little, and his hands found their way to my hips as he pushed against me.

I groaned as we rubbed together and took his mouth in a fierce kiss. His fingers tightened, and I allowed him to guide me, his hands and hips insisting we move faster. He was hungry and eager, a trait of his youth that I planned to enjoy thoroughly before I attempted to teach him some control. In mere moments, we were panting, moving in a quick rhythm which would lead to an inevitably quick end.

I didn't mind, really. We were due to be in the dining room for breakfast within short order.

It was sweet and intense, my lamb growling softly in his throat as he drew close. I heard the sound and gave him a growl back, mine deeper and more rumbling. His eyes met mine, dark and dilated, and I had a wicked idea. I rose slightly and caught at his hands, pulling them from me even as I kept moving upon him. Quickly, I drew them above his head, pinning him to the bed and holding his wrists with one hand.

Langton bucked against me, pulling at the restraint and crying out, his prick swelling even further against mine. I ground down against him and bared my teeth, then squeezed his wrists slightly, just enough to add some pressure.

His eyes rolled back, and he shuddered as he climaxed, his seed spurting thick between us. The sudden slickness made my movements freer, and I drove against him, chasing my orgasm as he panted my name and tried to kiss me. I took his mouth, muffling my groan as I finally spent, my seed mixing with his across his belly.

I smiled at the somewhat stunned look upon his face and kissed his nose. "Quite proper. One should always greet the day in pleasure, if at all possible."

Eventually, after much washing and a few delays in the process of dressing, we made our way down to the dining room to break our fast. There were surprisingly few gentlemen about, given that the house had been full, but as it was past nine o'clock, I assumed that those who could avoid their early appointments of the day were still in their beds.

We ate quickly and discussed the business of the day before; Langton was eager to return to the Hall and check his new theory on one of the investments against a file we had not brought. I was happy enough just to sit there and watch him talk, relieved that he was reacting so well to embarking upon the new turn in our relationship. He might not yet be completely sure of his feelings or what they meant, but he was, at the very least, up to presenting a solid front in public.

"Ah, Munrow!" Fitzhugh's voice called from my left. Langton fell silent as we rose to greet both Fitzhugh and Kirkland. Various morning wishes were exchanged, and they took the table next to us as we sat, Langton reaching for his coffee with a steady hand.

"We'd heard rumours that you were about the place

209

last night," Kirkland said to me. "I was rather surprised you didn't come to see the show. But all is explained now," he added, gesturing to Langton and smiling slightly.

Langton gave me a questioning glance but said nothing.

I leant back in my chair and considered the man. "I thought that the event might not be precisely what Viscount Langton -- my temporary ward -- would need to see, when what he sought was lodging for the evening," I said coldly.

Kirkland paled slightly, as well he might. It was one thing to tease about Langton when the lad was not present -- those sorts of liberties are not tasteful, but often taken, of course -- and quite another to be so presumptuous when Langton was present. The chastisement of Langton's social rank bit hard, especially coming from me, and when coupled with the reminder that Langton was not a member of the club and therefore should not even know of Daniel's debut... well, Kirkland crumpled rather satisfactorily.

"My apologies, my lord," he said to Langton. "And to you, Munrow."

Langton inclined his head, accepting the apology with grace, as did I. To Fitzhugh, Kirkland cast an uncomfortable look and got a glare in return. I was happy to know I'd not witness their private conversation.

"I trust you found the accommodations satisfactory, my lord?" Fitzhugh asked politely, saving the conversation. I wasn't terribly disposed to smoothing things over yet, and Langton was wearing a social mask that hid whatever he was thinking.

"Yes, it was a most pleasant evening, thank you," Langton said with a slight smile, and things returned to normal, even if a little more formal than usual.

After a few minutes conversation touching on business

affairs and idle gossip about unimportant people, Langton and I finished our coffee and bid Fitzhugh and Kirkland a good day. Our carriage and the journey back to the Hall awaited us.

We said almost nothing as we passed through the city, each of us lost in our own thoughts. I was watching Langton carefully, however, studying his face as he looked blankly out the window. He did not seem particularly troubled, but he was clearly weighing his thoughts and following one idea to the next. His brow was drawn in concentration, and his hand worried at a pleat of his trousers.

I wondered what it was that had captured his thoughts. Was it the previous night and the changes in our relationship? Truitt, or perhaps the three of us? Or was he focused upon the conversation at breakfast and what it meant in general or particular? I didn't wish to question him, as I had every expectation that he would raise the point himself when he wished; Langton had been very forthright to that point, something I appreciated. At his age, I was much more likely to rely on bravado than to speak up.

The carriage rolled over a particularly rough patch of road, jostling us and our belongings. I saw Langton wince as he shifted his weight, his eyes flicking to me and away again, his tongue slipping out to moisten his lower lip.

"Did I hurt you?" I asked, something I should perhaps have asked him earlier. It is possible that I should have considered our mode of transport the night before, but I doubted very much that it would have made any difference at the time.

Langton looked at me, his mouth curving into a smile. "I'm fine," he said softly.

I crossed the carriage to sit next to him. "That's not what I asked. Did I hurt you?"

He shook his head, looking at me through his fringe. "No. I have a... lingering ache, that is all." Colour bloomed on his cheeks, and he added in a whisper, "I like it."

I smiled and captured the hand nearest me, bringing it to my mouth so I could kiss his palm. "You won't object to trying that a second time?" I teased.

He laughed although his breath caught. "Did you think I would?"

I shrugged, keeping his hand in my own. "One never knows until it's happened."

Langton studied me for a moment, his head tilting to the side. "Do you not like it?"

I grinned at him. "I like sex. True, I don't often spread my legs, but that is more circumstance than anything else."

"Oh," he breathed, shifting again. "I should like to know what pleases you."

I brushed my mouth across his. Such a dear boy. "You will." I reached across him and drew the curtain across the window, blocking out the passing sights. He fairly fell into the kisses I pressed upon him, his lips parting easily to allow me entrance. I was careful to keep my hands from wandering any farther than his waist, spending ages caressing his face and neck, digging my fingers into his shoulders. He made lush, soft sounds, pressing close against me.

I found my impressions of the night before to be accurate -- my lamb was capable of magic with his kisses. Time slipped away without notice as we grew steadily more aroused, mouths hungry and hands moving more rapidly if not to new destinations.

The first tentative touch on my thigh made me

pull away from him, my eyes seeking his. He met my questioning look with one of such determination and heat it caused a thrill to race down my spine. "Langton?" I asked with a raised eyebrow.

"Do you suppose," he said in a low voice, "that my clothes would be much damaged if I knelt on the floor of your carriage?" His words were coupled with the tentative hand becoming much surer, the touch firm as it travelled along my thigh with serious intentions.

I embarrassed myself with the speed with which I retrieved a travel blanket from under the cushions opposite us. "No damage at all," I assured him. "However, I suspect that bumps, teeth, and cock would make an unfortunate combination."

His face fell, and he looked rather crushed. I tut-tutted him quietly and took his hand in my own, tracing his fingers for a moment before pulling it into my lap. "There are other ways," I said softly.

His eyes widened slightly and then he beamed at me, surging up to take another kiss as his hand reached its goal, his fingers quickly dealing with the placket of my trousers. In a moment he had me out, and what he lacked in experience was made up for in enthusiasm. Langton's clever fingers explored and rubbed over me in a most pleasing way, and I let him do as he would, content to encourage and experience.

I smiled at him, urging him to continue, although he really needed very little by way of coaxing. Langton's tendency to rush was still evident, of course, but that could firmly be blamed on his experiences at school where every encounter had to be stolen, as well as upon his age. It was something I could work with, given time. There was, however, very little else I would criticise about his technique.

His fingers were warm and quick, stroking over me

and exploring with a firm touch, his gaze fixed on what he was going. He played with my cock for long moments, tracing veins and slipping my foreskin back and forth until I couldn't hold back a groan. Delighted, he doubled his efforts and brought his other hand into play as well, cupping my balls and then starting to tug at my cock with long, even strokes, twisting his wrist every now and again.

I moved forward on the seat, my legs parting. I fear I was quite wanton, but he made me pant with need far quicker than I had expected; the fumbling touch Truitt had mentioned wasn't much in evidence as my lamb discovered how to touch me for maximum effect. I found myself wondering just how many pricks the boy had touched like that when he was at school. He really was more talented than I had expected.

"Langton. More," I said softly. Blue eyes glanced up at me, a palm moving over my thighs in sure motions. He teased the head of my cock with a gentle finger, his hand speeding and growing tighter. "Yes, like that," I sighed, my eyes drifting closed.

Langton made a soft noise and moved faster still, his wrist twisting and his fingers fluttering over the exposed crown of my prick. I groaned as he took me closer to coming, and had to still my hips from thrusting even faster. He worked me harder, his hands playing over me again and again, his fingers teasing once more. It did not take long before my balls pulled up and tension coiled in my gut.

"Yes," I hissed. "Lovely, lamb."

He slowed and the urgency retreated. I smiled.

Three times he brought me close to the brink before slowing and simply stroking my cock while I panted. Three times he stopped and checked my face for reaction, smiling up at me with dark eyes.

"Langton," I said hoarsely, driven nearly mad with lust for him, with my need for release. "Finish me."

He groaned and a shudder rolled through him as he pulled hard, his hand jerking faster over me. I tangled my fingers in his, unable to stop the sounds I was making as I thrust, my hips lifting off the seat. I panted his name, and he moaned, his head turn up until I finally took his mouth in a bruising kiss, spilling over his hand in long pulses.

It was a long moment before I could speak. Langton was calmly using his handkerchief to wipe me clean, and I sighed with utter contentment as he tucked me away and set my clothes to rights. He looked up at me, his eyes still dilated and his breathing harsh.

"You may well be my undoing, lamb," I declared as I moved him over and spread him on the bench opposite. If I'd had any thought of returning the favour by teasing him in a like manner, it vanished as soon as I tucked his waistcoat up and opened his flies. I'd barely taken his prick in hand when he gave a sharp cry and started to come; I dove, swallowing him as quickly as he spent and thus saving his trousers from awkward stains.

His face was scarlet when I lifted my head, and I laughed at him, not meaning to offend. "You flatter me," I said, rising to take a kiss.

He shook his head. "You overwhelm me."

I pulled him into my arms, and between the two of us, we were soon dressed and more or less presentable. "I do not mean to," I told him. "I am sure that many things are overwhelming you at the moment."

He inclined his head slightly. "I have much to think on, yes."

"Would you like to speak of any of it?" I asked, kissing his temple.

He hesitated, but a look at his face assured me he was merely looking for words, not shying away from the asking itself. After a moment, he relaxed against me with a soft sigh. "There is so much. My thoughts are scattered."

I nodded. "I cannot help with that, not really. But I will answer as best I can."

He made an agreeable sound and tilted his head for another gentle kiss. "Tell me," he said slowly, "what Kirkland meant. What was the entertainment you missed last night?"

I considered my answer. I would prefer not to break the confidences of the club, but that seal had already been well and truly broken. I had little fear of scaring Langton -- in fact, there were certain truths of which he had to become aware. It was only the phrasing which held me for a moment. "One of the members was showing off his partner, in a way. It is termed as a debut, when one chooses to share with the rest what they have accomplished together."

Langton looked at me, confused. "Accomplished?"

"Often it is a show of control," I explained. "The two men in question, according to what I know of them, have been exploring the depths of dominance and submission in their relationship; in this case, likely with the use of a flogger and bindings."

Langton's eyes widened. "I have heard of such things," he said softly, "but I doubted the truth of it."

I raised an eyebrow. "Oh, trust me, the implements are oft used."

"Not that," he corrected me. "I meant the... display. Did they really do that in front of others?"

I may possibly have blinked. The lad didn't turn a hair at the thought of bondage or flogging, but fucking in front of an audience threw him? Langton's depths deserved much exploration.

"That happens fairly often, too," I said. "Sometimes

flogging, binding, other toys. Sometimes sex. It depends entirely upon the couple -- sometimes it is an open invitation, sometimes restricted to specific people. There are others who never do anything in public. It is all personal choice, no demands are made."

Langton gave me a considering look. "And you? Have you... performed in public?"

I met his look and tilted my head. "Not often, but yes."

He nodded slowly but said nothing for a time. He settled again, or so I thought, his head resting on my shoulder. "And Truitt?" he whispered.

"I am unsure," I said. "I never showed him at the club; it wasn't part of our arrangement."

Langton sat up and turned to face me. "That is another thing, this arrangement. I don't understand what you mean, or why Truitt wanted you to discuss one with me. And I find myself wanting to ask why you qualified your answer."

I grinned at him. "Oh, you are a bright one, lamb."

He gave me a look that was very close to resignation. "You're going to call me that forever, aren't you?"

"Probably," I agreed.

"And Truitt does it now, too. Although I do find it better than 'pet'," he confessed. "What does he call you?"

I smiled. "At the moment, he calls me 'dear' and 'dear heart'. There was a time when he called me 'sir', but I suspect we've left that behind us."

"That was part of your arrangement?" Langton asked.

I nodded, then shook my head. "Not explicitly. Actually, our arrangement wasn't as terribly formal as it sounds. Truitt and I met at the club, through Lynch. We were attracted and spent some time together." I smiled at the memory, and Langton grinned. "At the end of the weekend, Truitt became rather... agitated; the reasons why are unimportant. I calmed him, ordered him to do certain things and behave in a specific way, and he responded very well. The next weekend he approached me and asked me to... well, to guide him, more or less."

Langton raised an eyebrow.

"Truitt wanted something rather specific," I explained. "He wanted to learn control, to learn his limits. He trusted me. So we discussed matters and decided that for six months he would submit to me alone. At the end of that time we hadn't reached... where we had wanted to be, so we extended the time."

Langton looked thoughtful. "I... Truitt thinks that you and I should do the same? I'm... I'm not sure if that..." He trailed off, now looking away from me and sitting straighter. "I'm sorry, if that's what you'd wanted -- "

I shook my head and tried to soothe him with a gentle touch. "No, lamb. That was what Truitt required, what he wanted. He had a need and asked me to fulfil it -- granted, I was willing. I think what he had in mind for you was more... setting boundaries, making sure that everyone is clear on certain things."

"What do you mean?" His eyes flickered around my face, perhaps seeking reassurance that I was not disappointed in him.

"I think he wants to make sure you see this for what it is. That you don't tie yourself so tightly to me that you lose sight of reality."

"He thinks that I'll be jealous?" Langton asked, his tone disbelieving. "That I'll not wish you to spend time with him?"

"Good Lord, no. Not with your already expressed desire for us both. I believe he was thinking more about time. You're only with me for the summer, after all, and then our lives will become... complex."

Langton's face cleared. "Oh. You both worry that I'll be broken-hearted. I... well, I understand the sentiment, but I'm afraid I can make no assurances." He pulled away again. "If that means you wish to keep a distance between us, I'll understand that as well, although I'll be... unhappy."

I smiled and touched his cheek. "As would I. No, I think that we should await Truitt's arrival on the weekend before we start talking of endings. We've barely made a beginning, lamb, and I find myself most reluctant to let you leave my arms, let alone my bed."

"You don't worry that I'll get too attached?" he asked with downcast eyes.

I closed my eyes. "It is not you I fear for at this point," I confessed. "I'm discovering all kinds of things about my heart of late."

Langton's eyes widened and then he smiled so shyly I had to kiss him again.

"There is one thing we must really discuss, however," I said when we broke apart. "Matheson."

"Matheson?"

I nodded. "Tell me honestly, how is he working out as your valet?"

Langton shrugged. "He's not done anything wrong," he offered. "He is respectful and seems to be making every effort. Why?"

"You might consider making him an offer to stay with you when you go back to London -- a permanent place as your man."

Langton's head tilted as he thought about it, and I took full advantage of the posture to nibble at his neck. "You're thinking that if he were to stop seeing me as a guest he would be more loyal."

"Servants see all," I agreed. "If he were yours, he would be less likely to tell below stairs about the state of your linens -- if you use them or not. I have no intention of stealing moments or riding out to the meadows to have you. There are beds in the Hall, yours and mine, and it would be a shame not to use them."

Langton nodded again, making a small noise as I returned my attention to his neck. "Yes. Beds."

"Big, soft beds," I said with a laugh.

"Which is not to say I object to stolen moments," Langton assured me. He sounded distracted.

"Oh, good." With part of my mind, I started making plans; the rest of me was concerned with more immediate needs.

Chapter Twenty Nine

We arrived at the Hall to be greeted by an open door and Dobbs waiting.

"Welcome home, sir, my lord. I trust your journey was pleasant?"

I did not look at Langton. "Most satisfactory, thank you," I said, walking through the hall to the private library. "Mr. Truitt will be arriving on Saturday, staying through Monday. See to a room for him, please, and have Cook send something to us -- just sandwiches, I think. Langton? Shall we finish the paperwork?"

"Of course. Dobbs, send Matheson to us as well, if you would." Langton followed along, and we were soon settled at the desk sorting files and discussing how various plans would be affected in the foreseeable future by outside influences.

Matheson and Dobbs arrived at the same time, Dobbs bearing a tray with sandwiches and a cold soup. He set the tray down and was dismissed, although I told him I might ring for him in fairly short order. He nodded and left, presumably to hover in the hall, poor man.

Langton straightened in his chair and regarded

Matheson, standing before us. "Matheson."

"My lord. Sir." The lad looked terrified.

"Mr. Munrow and I had reason to discuss your service to me and your place in the Hall whilst we were travelling," Langton began, but before he could go very much further Matheson had begun to pale. Langton held up his hand. "I am not displeased, quite the opposite, Matheson."

Matheson seemed to relax a little, and he nodded his head. "I had hoped not to be a disappointment, my lord."

Langton smiled and shook his head. "Not in the least. In fact, I wish to offer you a permanent place as my valet, which means that when the summer is done you shall, if you accept, come with me to London."

Matheson looked somewhat stunned but controlled it fairly well. He looked to me briefly. "Sir?"

"You have not displeased me either, Matheson. It would be a good position for you, if you choose to accept," I assured him. "Also, it would take effect immediately."

Matheson did not have to consider long. "Thank you, sir. My lord. I accept, with pleasure. Thank you." His eyes were bright now, and spots of colour were blooming on his cheeks.

Langton smiled and stood up. "Wonderful. Tomorrow we shall write up your new service papers and settle on a wage that is more suited to your new position."

"Yes, my lord," Matheson said, almost beside himself. "Thank you, my lord."

I stood and crossed to the door, finding Dobbs a few feet away as I'd expected. I motioned him in, and once I was seated again I said, "Matheson has left my service, Dobbs, and is now in the employ of the Viscount as his valet. Please see to the necessary changes."

Dobbs' eyes flicked to Matheson's, and he inclined his

head politely. "Of course, sir. Mr. Langton, we shall move your things to your new quarters immediately."

Matheson blinked at his new name and grinned for a moment before remembering himself. "Certainly," he said then bowed again to myself and Langton. "If there is nothing else, my lord?"

Langton shook his head, and they were withdrawing before it occurred to me that I should probably have given my own valet the consideration of having the gossip first. "Please tell Griffith," I said to Dobbs, "and then send him to me."

"Of course, sir," Dobbs said, and then they were gone.

"That went well," I said to Langton.

He smiled at me. "It seemed to. He'll work out, I expect -- at least I don't have to train any bad habits out of him. And it will be nice to have at least one person on my side when I return to my uncle's home."

There seemed little to say to that, so I leant across and kissed him, then reached for the tray. "Soup?"

Langton laughed, and we turned to our meal, talking once more of business.

That evening, Langton retired to his room before me, saying that he planned to go riding in the morning as the weather looked like it was going to hold. After some thought, I decided to join him and had Dobbs send word to the stables that we would need two mounts ready after breakfast. I tidied up a few papers in the library and then made my way upstairs to my room, where I found Griffith laying out my clothes for the morning.

Griffith had taken Matheson's new status in stride, reading between the lines quite nicely. I knew he would, and I trusted him to take Matheson on for a few weeks to teach him the finer points of being a gentleman's gentleman -- the things that had nothing to do with clothes, boots, fetching, or anything else that was tangible. I was counting on Griffith to make sure Matheson knew how to keep what he saw to himself and how to discourage rumours about his gentleman below stairs.

Of course, that also meant that as I got ready for bed, Griffith pointedly made sure that both pillows were acceptably plump and made a short comment about leaving a lamp burning in the hall so no one would get lost in the middle of the night. He left before I could throw him on his ear.

I had a very definite idea about how the rest of my night would go, and it didn't involve my bed -- for the most part because I doubted that Langton would take it upon himself to come to me. However, I had little fear that I would find his door barred to me, so at an hour that it was reasonable to assume discreet passage down the hall, I slipped from my room and went to him.

He was awake, which didn't surprise me in the slightest. A lamp burned low, and he appeared to be reading in bed, his night shirt tossed to the foot of the bed. He watched me come in with a smile upon his face, and the book in his hands was set aside with flattering haste.

"Good evening, lamb," I said, bending over to kiss him. "Reading something interesting?"

Langton shook his head. "No." His hands flew to me, one arm slipping around my neck and the other unfastening my dressing gown. He was as eager as ever, trying to pull me onto the bed with him, his mouth hungry and his body arching to me.

I laughed and shook his hands off, pressing a multitude of small kisses upon his mouth and cheeks and forehead. "Relax, Henri. Wait." I eased out of his embrace and soothed away the hurt look in his eyes with a lingering exploration of his mouth. "We have time, lamb, and I am going to teach you an important lesson tonight."

Langton's head fell back on his pillow, and he watched me as I stood to remove my dressing gown. "A lesson?" he asked uncertainly.

"Nothing difficult," I assured him with a smile. I draped my robe over a chair, walked around the bed, and pulled back the covers on the other side, rolling into the middle of the bed with a sigh. Langton's gaze roamed over me, taking in my awakening interest. I might very well have had intentions to take the night slowly -- indeed, slowing Langton down was my goal -- but there was no hiding my attraction. Nor was there any need to do so.

"Come here," I said softly, holding out my arms to him.

He still looked apprehensive, but he came to me, sliding into my embrace easily. His skin was warm, warmer than mine, and I pressed close to him with a happy sigh. "And now, we begin," I said, brushing the hair from his brow and kissing him gently.

He allowed the kiss and met it with another, his hand skating over my back to my shoulder. Within moments, he shifted as if to move against me, to rub and caress his body along the length of mine. I stopped him by the simple means of holding his hips still with a firm hand and making a discouraging sound. "Not yet. Just this, for now. In good time we'll seek more, but for now I just wish to feel you against me, to know your kisses and the touch of your hand on my skin. Let the need build."

"My need is built," he protested, but his eyes were happy, and he melted into me, his mouth sweet and gentle.

I had meant to kiss and touch him for a long time, for as long as I could stand not to move. He did not make it

225

easy. He held himself still as best he could, but the effort was costing him, and he began to make delicious sounds, tiny moans and whimpers that set fire to me. His kisses were intense, and that he was trying so hard to please me made me generous. I did not still his hands when once more he began to explore, his fingers teasing along my spine and over my shoulders until he was able to grip my arms. He pulled me closer, and I wound myself around him, eliciting a happy cry and a fevered kiss, his tongue quite taking over my mouth.

I found that what Langton wanted, what he seemed to crave, was to be enveloped. The more I covered him, the harder I pressed him into the mattress, the greater his need grew. He moaned into my mouth, whispered encouragements in my ear, and twisted in my arms until I was pinning him to the bed. He looked at me with wild eyes, his hair becoming damp with perspiration as we moved.

"Slow?" he asked, his breathing laboured.

"Perhaps tomorrow," I said with a shrug.

He laughed, one leg winding around my waist. "Please, Ned. I need you."

I shook my head. "Not that. Not tonight."

Outraged eyes met mine. "What? Why? I assure you, I'm not hurt -- "

"You're riding in the morning. Trust me on this, lamb. I'll not take you again tonight and watch you on horseback in the morn."

Langton glared at me. "I ride often." He wiggled against me, attempting to shift me a little lower, I thought. I grinned and pushed back, holding him still.

"And I'll take you often. Just not right now." Further complaints were stifled as I kissed him, grinding down with my hips and raking my fingers through his hair again. I was becoming almost fixated on his hair -- the texture, the colour, the length of his fringe. His hair, however, wasn't uppermost in my mind as I moved over him. He tasted incredible, heady and passionate, and all thought fled in the face of my hunger. I wanted to devour him.

Langton was panting when I broke the kiss, and I was no better. "Christ," I swore, taking his mouth again. Thought was all but gone as we moved, the only things that mattered were touch and sound; he filled my senses, stole my breath and returned it to me in gasps and pants, sweet sounds that shot through me like a bolt. I wanted to take him, wanted to bury myself so deeply in his body he would know not where we diverged. I wanted to blaze a trail down his body with my mouth, to ravish and bite him, mark him as my own. I wanted to take his cock into my mouth and feast on him until he cried my name.

Instead, I kissed him with my eyes open and watched his face as I wrapped my hand around him and learnt the weight of him in my palm. I watched his eyes as I stroked, listened to his breath catch and stop, tasted the salt of his skin as he tried so very hard to withstand my touch. I watched his eyes as they fluttered closed, his mouth opening but no sound made as his body tensed. I felt him tighten next to me, under me, and I groaned as he began to spill over my hand, the shudder of his body coupled with a low cry.

He was beautiful. Open, stunned, hedonistic. Mine.

Langton's eyes didn't open as he turned into my arms, his slick skin moulding to mine. He arched and curled, clinging to me, and I could take no more. I rolled onto my back, pulling him with me, and drove against his hip as I sought release. He bit down on my shoulder, and I came, fingers tangled in his hair.

My Henri. My lamb.

We said nothing; Langton lay upon me, wrapped in my arms, and shortly we slept.

Chapter Thirty

The next few days were full for Langton and me. We spent our days as usual, with a few discreet changes; the business of the Hall had to go on despite our new preference for spending as much time alone as possible. We spent a part of each afternoon combing through the financial records of the Hall so that we both could understand what resources I had available to me and what I would be able to use to help Langton when the time came. We found it distasteful to discuss, but there was no avoiding it -- he would be the next Duke, and eventually, he would inherit from me as well. It would fall to me to make sure that his mother and sister were cared for until that time, and I promised him I would not see him destitute whilst I lived.

I could not, however, find it in me to further curse Barrett. I had land and means and had gained so much more through his gift. With luck, it would not drain my resources to carry Langton until he had his holdings out of debt. We would not know the true state of his affairs until his uncle died and we could look at his complete records.

"He had a son, you know," Langton told me. "Illegitimate and sickly -- the child died before long, as did his mother. It is suspected that lying with her is the source of his own illness."

I was not surprised, nor, I suspect, was Langton. I did not ask him how he knew -- it didn't matter. I also kept to myself my utter lack of sympathy for his uncle; I was just eager for the bastard to die so that Langton could be free of his poison. Instead, I simply held Langton closer to me and set about taking his mind off such matters. I was most successful -- he had not been on horseback in days and had only just begun not to wince when he moved in the mornings. We were both disgustingly pleased with ourselves.

On the Saturday of Truitt's arrival, however, Langton was once more out riding. He'd been overeager and nervous all through the morning, and I finally made him go, lest he drive us both to distraction. I, myself, retired to the main library in search of something soothing and absorbing, finally settling into a monograph.

I heard footfalls in the hallway and set my book aside, looking at the rather unreliable clock on the mantle. It was mid-afternoon, and time for either Truitt to arrive or for Langton to return.

Dobbs came in with Truitt trailing along. "Mr. Truitt, sir," Dobbs announced, stepping to the side.

"Welcome," I said with a smile, going to Truitt and clasping his arm.

"Munrow," he said, his voice light and happy. "It is good to see you."

"And you. Please -- come in. I'm sure Viscount Langton will join us soon." I asked Dobbs to arrange for refreshments and waited for him to leave before I pulled Truitt to me, kissing him hard.

"That's better," he teased, crossing to a chair. "I do

like it better when we're informal."

"Liar -- you like the rules and being made to behave."

He laughed and nodded. "I do. Tell me, where is the lamb? Not hiding, I hope?"

"I had to make him go; he was... rather enthusiastic about your imminent arrival. I feared for my state of mind."

Truitt sat back in his chair, grinning. "Not having second thoughts, then?"

I chuckled and shook my head. "Oh, no. He's been most vocal about you."

"Really?" Truitt asked, looking pleased. "Do tell. Actually, tell me everything. I want to know what's happened. In great detail."

I smiled, willing to indulge him but mindful of where we were and how many bodies were moving about the Hall, ready to walk in at an inopportune time. "Well, we've taken a few measures -- he's given his man a permanent place for one, and I'm down a footman."

Truitt nodded. "Wise. Did it work?"

I shrugged. "Griffith tells me that the initial reaction downstairs was to congratulate Matheson -- he's from the area, and that he'll be working for a Duke in London stirred some envy. And then he became closed mouthed about certain things, and I suspect that while the details have dried up we have merely confirmed the fact that there is something to hide." I wasn't really concerned, really. None of us ever hoped to really hide anything from the servants; we could only hope to surround ourselves with people who would feel either personal loyalty or value their position.

"It can't be helped," Truitt said, echoing my thoughts. "I admit I'm unsure whether things will be easier for him now, with you so near, or later, when he is master of his own house."

"I don't know," I said, leaning back and closing my eyes. "To be honest, I'm not sure if it makes any difference. We spend our days planning for what will happen once he comes into his inheritance, and I find myself living today with my body while my head is in tomorrow."

"Planning your future?" Truitt managed to sound both curious and teasing, so I opened one eye to see his expression. He was looking at me with a slight, knowing smile, but I could see a note of concern behind his eyes.

"In a manner of speaking," I said. "His legacy is somewhat damaged, and it will be up to him to rebuild it. Between the two of us, we've been taking stock and testing his business sense -- for one of his age, he's doing very well. I only hope it is enough."

"Ah." If he had anything further to say it was stayed as Dobbs returned with a footman bearing a tray. Once the light meal had been laid out and we had drinks in hand, I dismissed them both, not wishing to have ears so near. As they withdrew, I had another thought and called Dobbs back, saying to Truitt, "Would you fancy a walk in the garden once you've eaten?"

Truitt didn't even raise an eyebrow, although I had never known him to be a great admirer of the out of doors. "That would be lovely, Munrow."

"Dobbs, please let the Viscount know where we are when he returns."

"Of course, sir. Will that be all?"

I nodded, and he left us to hurriedly enjoy our refreshment. I'm sure that Cook was flattered by how quickly we disposed of her offering, although as fine as it was, our eagerness had little to do with the flavours. Once safely outside, we could be a little freer with our conversation.

Truitt led the way, oddly enough, as we walked

through the gardens. He seemed to be somewhat pensive, although his body was relaxed and he strolled easily. He did not, at least, pretend interest in the plants -- that would have driven me completely mad, I think. Finally he stopped at one of the stone benches and sat, gesturing for me to join him. Raising an eyebrow, I did, not entirely sure what had brought on the change in him.

"Truitt?" I asked.

"Tell me, Munrow. Does he yet understand the scope of what he asks for?"

I lifted one shoulder. "I doubt it. We've discussed this, have we not? If you are having second thoughts -- let alone him -- we can stop. There is to be no pressure; I don't take reluctant lovers. Well, not usually."

He favoured my small joke with a smile and then shook his head. "Not second thoughts, dear heart. I merely wish to know... you said he's vocal about me?"

I stared and then laughed as the reason for his discomfort came to me. "Oh, pet. Feeling insecure in your place?"

He coloured slightly and looked abashed. "Not in particular, I merely... oh, damn it. I thought perhaps a week of being alone with you would banish me from his thoughts -- from yours."

I did not look around, for to do so would surely draw attention to us, I simply put my hand on his leg and leant close enough to whisper in his ear. "You are rarely far from my thoughts, pet. We talk about you in bed at night. I spin stories for the boy and touch him for you until he spends, calling your name. He's drawn images with words for me, of the ways he would like to have you, like to service you."

Truitt gasped, his eyes widening and colour actually rising on his cheeks. The man I knew would never have reacted thus, unless the circumstances were extreme --

an audience, a chance at being caught... high emotion. I smiled broadly and leant back, away from him.

"You have been spending your time pining," I accused happily. "Oh, Truitt. When were you going to let me know?"

He frowned at me, although it was not a denial. "Munrow, really. This is delicate, and there are other things to consider."

"Such as?" I was positively gleeful, which really just proves what a cad I remained; it's most unseemly to rejoice as one's fellow falls head over arse in love.

"Such as the lad who approaches and how soon we can get him alone," Truitt said abruptly.

I sat laughing as he strode toward Langton, arms out in greeting. Ah, yes, life was becoming most interesting.

By some miracle, we made it through the afternoon without any embarrassing incidents, although it was a close thing. Langton was as enthusiastic in his greetings as I'd feared he'd be, and Truitt barely escaped molestation. It should be noted, however, that he didn't actually try to avoid any of Langton's touches or suggestive smiles -- in truth, he actively encouraged them until I had to put my foot down rather firmly and insist that they maintain a respectable distance between them.

The afternoon passed pleasantly as we walked about the gardens. Every once in a while we'd note a twitch of the draperies or see a servant busily going from one building to another with no need which we could determine, but it mattered not a great deal to any of us that the spies were out in force. Once I'd restrained the two pups, we must have looked rather boring to the busybodies.

Dinner was relaxed; Langton and Truitt conspired between them to bore not only the footmen who brought our plates, but me as well. The length at which those two could converse about the smallest inflections of phrasing in a particular unknown French poem was really fairly stunning. Not being a huge reader of the stuff, I assumed they were making half of it up.

I did enjoy, however, listening to them speak the language. When Langton segued briefly into Italian to make a point, I very nearly called a halt to our meal and dragged him bodily up to my chambers.

Truitt also seemed approving, and if I recall correctly, the next two courses were eaten rather hurriedly.

We spent an hour or so in the library, for form's sake. None of us was terribly interested in cards, for there are few games which are good for three hands, so we talked quietly as we sipped our after dinner drinks. Langton drifted to the bookshelves, of course, and I sat back to listen as he and Truitt continued their dinnertime conversation, this time with reference material close at hand.

Alas, Langton seemed unable to find an excuse to slip into Italian. I admit I grew bored once more, although they seemed to be having a wonderful time. Truitt was speaking with his hands, his face and voice animated as he quoted books and recited stanzas from memory. Langton, either in agreement or not, was also vibrant and persuasive, his smile and eyes bright as he listened and countered. I found that if I ignored the dry subject matter, the pair of them were startlingly lovely.

Langton sat in his usual chair, and as I was in mine already, Truitt drew a third close, still speaking. Quietly, I arose and crossed to the shelf of black bound books and selected two. Langton's cheeks took on new colour although he didn't break off his conversation. Idly, I turned pages in the first volume until I found the image I wanted -- that which had so captured Langton in the carriage. In the second, I found exactly what I wanted -- one man, apart from the other two, watching.

Wordlessly, I handed the first book to Truitt and the second to Langton. Truitt, in mid-sentence, glanced at the page as he took the volume, and then looked again, his words drying up. Langton's cheeks were aflame, his eyes fixed on the page before him.

"Ned?" Truitt whispered.

I smiled at him, and winked. "The lamb fancies you in the middle, pet."

"Does he, now?" Truitt's look became smouldering as he turned it upon the boy. "And what's your pretty picture, Henri?"

Langton swallowed, but when he spoke, his voice was steady, if a little husky. "A very naughty man being a voyeur."

I laughed and nodded. "Very good, lamb. I suggest that we make this an early evening. If you both would be so kind as to join me in my rooms for a nightcap, I think we can send the house to bed for the night."

There was a noticeable lack of arguments.

If Matheson and Griffith were surprised to be dismissed after being rushed through their evening's work, they didn't show it. In fact, Griffith already had my night things laid out, my brandy in, and a basin of water ready.

"Will there be anything else, sir?" he asked as he hung my waistcoat, leaving me in my trousers and shirtsleeves.

"No. And I suspect a late morning as well," I said, struggling with my links.

He came to me and took them off, nodding. "Certainly. I'll make sure Cook knows." And with that, he took himself away, leaving me to pour my brandy in peace while I awaited my lovers.

For it could no longer be denied that they were just that. Perhaps not to each other yet, but to me, certainly. Not merely bed partners, for we'd all gone a shade or two beyond that, but something more, bound by affection and respect.

The only surprising thing was my lack of utter panic at the thought. The game had truly turned upon me; the lamb's teeth had made their mark.

Truitt was the first to arrive in my rooms. I had taken my brandy to my small greeting room, where Griffith had made sure the lamps were lit, and Truitt met me with a bright smile, his hand holding a snifter of his own.

"I've decided that brandy is one of your affectations I'll adopt," he teased.

"It's not affected," I assured him. "Merely a lingering effect of my weaning and the nights I spent keeping my nurse up with my croup." I set my snifter down on the table and pulled him to me, aware of the heat of his body and the hard length in his trousers. "Langton?" I asked, nuzzling his neck.

"I heard him as I passed his room -- he'll arrive shortly." Truitt moaned softly as I bit at the tender skin below his ear. "Ned. My glass -- "

"Get rid of it."

I was almost sure his glass made it to the table; I didn't check. I took his mouth, claimed him with a kiss so fierce it made him gasp and melt against me. We stood there, pressed tightly against each other, and I plundered his mouth, sucked on his tongue, and buried my hands in his hair.

"Oh, God," he whispered when I let him breathe. "Dear heart."

With one hand I held his jaw, kissing his lower lip, made swollen and full. The other I moulded to his lower back and kept him against me, one of my thighs pushing between his. He moaned again and moved on me, his breath a harsh pant.

From the doorway, there was a whimper, and I smiled into the next kiss. "Oh, pet," I said softly. "You are going to be so very well used this evening..."

Langton stood with his back against the door, his eyes wide as he stared at us. He seemed either unwilling or unable to speak, so I happily let him watch as I ravished Truitt's mouth again, my hands moving to divest him of his clothing. When I bared his chest, Langton moaned softly, and I glanced to the door, unsurprised to see my lamb avidly watching, his hand almost absently rubbing himself. He might even have been unaware, so intent was his attention on Truitt's body, on Truitt's sounds.

I wasted no time. I stripped Truitt gracelessly, my own clothes suffering a small amount of damage as we moved toward the bedchamber, leaving a trail of fabric and shoes behind us.

"Henri," Truitt gasped. "Here, lamb."

Langton came to us, to Truitt, who kissed the boy deeply as I fought a battle with the last of our garments. We all fell upon the bed, and I took Truitt's shaft in my hand. He and I were bare skinned with full, heavy pricks, and Langton remained fully clothed with wide eyes and harsh breath. The disparity made my cock throb.

"Henri," I said. "The oil. We shall have him, yes?"

Langton's eyes rolled, and he came in his trousers with a shudder. "Oh, no," he said softly, his cheeks reddening and his eyes tightly closed.

Truitt smiled and pulled away from me -- not an easy thing as I still held him in my hand -- and gathered Langton to him. "Silly lamb -- do you suspect that you're done for the night? You're lovely when you spend."

I let go of Truitt as he climbed over the boy, the two of them soon writhing and wrestling across my bed as Truitt removed Langton's clothes, the two of them trading kisses and whispers and scattered moans. I smiled and watched, completely delighted to enjoy the sight of them. Langton's colour didn't change, although the reason for his flush did, and I was unsurprised to see that Truitt had made sure the boy's hunger had risen once more.

I watched and waited, my fingers slicked with oil from the pot by the bed, and when I thought the time was right, when Truitt's hips began to thrust against Langton's in an unmistakable rhythm, I moved.

"Oh!" Truitt gasped as I breached him with my fingers. He thrust back hard and took them deeper, his head lifting. "Ned, yes. Please, dear heart. More."

Langton scrabbled out from under him, his eyes fixed on my hand as I fingered my pet open. "Ned?" he whispered. "God, Christopher. It's so amazing, you should see -- "

Truitt laughed, the sound choked and harsh as I massaged the hard spot inside of him. "I don't need to; I can feel... oh, God. I can feel it. Henri. Here. Please."

Langton looked to me, confused.

I smiled and oiled my cock with one hand. "Your picture, lamb."

His eyes widened, and his hand went to his prick. "Oh," he moaned softly. But he moved and didn't waste any motion in it. In front of Truitt he waited, staring at me. I grinned at him, and Truitt moaned, his arse wiggling in front of me, his mouth chasing after Langton's erection.

My lamb did me proud, moving just out of Truitt's reach. "Wait," he admonished with a fond smile before he looked back to me.

I nodded approvingly and winked, grasping Truitt's hip with one hand. I knew my pet, knew how open he was and what he could take; I admit, I was more willing to be rough with Truitt than with Langton, but with time

I knew that would change. As Langton watched and waited, I plunged into Truitt's body and made him gasp, made him cry out.

"Yes!" he sang. "God, yes."

And Langton, my wolf in lamb's wool, he waited until Truitt's eyes were closed, his head tipped back in bliss and his mouth open to breathe, and when the moment was perfect and unexpected... my lamb took his mouth. I imagined that Truitt's eyes flew open, but I couldn't see; I could feel it, however. The instinctive tightening of his body, the flutter of muscles around my cock, the tension in his shoulders as he opened his mouth farther and swallowed Langton's prick.

My pet loved to be used. He craved affection and thrived on it; he was at his best when he knew he was being cherished. But to be cherished and used at the same time was his reason for existing. He loved with all his being, gave everything entirely to his lover -- his body, his heart, his control. To be filled by my pounding into his arse and to have Langton down his throat must have sent him higher than anything I alone could have done.

I thrilled to it and knew I'd not last. It didn't matter; I had plans and this was mostly for Langton and Truitt anyway -- although I happily took my pleasure, I'll not deny. I leant forward and kissed Langton as he met me over Truitt's back, and with a gasp, I came, spilling into my pet with a grunt. Langton kissed me harder and rode it out with me, one of his hands on the back of my head. He whispered endearments into my mouth as I came back to myself.

Truitt was writhing, whimpering around Langton, and seemed to be trying to find a way to balance so he might take himself in hand. I pulled out of him and laughed at his efforts, dropping kisses along his spine.

"No, no, my pet. I said you shall be well used, did I

not? And that *we* were going to have you."

They both took my meaning immediately, Truitt wantonly rolling onto his back and spreading his thighs, Langton looking utterly panicked.

"I've not... I don't know -- "

"Shhh. There's a first time for everyone, and could you ask for better teachers?" I asked, kissing him gently.

Truitt raised his knees and smiled, his arms out. "Come and kiss me, lamb. You won't hurt me. Our Ned has seen to that."

Langton looked a little frantic still, but more than willing to try, so I got up and rounded the bed, seeking the oil. With my hand slick, I waited until Langton was between Truitt's knees and then returned to them, behind Langton. With a lazy hand, I oiled his cock, stroking him smoothly and kissed his neck.

"You're beautiful," I told him. "We're lucky to have you, you know."

He sighed and rocked his hips, pushing his slippery prick through my hand. "I'm lucky."

"At the moment, yes," I said with a smile. "Christopher has one of the best bottoms in England."

They both chuckled, but the sound was strained, and I knew it was time. I urged Langton forward and guided him, Truitt helping by baring himself utterly, legs over Langton's shoulders.

"So you can kiss me," he said to Langton with a tight smile.

Langton moaned and sank into Truitt's body. The moan grew louder and was joined by Truitt's; I merely sighed. I kissed them both and moved away, to the side of the bed. I could see them both better there, watch their faces.

Langton looked stunned, his eyes wide and dark. He shook slightly, and Truitt smiled up at him. "You can move; it's all right."

Langton nodded and then swore as Truitt rocked against him. "Please, I'll not be able to go slowly if you do that."

"And why would you go slowly, lamb?" Truitt whispered. "Take me. Do what you want, slam into me. Fuck me, Henri. Make me feel it, make me yell -- "

Langton moved, and I could hardly blame him. Eyes tightly closed with concentration, he thrust and stabbed and pounded into Truitt's arse, taking him hard and fast. It was not skilled love making, but there would be time for that later; it was what he needed, what Truitt needed.

I watched as they moved, as Langton opened his eyes and looked at his lover, as they began to work together. They sighed and swore and gasped, and Truitt pulled at his own cock, masturbated for Langton. Langton stared, his breath now coming in grunts every time he pushed home.

I joined them in spirit, my hand working in time, pushing and pulling, tight and there with them. With a cry, Truitt came, his seed fountaining up from between his fingers, and I joined him, unexpectedly. I'd not been close, had barely been aware of my own need as I watched Langton freeze, watched his eyes as he felt Truitt's climax roll through him.

"Oh, dear God," Langton whispered, and then his eyes closed, and I knew he was with us, knew the spasms that rocked him as mine did me.

Together we flew, and together we fell, and together we slept.

Chapter Thirty One

By common agreement, even if it was unvoiced by all, we passed the weekend without tension, worry, or touching upon delicate subjects. The matter of the Duke went unremarked upon, the state of Langton's expected estate was ignored, and the very idea that the three of us were enjoying a temporary and sheltered state of affairs was put aside.

We went riding and explored the grounds. We had a picnic away from the eyes of the servants and made love on blankets in a wood -- after we'd hunted the lamb down, of course. Langton and Truitt enjoyed their games; I enjoyed indulging them.

On Sunday night, the three of us lay tangled together in my bed, satiated and near sleep, the covers thrown off and the windows wide open to enjoy the rare heat of summer and the light of the full moon.

"Because it allows me to give up," Truitt said, in response to a question I'd missed.

"I don't understand." Langton pushed himself up on his elbow and peered at me. "Do you? From his position, I mean."

I rolled over lazily and stroked a hand down Truitt's spine. "What are we talking about?" I asked, feeling rather slow and sleepy.

"Being bound." Truitt grinned at me. "I haven't even got to the marking part. Or the spanking. The teasing. The begging."

I groaned and rolled onto my stomach, pushing Langton into the middle. "You two will be the death of me. Go to sleep, we'll discuss perversions when I'm not weak from entertaining you both for hours on end."

Langton giggled, and Truitt reached over him to pat me on the head. "Poor man, getting on in years. Good thing I have this strapping young one to keep me satisfied."

I merely snorted and closed my eyes, dismissing them both as sleep tried to claim me.

The moon hadn't moved very far in the sky when I awoke to feel the bed shifting as they fucked beside me, Langton straddling Truitt's hips and sitting up, taking a pounding from below.

"The very death of me," I reiterated as I moved over and claimed my kisses and a free hand.

The carriage was ready for Truitt by mid-morning, and we both walked him out, his man loading his cases.

"Munrow, I was thinking..." Truitt said slowly.

"Oh, dear."

Langton snickered and swayed away from Truitt as the pet tried to land a blow.

"Children," I sighed, trying very much to sound as my mother had just before scolding Arthur and me. They took no notice. "Truitt. What were you going to say?"

They both straightened up and looked at me, and with a sinking feeling, I knew they'd been planning something. Oh, dear, indeed. "Out with it," I ordered.

Truitt smiled slightly. "I would very much like it if Langton came to London on the weekend."

I raised an eyebrow but said nothing. Truitt said nothing as well, too used to my methods. Langton, the poor lamb, was new to our games and promptly spilled his guts all over the drive. Discreetly, of course.

"There are things I'd like to see, which you've already explored," he said carefully, looking nervously at Truitt for approval. He got a nod, and encouraged, he added, "Truitt can guide me, and this way I can be out of your way for a weekend -- I'm sure there are things you'd like to tend to, and if there are any papers to go to the city, I can take them for you."

At least he knew when to stop talking; any more and he'd have embellished it all out of recognition. As a simple request there wasn't anything wrong with it. And honestly, if he wanted to be tied to a bed and fucked silly, there wasn't a better introduction to the activity than Truitt. He'd be gentle, discreet, and make sure the boy was both safe and had a good time. I know myself well enough to know that I get bored with ropes and move to the torture and marking a little too fast for a beginner.

I wouldn't have minded watching, however.

Truitt shrugged one shoulder ever so slightly and slid a glance at Langton. Ah. The boy was eager. Of course he was; how I missed it I'll never know. With a sigh, I nodded.

They both smiled at me, and Truitt promised to make arrangements at the club. A few moments later he was in the carriage and off, down the lane.

"So you want to learn it all," I said to the boy.

He looked abashed and nodded. "I'm sorry?" he offered tentatively.

I laughed. "You are not. And you owe me, lamb -- I'll expect something wonderful on Thursday as a goodbye.

And an amazing greeting on Sunday when you return."

"Oh, of course," he assured me with a broad grin. "I'll do my best."

As if I'd doubt it.

And that is why he was not at Red Oak Hall on Saturday afternoon when Dobbs appeared at the library door and said, "Lady Julia Langton is here to see you, sir."

Chapter Thirty Two

I did not panic. I will admit to a certain level of surprise; the unannounced and decidedly unplanned for arrival of Lady Julia would have been one of the very last things I'd ever have expected. I sent Dobbs to see to her comfort and immediately went to my rooms, where Griffith did his level best to make me perfectly presentable on short notice.

It was not until I was descending the main stairs that I really -- completely and finally -- became aware that not only was Lady Julia my intended bride... but she was also my lover's mother. I sighed and prayed that a small portion of Barrett's affection for me still lingered in the very walls of Red Oak Hall. Never before had I made quite so startling a mess of things.

I found her in the morning room. Her back was to the room as she gazed out the window, but as she heard my step, she turned to face me. She was dressed in the purple and lavender hues of mourning, the black and brown of the early days since her loss gone. The colour suited her, and her hair glittered gold under her hat; I suspected that if it tumbled free it would curl just as Langton's did.

"My lady," I said politely, inclining my head. "I regret the delay; thank you for your patience."

"Of course, Mr. Munrow," she replied, equally as polite. "Thank you for seeing me."

As if I would have turned her away.

Dobbs moved silently into the room, a tray in his hands and a footman at his heel.

"Unfortunately," I went on, folding my hands in front of me, "I'm afraid I also have to inform you that the Viscount is not here. He's in London, taking care of a few small matters for me. I'm sure he will be very disappointed to have missed your visit."

Oddly, she looked more relieved than disappointed. "Oh, I am sorry to hear that," she said. "I would have enjoyed seeing him; however, it is you with whom I wish to speak."

"I'm at your disposal," I said. "Please, let us sit." With one hand I indicated the chairs, waiting for her to settle.

She hesitated and looked to the window. "May we perhaps take a walk in your garden?"

I took her meaning immediately. She wished to impart some information to me, or to speak rather freely, and did not want anyone to overhear.

"Of course," I said smoothly. "Your wrap?"

"I'm fine," she assured me.

I nodded and led her out the garden doors, leaving her footman and my house of ears behind. We walked for some few minutes without speaking, until I finally couldn't hold my tongue any further. "My lady," I began, "I can only assume by your unexpected arrival that you have something to tell me. Is the Duke's condition worsening?"

She stopped to examine a hosta, bending low as she touched its wide leaves. "Mr. Munrow, I am afraid I must be blunt; I am well aware how unseemly my behaviour is in coming here like this and how vulgar it may appear to you that I am so... plainly spoken at the moment. I have little choice, I feel, and in truth I grew accustomed to being able to speak freely with my late husband."

Somewhat bewildered, I nodded. "Speak as you feel best," I invited.

I can only assume she saw my confusion, for she smiled at me rather sweetly with a good humour. "I believe that you and I can come to an agreement, if we are honest with each other -- or at least frank." She began to walk again, her steps measured. "My brother-in-law is dying, and I suspect he'll be gone sooner, rather than later."

She did not sound particularly upset.

I nodded. "He's looking worse. Does he have until Christmas, would you say?"

"No. I think he's doing all he can merely to survive the summer. I believe the end of the season has a particular significance to you?" She looked at me out of the corner of her eye.

I coughed discreetly. "It does, and I'm sure you're not unaware...?"

"That you'll swoop in and wed me? I'm well aware." She stopped and turned to face me, her hands in the folds of her skirt. "Mr. Munrow, I know you are being forced into this. I also realise that it would be foolish in the extreme for me to refuse. If nothing else, a marriage to you will mean security for my children -- and my late husband would wish that. Marrying you will allow my son to retain his family holdings and lands, and it will enable my daughter to pick her suitor instead of having to settle for the first man who would take her. There is no logical or practical reason for me to refuse."

I could hardly argue with that.

"But I don't want to," she said softly, and suddenly

she looked terribly sad. She bit her lip and looked around, blinking rapidly. "I'm sorry," she apologised, although I was unsure if she meant for the emotional display or for not wishing to marry me.

"It's quite all right," I assured her, for I had to say something -- and it was all right. Why on earth she should be eager to be joined with a man she'd never met, a man who was being blackmailed into marrying *her*... honestly, the entire situation was horrid and getting worse the more I considered the reality of it.

We walked again, and she said, "I've spoken to a few people, Mr. Munrow, and while I've been unable to discover precisely what hold the Duke has on you, I have a fairly good idea. I would like to make a proposal which would enable us both to have at least a tolerable existence under this betrothal which has been pushed upon us."

That gave me reason to pause, and I actually stopped walking. "Madam?"

She looked up at me, her tiny face more determined than I had ever seen even Langton's. "Mr. Munrow. You wish to live your life, no? I do as well. There is a certain situation I would like to see continue, and a marriage could seriously wreak havoc with it. Am I speaking plainly enough?"

I stared at her. "A situation."

"Yes."

My mind was reeling. "And a marriage..."

She sighed. "Do you have a lover, Mr. Munrow? Would it make your life easier if I didn't live here at Red Oak Hall? In fact, would it not make your life easier if we rarely saw one another and maintained a civil and friendly relationship? I will, of course, meet a reasonable number of social obligations, both here and in London, but in exchange for staying out of your way, more or less, I'll expect the same courtesy."

I may have looked like a fish out of water. I hoped I did not actually gasp.

Calmly, she turned and began to walk again. "I suggest you contact the Duke as soon as possible and make arrangements. He'll want us wed before he dies, and I don't trust him to change his will until it's done. If you wish to marry soon, I have no objection as long as you're agreeable to what I've suggested. I know it will be futile to object in any event, but I did need to make myself understood. Oh, and one more thing, Mr. Munrow." She dropped her handkerchief as she walked, and I automatically stopped to pick it up. Twisted in the fine linen was a gold band. "That is the ring you will give me."

I slipped the band into my watch pocket. "A commitment to you by proxy?"

"And me to him," she said coolly. "I will, of course, consummate our marriage; I'll even keep most of the vows. But the promise I'll make to you, the important one, is that I'll protect you if or when you need me to. I have no wish to see you destroyed, Mr. Munrow; I only ask that you not embarrass me or my children."

It had taken me a while to get past the initial shock, I admit, and longer to realise all the nuances of what she was proposing. "My dear Lady Julia," I finally said. "It will be an honour to marry one such as yourself. I think we'll be quite happy apart."

She smiled at me and even laughed. "Don't lose my ring, Mr. Munrow. It's very dear."

I bowed to her, smiling myself. As marriages by blackmail go, ours was shaping up nicely.

Chapter Thirty Three

Langton was not happy with me.

"But I've just come back!" he said loudly, pacing through his room until I caught him about the waist. "Must you go? Can't I come with you?"

"I have to see your uncle," I explained, hoping that he wouldn't press the matter. I added further distraction by tweaking his nipple, but the boy would not be dissuaded.

"Why? He'll send you word when he's ready to force your hand," Langton said, glaring at me as he swiped my hand away. "I wanted to tell you all about last night."

"And you shall," I promised, licking a trail up his neck. "I'm not leaving until morning, and, frankly, I'm a little upset that you keep talking."

He moaned softly as I attempted to ravish him. "You're trying to distract me from the fact that you're leaving."

"Yes."

"It won't work," he said as I undid the placket of his trousers.

"No?"

"No. Oh, yes. I mean, no. Why do you have to see him?" His eyes were a little crossed as he attempted to look sternly at me whilst I stroked his rampant erection.

I sighed. "Because I suspect I'll have to marry your mother within the month, if not the fortnight."

"Oh," he said with a gasp. I would have liked to take credit for his breathlessness, but as his erection withered at the same time, I doubted it was me.

"Oh, no, you don't," I said, tossing him bodily to the bed.

"Well, if you would refrain from mentioning my mother when you have my cock in your hand, there wouldn't be a problem, would there?" he accused.

"And if you would mind your own business, we could be having a much better time," I shot back, not really meaning it. As I was busily stripping his clothes away, I could only assume he took it in the spirit it was intended.

"It is my business," he insisted, rolling away. "You are going to be marry her. Which means you'll be my--"

"Don't say it," I said clamping a hand over his mouth. "Let it be, lad. We'll all rest easier without those words spoken aloud."

He wiggled an eyebrow at me, and I sighed. "We're going to talk about this, aren't we?" I asked, more or less rhetorically. I let him go and went to fetch a glass of water off his table.

"Ned," he said quietly. "I know it must happen. And I even approve of it, from a practical point of view, since I'll be the one to benefit the most. However…"

I nodded, not looking at him. "It's become somewhat awkward, hasn't it?"

I heard him sigh. "I didn't mean for it to. And I know you didn't -- "

I laughed. "Oh, I most certainly did. I was going to

seduce you, lamb, and make a mockery of your uncle on his deathbed. I was going to send him to his grave knowing I'd buggered you and made you beg for it."

There was dead silence behind me, and I turned to look at him. His eyes were wide, stunned. "You -- "

"And then I fell in love," I said softly. "And Truitt... Oh, lamb. We're going to be paying a high price."

He flew into my arms. "Don't do that to me; I thought my heart had stopped. You love me?"

I smiled at him. "I do."

He kissed me, and as I felt his interest grow against me, I decided to let the subject of my impending nuptials drop in favour of divesting him of the rest of his clothes as well as removing my own. In short order, we were happily naked, rolling on his bed, until he was astride me, smiling down.

"Tell me of Truitt," I said, looking up at him and reaching for the oil.

He shuddered, his eyes slightly glazed. "He made me spend in the dining room again, without even touching me. He merely talked, made promises, and told me such stories..."

I grinned and slipped my wet fingers between his cheeks. "I'm sure that delighted him."

"He dragged me up to our room immediately," Langton said with a smile. "Once there, we... well, we were rather eager. We kissed and stripped, and he cleaned me. Then he distracted me by taking me in his mouth."

He groaned as I breached him with my fingers and started to ready him; or perhaps it was in remembering Truitt's mouth on him.

"Yes?" I encouraged, pushing my fingers deeper. "And what did he do when he had you distracted?"

"He had... he had a soft rope. It was so very long; I had no idea why he needed so much. But as he sucked on my prick, he tied my right ankle to the bed, and then he wound the rope up, around my thigh."

I growled a little and pulled my fingers free then lifted Langton until he could take me. We both moaned as he slid down on me, his arse tight and hot around my cock. "Oh, God," I said softly. "Then?"

"He teased," Langton said, his voice strained. "Just tied like that I could move, and he wouldn't tie anything else until I'd come again. Finally, he tied my right arm, the same way, winding the rope to my wrist and then fastening it."

I thrust up, and Langton rocked back. For a long moment we left Truitt behind as Langton rode me, and we moved closer to our mutual pleasure. I pulled him down and took a deep kiss, keeping him there until he pulled back, gasping.

"It... it was a long time until I was tied down," he said, grinding his hips down on me. "Oh, God, Ned."

"Tell me," I ordered through gritted teeth. I could feel myself moving faster and faster toward completion.

Langton groaned piteously. "I begged him to fuck me, to take me. He knelt above me, and I sucked him until he was close, until his breath was catching, and then he moved away, down my body."

I stared up at Langton, lost in the image and knowing full well where it was going. Even when he topped, Truitt liked to bottom. "He rode you," I whispered, thrusting up hard. "Like this."

Langton came, shooting his seed across my chest in long pulses. "Oh, God," he cried out, slamming himself down on me.

I rolled us over, tucking one of his legs up over my shoulder so I could stab into him again and again until I came with a roar, my cock pulsing madly in him.

Panting, we remained like that for a long moment

until I had the sense to pull out of him and gather him into my arms. "Welcome home, lamb," I whispered.

"Let me come with you," he whispered back.

I sighed. "All right."

Chapter Thirty Four

The journey to London was spent mostly in staring out the windows, both of us too busy denying what was happening to concentrate on anything else. Eventually I moved to Langton's side of the carriage, and we held hands for part of the way; the contact was needed.

We were met at his uncle's door by the butler and two footmen; our admittance was rushed, the footmen sent to fetch not only the Duke but Lady Julia as well, who was in residence.

"Lucy?" Langton asked the butler.

"Miss Lucy is not here, I'm afraid, my lord. She's visiting friends for the afternoon but will be home for tea."

Langton nodded, and we dutifully followed the butler into the drawing room, where we were left to our own devices for a few minutes.

"How long do you think we'll wait?" I asked Langton as I walked around the room picking up items and setting them down again.

He shrugged. "I suspect Mother will arrive first."

I gave him a long look. "How are you?"

"I'll be fine," he said softly. "Will you go to your brother's tonight?"

I shook my head. "Not unless I have to."

"The club?"

"Maybe," I said. "Probably."

He nodded and sighed. I was about to go to him, to offer some comfort if I could, but the door opened and his mother swept into the room.

"Henri!" she said happily, holding out her arms.

"Mother." He smiled and went to her, accepting a kiss on his cheek and returning it. "You look wonderful."

"Thank you," she said, her cheeks dimpling. "As do you. And this must be Mr. Munrow."

I sketched a quick bow. "My lady."

She nodded, and when Langton moved to pull a chair closer for her, she winked at me.

"It's good that you've come," Lady Julia said to Langton. "I don't think your uncle has very much time left, to be honest."

Langton said nothing. I moved to the other end of the room, allowing them a chance to talk without me being in the middle of their conversation.

"Tell me," she said. "How has your summer been? I've missed you being here, Henri. Lucy has missed you as well."

"It's been wonderful," Langton replied with a smile. "Mr. Munrow has taught me so much."

I looked out the window and tried not to smile; the boy did know how to be discreet, to be sure, but he seemed to have picked up some bad habits from Truitt. His phrasing was no doubt aimed to leave me choking. The lamb had teeth, indeed.

Langton and his mother spoke quietly for a time, and I kept my vigil out the window. I'm sure that the entire scene was bordering on the ludicrous; not one of us was in any way maintaining the roles assigned to us by society and training, and each of us was happy to shed those roles.

The door opened slowly, and the three of us turned immediately to watch the Duke come in. He walked painfully slowly, and it was obvious to me that he'd not been out of bed for some days. He was clean enough and dressed presentably, but his ravaged and hollow body was stiff, his movements jerky and clearly painful. He looked, quite simply, like a dead man. I half expected him to keel over at any moment.

Not one of us moved to help him as he made his way to a chair.

"Munrow," he said, his voice ratty and torn. "What do you want?"

I stood before him and looked down upon his withered body. "The letters."

"No."

I shrugged and glanced at Lady Julia. She gave me a tiny nod, and I looked to Langton, who merely raised an eyebrow.

"In that case," I said, "I wish to know if you've made changes to your will."

He turned his head and looked at Lady Julia. "Out," he ordered harshly. "And take the boy with you."

I spared a glare for him and walked Langton and his mother to the door. "Don't go far," I whispered to Langton. "This won't take long." I nodded to Lady Julia. "My lady."

"Mr. Munrow," she said, nodding her head. "Come, Henri. The morning room."

I waved off an approaching footman and closed the door softly then paced back to my spot before the Duke. "You look like hell." I admit I took a little pleasure in being so blunt.

"I'm dying," he said acidly. "I apologise for looking like it."

"Apology accepted," I said. "Now. You won't change your mind?"

He stared at me, fire in his eyes, which was my only hint that the old bastard really was in there; his condition made him look entirely helpless. I found myself wondering at his lucidity; I'd half expected to find him raving. The thought scared me a little -- I feared marrying Lady Julia and then discovering the Duke had made no changes to his will and that some distant cousin would steal Langton's land.

"Fine," I said, reluctantly. "I'll meet your demand."

"Of course," he said, reaching for a bell by his chair.

I snatched it away. "I have, however, my own demands."

Again, he stared at me.

"We will marry as soon as possible," I said. "And the very next morning, you and I will meet in this room with your solicitors, and you will change your will to reflect Viscount Langton's inheritance."

He glared and me and nodded. "Acceptable," he said, his tone indicating that it was anything but.

"And," I went on, "I have one or two matters of business involving Red Oak Hall to which Langton has been party. He will return with me for the duration of the summer, so that he might see them out. If nothing else, he will gain by the experience, and he'll be out of your hair. You can die in peace, then."

The Duke snorted at me. "You'll take your wife and daughter as well."

I shrugged, "If they wish it. If not, they can go visit relatives."

"You don't care?"

"Why would I? I'll not pretend to love her. Not for you." He growled at me, and I held his bell out to him. "Agreed?" I asked.

He took the bell and rang it fiercely until the door opened and the butler looked in.

"Your Grace?" the poor man asked.

"Please tell Lady Julia we'd like to see her," I said before the Duke could say anything. "If, of course, it is convenient."

"Certainly, sir," he said, and with a bow of his head he left us.

The Duke and I contented ourselves with glaring at one another until there was a polite rap at the door and Lady Julia came in. She said nothing at all but went right to the chair she'd sat on before; the Duke went even paler at the slight of courtesy. Personally, I rather liked the display of wilful rudeness.

"Mr. Munrow has agreed to take you," he said, and my hand flew up.

For a horrifying moment, I thought I might actually strike the man, but I managed to control my baser instincts. There was no way on God's earth I would allow him to start my marriage -- sham though it was to be -- off on that particular note.

He fell silent, and I went to Lady Julia, thankful that Langton was not in the room. "My lady," I said gently, kneeling down so that our eyes would be at a level, if not for the grand gesture. "It would please me greatly if you would consent to have me as your husband."

She nodded stiffly, and if her eyes were not warm with love, they were not at least as hard as stone. "It would... honour me," she said quietly. "I accept your proposal."

Together, we turned to look at the Duke. I was well aware that not a one of us was smiling.

"Well?" I asked.

"Two days," he replied, with a mirthless smile. "I doubt either of you wants a large wedding?"

"The banns -- " Lady Julia began, but he waved it off.

"They will be entered later."

I didn't ask how he was going to manage that; some things even I would rather not know about.

Lady Julia stood and nodded to him. "I'll let you see to the arrangements, then." She turned to me and nodded again. "And you as well. Good day, Mr. Munrow."

I rose and bowed. "Good day, my lady."

The next time I saw her was at the church. She was dressed in cream, a lovely frock, and had a piece of lace clutched in her hand. At her side was Lucy, a very pretty girl who looked rather terrified, and Langton, who looked pale.

Truitt stood beside me, and the Duke looked on as I married Lady Julia and became a legitimate gentleman. No one cried. No one laughed. Lady Julia did smile, once, when I slipped her ring onto her finger, and I looked up in time to see a tall figure leaving the church. Even then, she did not cry.

After the service I had Truitt slip away with Langton in tow. I wouldn't see either of them until the next morning; I had a duty to fulfil.

Chapter Thirty Five

I feel as if I should make mention of our wedding night, but it is the morning after I remember best. Oh, the evening passed in the usual way -- terror on both sides and rather inexpert fumbling, but Julia proved to be a humorous woman, and if not for the fact that we were forced to be in the same bed together, I rather suspect we'd have got along well.

That is not quite true, I must admit. The entire situation caused me near physical pain, and even in the remembrance I find myself wishing to skip the telling. Conscience will not let me, however, so to be quite plain about it, I find myself forcing the words out.

The inexpert fumbling began with both of us in the bed, her in a long frock and me in my robe. We said nothing for a long time, and finally, I had to look at her and confess that I'd never lain with a woman before, and if I were to be utterly truthful, I wasn't sure I could. She was, I assured her, a perfectly lovely and attractive woman; it just didn't seem to be enough.

She bit her lip, and in hindsight, I believe she was holding back laughter. I tell myself that she was nervous and near hysterical -- not simply amused. She looked at me with wide blue eyes and offered to... help me.

At which point I decided brandy would be help enough. A drink later and I got back into the bed, not terribly amused to find her giggling at me. She raised an eyebrow and reached for me, untying my robe without saying a word.

When it became clear that I was holding my breath, she poked me, rather sharply. And then she touched me. Her hand was on my sleeping cock, and it was all I could do to stay in the bed.

Her eyebrow remained up while she explored me, her touch light and teasing, dancing over my prick and balls. "You really would prefer not to do this, wouldn't you?" she asked, sounding curious.

I cleared my throat and yet remained unable to speak, so I merely shook my head.

She looked thoughtful. "Think of your lover," she suggested. "What is... he like?"

"Lovely," I gasped, refusing to think of her son and concentrating only on Truitt. "Beautiful."

She peeked under the sheet and squeezed my cock a little. "But not a miracle worker?"

"Apparently not," I said. "I apologise."

She smiled at me and withdrew her hand. "I think I should be rather grateful," she said. "We can simply say we consummated our marriage if anyone is bold enough to ask. A worthy lie, on top of all the others." She gave me a look of sympathy. "I don't really wish to sleep with you, either, you know."

Oddly, I was rather insulted. "Oh."

She laughed at me. "Does that shock you?" she asked, still giggling. "I love another. I lie down with another. You and I have promised to each other to avoid just this very thing. Forgive me, Mr. Munrow, but I have no desire for you at all. The fact that you are being... kind about this, is a gift."

Yes, I was being kind by being unable to achieve an erection. The notion appealed to me. "Are we done then?" I asked brightly.

She nodded. "We were in bed, there was touching, drinking, laughter... a very successful wedding night, I think."

I smiled and got out of the bed, reaching for my clothes. I was dressing almost happily, ignoring my complete embarrassment, when I happened to see her looking at me. Her eyes were not unfriendly, and I took a chance.

"May I talk to you?" I asked, buttoning my waistcoat.

She looked a little surprised, but nodded. "I can't imagine why not," she said dryly. "Is it about Henri? He seems to like you -- and he certainly appreciates being away from here."

"He's fine," I assured her, moving past the subject as quickly as I could. "He's smart and learns fast; he'll do extremely well for himself, I should think."

She nodded, and I sat down on a chair. She remained where she was, in the bed, covered from chin to the tips of her toes in sheets, blankets, and the plain cotton gown. I confess, I had managed to muss her hair, mostly by accident, but the rest of her was in fine shape.

"We need to discuss housing," I said easily. "You will, of course, keep this house -- it will go to Langton, and I can't see him moving you out. I will have Red Oak Hall, and you will be welcomed there as its Mistress; Langton will also inherit it. Oh, that reminds me, you and I will have to sit down with your son in the near future and work out a dowry for Lucy."

She nodded, looking faintly queasy. "So much," she

murmured.

"There is," I said sympathetically, "but we'll figure it out. My point, however, is that for you and I to... stay out of each other's way, as it were, it might be an idea for me to purchase another home in London -- nothing like this, of course, but a house nonetheless."

"People will talk," she pointed out. "No matter what servants you hire, people will talk. And it will all be for naught. The inheritance will be secure, but we'll both be ruined in society as the rumours start."

I sighed. She was right, of course.

"What of your... your lover?" she asked. "Perhaps a house can be purchased that way?"

I stared at her. Langton could not buy a home -- in fact, Langton would have to buy *her* a home when the time came for him to marry and produce his own heir -- but Truitt could.

Truitt should.

Truitt would.

"Thank you, my lady," I said, standing up.

She beamed at me. "I must say, I never thought being married to you would be quite like this."

"What? A quick, disappointing tumble, some real estate talk, mention of my infidelity, and smiles all round?" I teased.

"Yes, like that." She laughed and pulled the blankets higher. "Goodnight, Mr. Munrow. I'll see you in the morning."

"Goodnight, Mrs. Munrow," I said softly.

She threw a pillow at me, and, laughing, I fled.

* * *

The morning saw us in the Duke's company once again as he made good on our gentleman's agreement, making changes to his will and to various business enterprises which would enable Langton to take over as soon as the Duke died. He allowed me to read through the documents, which took rather a long time, and in the middle of it, Lady Julia asked me to give her a moment's conversation in the morning room.

I crossed the hall to her, leaving Langton with his uncle, and she told me that she and Lucy would like to visit her cousin in Essex for a week, if it was agreeable with me. I said of course, naturally, and we agreed that she would come to Red Oak Hall in a fortnight, so that she might know the place. She went to pack, and I returned to the drawing room and to business.

Langton had been very quiet, and I had not been able to be alone with him at all since our arrival in London. I prayed Truitt had taken good care of him, and the care Langton took when he sat encouraged me. I made an effort to ask his opinion several times and to lean close to him when we were reading the same pages. Within an hour, he was noticeably warmer to me.

In two hours, I was fending off his fingers under the table.

At the end of the third hour, everything had been signed and we made ready to leave. Langton and his mother exchanged farewells, and Lady Julia and I had another very quick exchange about her journey. Langton seemed to approve of her trip and even suggested we delay our own departure for an hour so he could see them off.

So we had another pot of tea, and I watched while Langton and Lucy and talked quietly in the corner. The Duke glared at all of us and was roundly ignored. At long last, Langton and I walked Lady Julia and Lucy to their carriage and waved them off. I was more than ready to stand on the step and await our own carriage, and I said so.

"No, no. Come back with me and say goodbye," Langton said.

"Langton..." I really didn't like the look in his eye.

He grinned and walked back into the house, into the drawing room. I followed, mostly hoping to stop whatever he was going to do before it could go wrong and land him in a world of trouble.

He closed the door behind me and then walked to his uncle. "Congratulations," he said. "You won, and you saved me personally from a life of utter destitution. Thank you, really."

His uncle glared up at him. "You should be grateful."

"Oh, I am. I have a secured inheritance, you're going to die soon, and I... oh, right, you don't know that part yet." He clicked his tongue and turned to me.

"Oh, no, you don't," I said, putting a hand up.

But he was too fast, too determined, and I don't think I was really all that interested in fighting him off. Langton launched himself at me and kissed me so deeply and thoroughly that, by the time I'd peeled his hands off my arse and got his tongue out of my mouth, we were both panting. And hard.

The Duke was gasping as well, but his pallor had become a shade of crimson, and I wondered if he might die on the spot.

Langton bent down in front of him. "I love him, you bastard, and you're the one who ensured it. He fucks me, and I beg him to do it. And if you tell anyone, they won't believe you -- you're too sick, and he just married my mother and took your land. No one in London would believe you. Congratulations. I win." He stood and walked away, right past me to the door and out.

I looked at the Duke and shrugged one shoulder. "Would you like a doctor?" I asked as solicitously as I could.

"Get out!" he roared.

I left. The carriage, thankfully, was at the front of the house, and Langton was waiting for me; as soon as the door closed he was in my lap, squirming like a puppy.

"You are in so much trouble," I whispered to him, fending off his hands.

"Let me make it up to you," he whispered back. And then he was on his knees between my spread thighs and I gave up any form of argument. It was fast and dirty and by far the most satisfying five minutes I'd had in a few days. After I'd spent in his mouth, biting my lip to keep from yelling, he fell back and wiped his lips.

"Forgive me?" he asked with a grin.

"Eventually," I allowed. I tugged him back up onto the bench and kissed him until I could no longer taste myself.

We were having an early lunch in the dining room three days before Lady Julia was to arrive at Red Oak Hall when Dobbs came in holding the silver tray we used for calling cards.

"Yes?" I asked curiously.

"Sir," he said, inclining his head to me before turning to Langton and bowing a little lower. "Your Grace. Your mother requests you return to London immediately. She requires the attendance of her husband as well, in order to deal with matters of your late uncle's estate."

And thus, my gentleman's agreement with the Duke reached its inevitable conclusion.

Epilogue

Five years later....

"You didn't just leave him there?" Truitt demanded from across the dinner table. His eyes were narrow and his jaw tight, and I was fairly sure I was in a great deal of trouble.

"Of course not!" I protested, my hands up and palms out to placate him. "Well, not really."

Truitt glared at me, and I sighed.

"Drink your wine, pet," I said. "He'll be here as soon as he can be." Which, if I knew our Langton, would be far sooner than even Truitt would have expected. Langton's mind for business and negotiating was keeping him in fine form, and acquiring a bride, if approached from that standpoint, wasn't overly upsetting to him.

Truitt, on the other hand, was having fits at Langton's proposed nuptials.

"You couldn't stay with him?" he asked again, poking at his roast and starting a fine sulk.

"No, Christopher," I said patiently. "I am merely Henri's stepfather -- "

Truitt shuddered, and I admit to squirming slightly as

the words were formed in my mouth. It was an unwritten rule to never mention that among the three of us unless it couldn't be avoided.

" -- and he's a Duke," I went on. "He's capable of handling this himself, and my presence was neither needed nor wanted. So, I came home to wait with you."

Home was, of course, the house to which Truitt held the deed and which all three of us called ours. After I'd married Lady Julia, Langton and I were naturally encouraged to spend even more time together as we merged our households and business dealings as best we could. I spent long hours and days in London following the old Duke's death, finding out just how horrible Langton's financial situation was and making plans with him to fix it. Ideally, we'd hoped to recover his solvency without having to strip my own assets to do it; that, at least, seemed to finally be coming to fruition. The house became a stopping point for me to stay at, which we'd planned for, and Langton was always welcome.

We spent so much time together, in fact, and were so neatly tied to one another that no one seemed to raise an eye when we began to socialise together, attending the same parties and visiting one another regularly. As I was already known to be close friends with Truitt, the three of us keeping company, as it were, wasn't even mentioned.

All in all, we three managed to find a place for ourselves and our relationship. Discretion was key, and we'd all learned that. Our house was staffed by one housekeeper and cook we'd tempted away from the club, and our own gentlemen. That was it -- few people to keep secrets with, and those who needed to keep them were well paid and loyal. It was rare for the three of us all to be home for more than one night at a time -- typically, Truitt lived there full time, and Langton and I stayed when we could -- but if Langton's discussions with Mr. Peters about his daughter, Sophie, went according to plan, I suspected that the three of us would be spending a day or two hiding from the world and soothing each other.

Truitt in particular was upset and troubled, I thought. He had no need to marry, having no need for an heir to take over. His holdings were his, and as a third son, he had no expectation for land. As a single man, he was quite well off; a wife and family would actually have proved a burden, if he'd been of the sort who desired the same. Luckily for us, all he wanted was what he had. There were enough nephews and cousins and nieces around for him to know that what estate he had would be well used, and that was all the comfort he needed when we chanced to talk of such matters. However, when it came to my marriage or Langton's, he was given to moods.

It made sense, I supposed; not so much with my situation, for Lady Julia was a remarkable woman who only required my presence a handful of times a year. But Langton... it was unlikely that he would find a wife so understanding, and that weighed heavily upon us all.

"I don't see why it has to be now," Truitt said as he sipped his wine. It was a refrain I'd heard many times over the last few months. "He's not even five and twenty; he has plenty of time to choose a wife."

I sighed again. "You know why, pet."

Truitt pouted, although he'd be loath to call it such. "Is he really so sure that her father is about to come into a fortune?"

I nodded and picked up my own glass, ignoring the meal before me. "He is. You know how Henri is; he can spot a good investment. He's doing what's best for his estate. Sophie's family isn't titled; they have no land... she's young. Henri knows what he's doing."

Truitt looked at me intently. "How young?" he asked.

I smiled to myself, surprised it had taken him this long to work his way around to the actual wife in question, for him to get beyond the concept of Langton being married. "She's barely fourteen. They won't actually marry for years yet."

Truitt raised an eyebrow. "Her father can do that in this day and age? Simply... set her life out for her? How utterly horrible."

I shrugged. "We'll see. If it all falls apart, Henri will simply find another father with what he needs and start all over again. Like you said, he has time. He needn't fall in love -- that's what we're for."

My words were so clipped and cold that it gave me pause, and Truitt had good reason to stare. I fought to create a smile for him and shrugged one shoulder. "Perhaps I'm not as pleased about it as I try to pretend," I admitted.

Oddly, this seemed to cheer Truitt. Not that he was happy to see me displeased and uneasy, but he seemed to find comfort in not being alone. Why on God's earth, really, should either of us be happy for Langton? There was no reason for us to be cheerful about his plans to be married.

With a frown, I pushed away my plate and stood up, taking my glass of wine with me as I paced about the room. Truitt was silent and didn't make any move to finish his meal, either. He stood up when we heard the outer door slam shut and the sound of Langton's step upon the floorboards, and we were both moving to the dining room door when it opened and our lamb came in.

Langton stopped short, looking at us both in surprise. "Is something the matter?" he asked.

I shook my head, and Truitt advanced on him, pushing Langton into the wall as he kissed him.

"Oh!" Langton gasped when our pet released him. "I see. I have to say that such a welcome is just what I needed." His face was flushed, and his hand had already clamped down on Truitt's arm, not letting him go.

Watching them, still more than an arm's length from me, I was struck by a terrible hunger, an anger against those who stood between us all. It was irrational and something I purposefully ignored at most times, but there were times that it reared its ugly head, and I envied Barrett his flight to France.

It must have shown on my face, or something did, for they both turned and as one took a step towards me. "Ned -- " Truitt said.

I didn't want to hear whatever it was he was going to say in order to soothe me. I didn't wish to be soothed. I accepted the feeling in me and let it run through my body, let it heat my blood. I shook my head at him and backed up a step. They advanced again, Langton still holding Truitt's arm.

I ached for them. I ached to feel them, to have them. To possess them and to be possessed.

"Do you want me?" I asked them both, my voice deep and so hoarse I had to clear my throat.

"Always," Langton, our sweet lamb, said. His eyes were troubled, and he looked to Truitt.

"You don't have to ask," our pet said, his eyes intent, darkening and narrowing. The years before Langton seemed to have given him an added insight to my soul, or perhaps his perversions matched mine to a degree where we were beginning to think alike. He took a step forward, and I moved around the table. "You'd flee me?" he asked, amused.

Langton's gaze darted back and forth, and the confusion in his eyes cleared away as he understood we were starting an impromptu game. "Perhaps he feels a need to be pursued," Langton murmured, stepping back to come to me from the other side.

I held up my hand and they both froze. "You want me, you must find me," I said, starting to smile. "Pursue, indeed. You must hunt."

They exchanged a look. "Territory?" Langton asked shortly. That was our lamb. So smart, so quick. So willing to play.

"Just the house," I said. "I'm not prepared to take to the streets of London this night. Perhaps another time."

Truitt nodded and picked up his wine again. "You'll want some advance time?"

"Only a count of one hundred," I said, flying to the door. And as quick as that I was off, hurrying to the kitchen. As I'd expected, the men who took care of us were just sitting down to eat their meal.

"My apologies," I said as I ran into the room. "This is one of those nights were you can either stay and pretend yourselves blind and deaf, or you can flee now." I tossed coins onto the table and dashed out the far door, not staying to see their reactions. I did, however, hear the laughter and the sounds of their chairs scraping on the floor as they got up. There would be hell to pay in the morning for the uproar caused, I knew, but it was going to be worth it.

The key to this game, I decided, was timing. I wanted them to hunt, so it was a mobile game of hide-and-seek, but I also wanted to be caught, or there would be no point. If I knew my lovers, they would stay close together for a short while, and then Langton's mind for tactics would force them to split up.

I went from the kitchen up the backstairs to the bedrooms and hurriedly grabbed a bottle of oil, only pausing to make sure it was stoppered well before returning to the hall. I waited at the top of the stairs but couldn't hear them, could not, in fact, hear anything for a long moment. Then a creaking behind me warned of their ascent on the backstairs, and I nearly flew down the main staircase, darting into the morning room. I didn't hide in there, for there was little point at that stage of the game. Instead, I removed my coat and draped it over a chair.

In the parlour, I removed my waistcoat and collar.

I left my cufflinks on the silver card tray in the hall.

In the library, I stopped and stood in the middle of the room. I listened intently until I heard movement overhead, in what was nominally my bedchamber, and then I selected a few volumes from the books hidden behind Truitt's desk. They were not Barrett's black bound volumes, but they would serve just as well. Leaving them on Langton's reading chair, I removed my shoes and crept into the kitchen once more.

I was just walking past the table, a grin on my face as I viewed the remains of the uneaten meal, when I heard a booted footfall on the backstairs. I slid into the pantry and edged the door closed, hoping they would pass by, and was in luck -- Truitt barely glanced around the room as he hurried through to the dining room.

Langton was not with him. This surprised me, really; I'd expected them to take a turn about the whole house before splitting up. A thrill went up my spine as I realised the game would be much faster than I'd intended.

I crept after Truitt, walking softly and keeping most of my attention alert for sounds behind me. I peered into the dining room and found it empty, so I went through it and into the main hall, quickly picking a room almost at random as I tried to find cover. Once more in the morning room, I swallowed a curse -- there was only the one door and I'd effectively trapped myself until I could determine that the coast was clear.

Carefully, I made sure that I really was alone and then

stationed myself just inside the door so I could look out at the hall and the doors to both the library and dining room. I could barely see the end of the stairs, but they were not hidden, at least, and in order to get to the drawing room, my hunters would have to pass by me. Really, aside from the lack of escape, it was an ideal spot.

In moments, Langton appeared at the very bottom of the steps and I was forced to grin. I'd not heard a sound. The lamb, it seemed, had a very soft step. He slipped into the library, and in a second, I heard a soft cry from Truitt as, no doubt, Langton scared him out of five years of his life.

I waited for almost two minutes, and they didn't reappear. I could hear nothing. I could see nothing. Frustrated and tense, I considered my options. I could make a run for it and head upstairs. I could secret myself in any of the other rooms -- one with an escape built in would be a fine choice. Or I could figure out a way to see what they were doing.

I really do make a much better hunter than prey.

Deciding that if they spied me or came out of the library as I was crossing the hall I could simply turn tail and run like mad, I left my place of relative safety. My heart was sounding loud in my ears, and I scarcely drew breath as I crossed the few steps to the library doors and looked in.

If I hadn't already been stiff in my trousers, I would have been made so as I looked at them.

Langton was sitting on the desk, his legs spread wide with Truitt standing between them. As far as I could see, they were both dressed, but they were kissing deeply, passionately, and fingers were quickly undoing buttons. Truitt's hips were moving in an unmistakable rhythm, and I could see Langton's arm move, matching him as Langton stroked Truitt's cock.

I must have made a sound; I know for certain that my own hand was clamped tight on my prick, even through the layers of cloth. Langton's head turned, and we all three froze for a moment.

I don't know why I didn't simply go to them. Perhaps it was simply that I wanted to play, that I wanted to be the chased; more likely, it was simply because the game had become nature -- I was tuned to flee, so I did.

I turned and ran, laughing as I heard Truitt curse and the sound of something solid being banged. I dashed into the dining room and made sure the door swung shut behind me, but I could hear Langton moving quickly, his laughter louder than Truitt's.

"The kitchen!" he cried. "He'll try for the kitchen!"

As I was already pushing the door to the kitchen, I had to grant him that. I turned and stood, waiting for him to choose which side of the dining room table he was going to circle, but he merely smiled at me and remained by the door.

"You're stuck," he said.

"One would think so," I said, hearing Truitt knock something over in the kitchen. I grinned and stepped to the far side of the door, just as it swung open and Truitt ran in.

"No!" Langton shouted as Truitt took two steps too far and I got behind him and into the kitchen.

"Damn!"

"Backstairs!"

I laughed and moved through the kitchen; there was no way one of them would be able to cross the hall, run upstairs, the length of the house and back down the other flight before I could get upstairs and hide.

Unless, as it turned out, the one doing the running was Truitt, leaving Langton to chase me through the kitchen. I was halfway up the stairs when he caught me, right on the corner landing, and then there was a hand clamped on my ankle and Langton's grinning face looking down on me as I fell.

"Caught," he whispered triumphantly, just before he kissed me, his body plastered over mine on the stairs.

It was uncomfortable, to say the least, but as I tasted his kiss and heard his moan, and felt his hand start to rub at my cock, I didn't care. I leant back against the wall and let him do as he would, my mouth opening to his, my legs parting to give him access. "Yes," I said into the kiss. "My lamb."

"Your hunter," he corrected, his hand fitting around my prick and stroking gently. "Say it. Say I won."

"You won." I couldn't deny it, had no wish to. All I wanted was more of his touch, more of his mouth. "Suck me," I said.

He shook his head, smiling. "I have another idea."

His hand pulled at my cock, his palm hot and smooth on the head, and I groaned. "Anything."

I heard Truitt's step above me, and both Langton and I looked up to see him watching us, his smile bright.

"Wonderful, I'm so glad to hear that," he said. "Henri? As we discussed in the library?"

"Of course," Langton said, stroking me again.

I moaned and spread my legs wider, my hips rocking. I needed. I hungered. I wanted. "Discussed?"

Truitt sat on the step just above me and nodded. "We had just finished discussing the finer points when you found us," he said, undoing the placket of his trousers.

My cock leapt at the memory and at the sight of him happily masturbating right in front of me. Langton's hand left me, however, and I turned back to frown, only to discover him fishing the oil from my pocket.

"I knew you took it," he said with a grin. "Now. You were the prey, we caught you, and you are at our mercy."

I raised an eyebrow and tried to reach my cock, only to have my hand swatted way and to hear Truitt tut-tut me. "You'll show me mercy?" I asked.

"Not at all," Langton said with a wicked grin. His hands darted out and Truitt grabbed me, turning and manhandling me most expertly, and the next thing I knew, Langton was laughing evilly.

From behind me.

I was eye to prick with Truitt, my trousers and underthings were around my knees on the stairs, and I was completely trapped. Neither flight nor fight seemed like a pleasant idea, and to be completely honest, I was quite possibly more randy at that very moment than I'd been in years.

I was going to be taken. Thoroughly. It was a rare thing, something that wasn't withheld from them at all, just not common among us. When Truitt's need came to the fore, it was most often Langton he reached for; Langton, in turn, seemed to reserve taking me for special occasions only.

With a low moan, I gave myself up to it, to the them, to my lovers, and I opened. My mouth, my arse, my soul; I was theirs. Always.

Truitt slid his prick past my lips and gave a choked cry. I moaned around him, the taste of his skin and his excitement exploding across my tongue as I began to suck him. He was swollen and huge in my mouth, his cock rock hard and hot, utterly perfect.

"Oh, God," I heard Langton say as I suckled. "Dear God."

In a moment, my concentration was shattered as slick, nimble fingers breached me. It was far from the first time that Langton had done this to me, but it was rare enough that I gasped, and he slowed his touch; used to Truitt more than me, he took care when he felt me tense.

Truitt pushed into my mouth, and I was soon lost. I sucked and licked and felt Langton play with my arse, and I drifted on the sensations. I relaxed and let Langton in, let Truitt into my throat. There were sounds all around me: wet sounds of suction, the moans Truitt made as I lapped at the head of his prick, the sound Langton was making, and the added groans of my own pleasure.

My cock was aching, swinging between my thighs as I moved on Langton's fingers. I moaned and groaned and begged with my body as he massaged the spot inside of me that would have made me scream had I been able.

"Soon, Henri," Truitt begged. "Take him. God, hurry!"

I nodded as much as I was able and groaned and tried to part my knees.

"Ned," Langton breathed. "Oh, my Ned."

The head of his cock breached me, and he pushed in, filled me, stretched me and made me groan. Truitt moaned, and Langton cried out, his legs shaking. I could feel all of us tense.

It was in the backstairs of our house, and I was certain that it was about to be the shortest, most intense fuck of our lives.

Langton thrust. I sucked. Truitt yelled and thrust back, driving his cock into my mouth and shoving me back onto Langton. It was primal and without rhythm, and it was utterly without grace.

When Langton suddenly gripped my prick, I cried out around Truitt's shaft and came, my body jerking as I shot ribbons of come into Langton's hand. He swore and pushed deep; even in the throes of my orgasm, I could feel him pulsing within me. I felt every twitch of his cock, every throb of it as he filled me. Poor Truitt had to pull away; we were too wrapped up in our mutual ecstasy.

As soon as I could, I reached for him, sucked him quickly and harshly while Langton moaned, his cock still buried in my arse. It took almost no time before Truitt came, just as Langton was describing what we'd do when we made it to bed. From what I could make out around the gasps and grunts, it was going to be a very long night.

I swallowed Truitt's pleasure, revelling in the praise he heaped upon me as I suckled and licked him in the aftermath. Langton finally slipped from my body, and I groaned, reluctant to let him go. The three of us traded kisses and touches for a short time, the steps quickly becoming an annoyance.

"Take him upstairs," Langton told Truitt. "I'll clean up here and bring up something to drink. Wine, I think."

I nodded and let Truitt pull me up. "Are we celebrating?" I asked as I put my clothes to rights.

"More or less," Langton said. "He said no."

We all smiled.

"To another few years of love, uninterrupted," I said as I turned to go upstairs.

"A lifetime of love, though," Langton replied, calling up from the kitchen.

Truitt smiled at me and whispered, "Amen."

Indeed.

The End.

An Agreement Among Gentlemen

Chris Owen

An Agreement Among Gentlemen